Jingle Balls

Participating Authors

Annie Mick

Kayla Baker

Melony Ann

Nikki A. Lamers

Samantha Michaels

Copyright

First Edition, November 2023
Copyright © 2023 by Nikki A Lamers

Paperback ISBN: 978-1-951185-24-4

Disclaimer

The five authors in this anthology have come together to raise support for the National Safe Haven Alliance, a charity that helps children in domestic violence situations.

100% of the royalties the authors involved in this anthology get will be donated directly to the National Safe Haven Alliance.

The authors would like to send you their thanks for being so kind as to purchase this book and wish you all the happiest of holidays.

Donner's Vixen

by Annie Mick

Blurb

~ Rudolph may have saved the night, but let's not forget the rest of the team. ~

It started with a simple traffic stop…

Get her name, ask her out, have a little fun.

But Officer Donner got a whole lot more than he expected when presented with a frozen body in the trunk.

While he attempts to unravel the mystery, he has to fight the pull the sassy little vixen has on his heart.

~ A short, steamy romance to make you laugh, melt your heart, and warm a few. . . body parts. ~

Chapter 1

❄ Haley ❄

"Blowing your horn is not going to make them move, you moron!" I white-knuckle the steering wheel in frustration. "The light may be green but if the intersection is blocked, he can't go anywhere!"

My scolding might be more effective if my window were down, but I'm not in the mood to get shot today. The groceries in my trunk are going to spoil if I don't get home soon and melted Cool Whip and ice cream is going to suck. Refrozen ice cream is the equivalent of Elmer's glue and tastes just as bad. Not to mention good ol' Tom needs to thaw in the fridge over the next two days; not in my trunk in the next two hours. I doubt Myrtle, Stanley and Frank would appreciate salmonella as a gift. Now, a gift of *Sam* for Myrtle and an *Ella* for Stanley and Frank to share might be another story. But alas, Amazon hasn't stooped to selling one-night stands for horny senior citizens, so I'm shit out o' luck for getting off easy this year. It's all copasetic. I still have a month to choose their gifts. This is Thanksgiving dinner in my trunk.

Now that he's been granted it, I wait for Mr. Moron to move up a few feet so I can whip Myrtle's zero turning radius Hyundai off to the right around him.

Honest to God, you'd think this guy was begging for doggy style the way he'd been crawling up the ass of the car in front of him. If my horn didn't sound like a sickly VW from the sixties, I'd be tempted to lay on it just to give him that little jumpstart. However, if I blow my horn, he won't move. This is his battle. Take no prisoners, king of the road, he owns it. Out of sheer stubbornness or assholery – depends on your outlook – if I were to honk he won't budge, even if traffic does. So I sit and wait.

Bingo! With a mere few inches to spare, I veer around him and take the small space I'm awarded – give or take a kiss or two to the curb – and head toward an alternate route. Might not be my brightest move today – it's a busy four-lane to cross from a side street sans traffic lights – but anything is better than the standstill I'm stuck in.

Three miles through a vintage neighborhood with stop signs every couple blocks, two-story houses in varying degrees of upkeep, and I'm finally at the intersection of 10th Street and Sterling. The sun is in the southern sky at this time of day and I'll be turning north; shouldn't be too hard. One left turn and I'll be homeward bound to my tiny little paradise of Gator Springs.

Straight ahead on the other side of the intersection is a cop waiting to cross. Finagling the intersection isn't so bad if you don't have another vehicle to contend with. However, there are some drivers who should have remained pedestrians. But this is a cop. He'll know the laws, right? He won't sit there struggling to recall rules from the driver's manual regarding who goes first, will he?

I flick the bar on the steering column, indicating my intentions to turn left, and wait for traffic to clear. The officer on the other side of the intersection has the right-of-way so I wait for him to go first. I watch the traffic cautiously, my head flitting left to right and back again. Finally, an opening appears – for him anyway. I'll have to wait for the next one. So I do just that. I wait...and wait. As does the officer. I honk the wienie horn on this car to give him a heads up. And the opportunity has soon eluded us. My hands grip the steering wheel in frustration and I growl to myself.

If I turn right, it will take me into no man's land and getting turned back around is five miles out due to an inconvenient median in the road. So not worth it. If I go straight, it leads to an entrance ramp onto the highway and I am totally screwed. Again, so not worth it. As I ponder these thoughts, another opportunity becomes available. I wait. And so does he.

Are you kidding me?

I raise my hands in frustration and scream, "Move it, Captain Crunch! You have the right of way!!!"

My groceries have been in the trunk for nearly an hour. Tom has approximately one hour left before he goes into a meltdown and I'll be questioning his worthiness for dinner. The Cool Whip and ice cream are probably already a lost cause. Oh shit! I have frozen pies back there as well!

Why didn't I put everything in the backseat? At least they'd be in the air conditioning I'm enjoying the benefit of at the current time.

I glance in both directions once more and spot my chance. "You snooze, you lose, pal." I pull out into the intersection whipping left, one hand in the air as I resist flipping him off – failing miserably – the other on the steering wheel.

Yes! Success!

"Nooo," I release a low, drawn out groan moments later as the lights flash in my rearview mirror and the ear piercing single whoop of his siren blows. "You've gotta be kidding me."

Yanking the steering wheel to the right, I pull over into the parking lot of a convenience store and slam the gear shift into park. Without ceremony, or forethought, I throw open the door and hop out of the car, approaching the officer who is now exiting his own. Whoops. Way to go, Haley, that's two laws you've broken today. You're supposed to stay in the car!

Well, at least he doesn't have his gun drawn. I don't think so anyway. I'm so mad at the current time, I'm not sure I care. There are witnesses here. He wouldn't shoot me, would he?

Once in close proximity to each other, I whip my shades off my face, holding my hands in the air so he knows I'm unarmed, and shriek, "Why did you pull me over?!"

"I thought you needed me." His voice is so low it makes the ground beneath my feet rumble. Oh wait, that's my chest. And what do we have attached to that chest? Ah, nipples. Stand down, ladies. We're mad at him. Though it is a challenge; he's gorgeous.

"What?!" I snap harshly, an octave higher than I mean to. "Why would you think I needed you?"

I've never seen a cop with mischief in his eyes before, but I swear I'm looking at one right now. "Because you honked and waved at me. I took it as a distress signal."

"A distress signal?" Oh no. He's not going to get away with trying to make me look incompetent behind the wheel. I press a finger to his chest. "I was waving my hands in frustration. I was pissed because you were not following the law. I was trying to be good and you made it impossible."

He dips his chin to glance at the finger I have pointed in his chest before clamping his huge hand around my wrist, applying a gentle pulsing pressure with his thumb to the center of my curled palm. Damn! Now that's an innuendo if ever there was one. He arches a brow above a wicked gleam in the iciest blue eyes I've ever seen. "Are you always good, Miss...?"

My knees nearly buckle as my breath stutters and I swallow hard to hide the whimper that begs to leave my throat. *Food, Haley!* It's melting faster than you are right now. Besides, you swore off men for a year. You have five months to go.

"Are you arresting me?"

He grins puckishly. "Not yet. You haven't given me your name."

I glance over my shoulder at the Sonata screaming for me to unload groceries from the trunk. "Sorry, officer." Pasting on a saccharin smile, I finish, "Tom is going to thaw if I don't get him home soon. Frozen bodies don't do well in this heat. I really should have loaded him in the backseat but I stuffed him in the trunk instead. Probably not my wisest decision. If we're done here, I really do have..."

Word of advice people: DO NOT NAME YOUR TURKEY!

I am whirled around and cuffs are slapped on my wrists before I can blink.

Way to go, Haley. Play nice.

"Jesus," he mumbles behind me as he fast forwards me toward the car. "And I thought you were cute."

"You thought I was cute?" I say coyly.

"Shut up," he orders harshly, reaching into the car to grab the fob while roughly holding my elbow. "Let's see what you got in the trunk, lady."

Playing it for all it's worth, I nearly sing, "You think I'm a lady?"

"You don't want to know what I'm thinking right now," he growls.

"You're not going to tell his family, are you?" I cry on the way to the back of the car, digging my heels in the concrete to halt his footsteps. "You have no idea how mean they can be. They flock together. Get them in a group and they will literally *gobble* me up. Don't do this. Please."

He pushes the button on the fob for the trunk and yanks on my arm once more to pull me with him. He studies the contents inside; frozen pies, Cool Whip, and ice cream; all covered in condensation indicating the melting process started quite some time ago. Potatoes, various produce for the veggie tray, and...Big Tom – thank you, Butterball – my turkey; now defrosted probably an inch into his big fat breast. At least the little red button hasn't popped up through the plastic wrap and out of his boob yet.

I look up at the man in blue's scowling face and bat my lashes. "Meet Tom, officer." I bend a little and squint. "Nineteen pounds and four ounces. If he had a hand, I'm sure he'd shake yours in gratitude. You know…" I wink "…trying to rescue him and all."

He spins me until my back is to him and unlocks the cuffs. Then, the oddest thing happens. He gently caresses my forearms once before he guides my hands around in front of me – his chest pressed to my back – massages my wrists and inspects them to ensure there's no damage from the cuffs. His mouth is so close to my ear, I feel his breath whisper across my skin as he presses the fob into my hand and says, "You are trouble. Go home, before I figure out exactly what it is I want to do with you."

Chapter 2

❄ Donner ❄

She whips out of the parking lot as if her ass is on fire, but sends a little wave accompanied by a cocky smile in my direction before she's gone. God, she's beautiful. It's why I was frozen at the intersection. The trees shaded her windshield and gave me a view to the driver inside, literally stealing my breath. I knew I had the right-of-way – straight versus turning traffic – but I was having too much fun watching her. That mass of wild blonde curls surrounding the face of an angel; her head bobbing with either extreme impatience or to music playing in the baby-shit green Hyundai Sonata I'd seen her climb into before. At those times though, it was a temporary plate on the back with small numbers, and I was still inside the store. Who in the hell drives such a butt ugly car? She must have bought it at one helluva discount. That, or the woman is severely colorblind.

Then the traffic cleared and it was time to go. I shouldn't have taken such delight in her frustration, but damn, that girl is hilarious when she gets riled. Hands flailing, screaming obscenities as if someone could hear. I had to pull her over, seize the opportunity. I had no intention of giving her a ticket; I only wanted her name.

The two times I had seen her before was at the grocery store with who must have been her grandfather, and the other at a pharmacy with most likely her grandmother. Eyes as blue as sapphires but more sparkle. Pert little nose that crinkles when she smiles. And that mouth. Oh, the things I could do with that mouth.

If sunshine had a sound, it would be...her laughter.

Sassy little shit. Frozen Tom in the trunk. What was I thinking? An old boyfriend? An ex-husband? A body she was preparing to bury?

She may think she got away, but I got her license number this time. With a few clicks on a keyboard I'll have her name and address in no time. I wonder who she's fixing that 19-pound turkey for. Correction: 19 pounds, four ounces. About the size of her ass. Perfect fit for my palms.

Seeing her in passing was one thing. Up close, exchanging the same air, my front to her back even with clothes on? Exhilarating. Definitely peach-shaped ass. *The one the little fireball rubbed against my crotch for good measure right before I let her go.* Buckle up, Miss whatever-your-name-is. We'll be seeing each other again soon.

I'll wait until I get back to the station to pull up her info. I've got six hours left on my shift. Work first. Play later. Damn, she's going to be fun.

❄ ❄ ❄

"Myrtle Beatrice Bainbridge?" I mutter to myself in disbelief as I stare at the monitor in front of me. No way. That woman's name is not Myrtle. Not if she's still speaking to her parents, anyway. Who names their kid Myrtle in this day and age? That's borderline cruelty. At least with names like Agnes or Edna you can derive a nickname of Aggie or Eddie. Kind of cute really. I had an aunt named Ida. Nobody liked her. We called her Ida-ho. Nothing to do with the state, mind you. It just was what it was. But what can you do with Myrtle? Yet, here it is in black and white.

Myrtle Bainbridge

165 Pelican Court Apt. 2C

Gator Springs, Florida

"Hey, Donner," Eric calls out from across the squad room. "We're headed out to Spanky's for a few. Want to join us?"

I jot down the name and address, log out, and tuck the paper in my pocket. "Yeah, let me change. I'll meet you guys there."

"Maybe she goes by her middle name," I whisper to myself as I change out of my uniform and into street clothes. "Bea or BB. That wouldn't be too bad." I roll my eyes and slam the locker door shut. "Get over yourself, asshole. What's in a name?" Not that I have a lot of room to talk. *Donner.* Once we hit junior high and studied the famous wagon train tragedy, I suffered my share of jokes and ribbing. If it didn't center around reindeer at Christmas, it was the age-old questions of:

13

"Did you want the toes or fingers for dinner tonight?"

"Got a heart left over if you're extra hungry."

Or the classic call in the cafeteria: *"Donner, party of ...wait! Didn't you guys eat each other?"* Or *"Sorry, it's a vegetarian menu today. Beggars can't be choosers."*

Didn't find it funny back then. Definitely not humorous these days either.

The bells hung on the door of Spanky's ring loudly as I open it. Why they couldn't wait until we're a little closer to the actual holiday, I'll never know but the damn things go up the day after Halloween and don't come down until the middle of January. A bit like Walmart, but these guys serve beer...and wings.

"Donner!" Jizz yells from the far corner. Nope, not kidding. Proper name is Lance Jizzman, but in keeping with the crudity of guys who work a stressful job, you seek entertainment where you can find it.

There's Eric Campbell who we call "Soup". There's also "Nad". He had an unfortunate run-in with a knife wielding perp and lost one so...self-explanatory. He's cool with it. He's gotten married and had twins since the incident. Single chamber – double barrel apparently.

Pulling a twenty from my wallet and tossing it on the table first, I take a seat at one of the three tables they've pulled together into one long one. Jizz slides a pitcher of beer and an empty glass to me and I pour the first of my limit of two.

"Who's off the rest of the week?" Eric asks everyone within hearing range.

Ha! It's only Monday night. A holiday week. I'm on until Friday. So much for Thanksgiving dinner with the family...on Thursday anyway. I'll be working a 12-hour shift. My mom will offer to postpone, I'll demand she not, she'll eventually concede, and I'll end up with leftovers for a week. Being single, I've never minded working the holidays for guys who have wives and kids to spend them with. Various yeas and nays come from around the table; some with grumbles.

Hot Rod holds his glass high in the air. "I am!" Rodney Gasman. Young, horny, easily lit, never goes home alone. Need I say more?

A flash of blonde curls catches my eye as she breezes past us on her way to the ladies room. Hot Rod whistles between his teeth as he nearly falls out of his chair leaning over to watch her walk down the hall. "Hot damn," he breathes out a low growl. "Think I just figured out how I'm spending my time off." He bobs his eyebrows and starts to rise from his chair. "See you around, Donner. Happy Turkey day."

"Sit down, asshole." I'm out of my seat before he can straighten his legs. "She's under my surveillance. Don't screw up my case."

His ass plops back down in the chair as he raises his hands in defense, as well as his eyebrows in surprise. "Whoa. I had no clue, Donner."

"Now you do." I turn toward the hall that leads to the restrooms, leaving Hot Rod behind. It wasn't a total lie, just a little white one. Maybe gray. If I have my way, she and I will be making those 50 shades look like child's play.

The door to the ladies room flies open and approximately five feet, six inches of sheer beauty steps out. She missteps when she sees me standing so close but catches herself quickly. Her quirky expression as she studies my face is adorable – tilting her head slightly – but then a smile lights her face and her sass is in full swing.

"Officer Friendly," she singsongs. "I almost didn't recognize you out of uniform." She holds her fisted hands out, wrists up. "Did you come to cuff me again?"

Her eyes are captivating; lit with mischief. There's a flicker of innocence with a side order of determination; both of which are heightened by the sparkle as she refuses to be the first one to break our gaze.

If sparkle had a color, it would be...her eyes.

Her scent is disarming in this small space; a hint of coconut and vanilla spice. Sweet and delicious. Damn, I'll bet she tastes good. With that thought, my eyes drop to her mouth and I realize I've lost the battle. Her tenacity has won her this round.

"I came to get your name." My voice is low as I fight reaching for her; wrapping my hands in those curls, tasting those lips.

Her eyes fly open wide and her jaw drops as she presses a hand to her chest. "You don't remember it?" she nearly cries, feigning shock.

"You didn't give it to me."

"No, you gave it to me."

Confusion causes my brow to furrow. "What?"

Tongue in cheek before she smiles again and bats her lashes. "It's Trouble. I'm crushed. I'm also late and need to get home." She winks. "Tom's waiting for me. Good night, Officer Friendly."

"But..."

She wiggles the fingers of her bare left hand as she departs with a giggle. I had carefully noted the bare left hand earlier today. I'm observant that way, and *I'm not an asshole.* I watch as she takes her leave out the front door; the jingle bells rattling above. She climbs into a waiting Lyft out front and the car pulls away from the curb.

Have it your way, Ms. Bainbridge. I know where you live.

Hot Rod eyes me curiously, a knowing smirk tips his mouth as I take my seat at the table once again. "Surveillance, huh?"

"Yup." I sigh and take a pull of my beer. "She's a little slippery."

He laughs heartily. "Oh, Donner, the thoughts you just put in my head."

"Shut up, asshole."

Chapter 3

❄ Haley ❄

My slow crawl to the third floor is exhausting. It's been a long day. A big presentation this morning, grocery shopping this afternoon in 95 degree heat with equal humidity index, then meeting with those same clients this evening at Spanky's to sign the contract to be the new influencer face for *Keep It Real* cosmetics. Lest we forget Officer Friendly...twice! The face of a model and a butt Tom Ford and Levi's would pay double for. Hell, I'd take him to dinner myself, *if* I weren't on a hiatus from men.

I could take the elevator, but taking the stairs gives me the opportunity to check on my MIPs. Myrtle, Frank and Stanley live on the second floor of our building; I'm on the top. The entire third floor that covers the expanse of their apartments below. I'm the woman who can hear them if they pound on the ceiling with a broomstick. Should they suffer an accident in the night, I'll be at their beck and call. If they holler out, "Help! I've fallen and I can't get up!", I'll be their medical alert person because they're too damn stubborn to wear the button. *"Buttons are for old people"*. I keep three baby monitors – one for each of their apartments – in mine so I can hear them. They drive me crazy and keep me grounded at the same time.

They adopted me nearly seven months ago when I moved into this building. I'm their *foster wild child* and they're my *bonus grandparents*. *Stubborn, feisty, lovable grandparents.*

Nighttime is my typical time to work. No interruptions – short of Frank's and Stanley's snoring – but I can turn the monitors down to virtual silence and I would still hear them. I'm an influencer for six cosmetic companies and three clothing designers. I make bank – well enough to live quite comfortably and stash away a very nice cache of savings every month.

My comfort zone is small – my circle of friends even smaller. I'm not really a people person. It's easy to smile for a camera, make videos; knowing you can fix the flaws, do it over, make it perfect if you fail the first, second, or even third time. It's like visiting with a long lost friend when you speak to your followers, show them the latest trends, share secrets for tricks of the trade. You wanna shrink those pores? Here ya go. You want to eat the muffin, but not wear one? Check out these new control top jeans. They're like family. I love my job!

I tap lightly on Myrtle's door first. "Come on in, Skeeter!" Frank calls out from inside. I smile at his nickname for me, until the pungent odor of cigar smoke hits my nose.

Turning the knob, I open the door and nearly gag. "What are you doing?!" I scowl when I see him blow a heavy cloud of lung killer into the air. It's not a question. He knows it, so doesn't bother to reply. I step forward and snatch the disgusting stogey from his chubby fingers and snuff it out in the ashtray.

The three of them sit at the table with cards in their hands. *Guess I only have one door to knock on tonight.* Myrtle lifts a lady cigar to her mouth, pulls a long drag and blows perfect smoke rings toward the ceiling. "Poker," she says lightly after three rings have left her scarlet lipstick stained mouth. "You in for a hand?"

"Stanley!" I scold when I see his bare chest. The air conditioning is set to 75 degrees in here. It certainly doesn't warrant stripping your clothes off. "Where the hell is your shirt?"

He tips his chin toward his poker pal. "Myrtle's got it. Won it fair and square in the first hand. Full house to my two pair." He looks up and grins. "Frank ain't got no pants on."

"Myrtle!" I glare at her in disbelief. "You didn't say *strip* poker."

She moves her bare foot out from under the table and lifts it proudly. "They only got one shoe outta me. I'm not showing these idiots the goods."

Pressing the heels of my palms to my eyeballs, I groan a little. "Stanley, put your shirt on. Myrtle, put your butt out in the ashtray. Frank put your butt back in your pants. Shame on you. You've had a heart attack. You know better than to smoke."

"I didn't inhale," he argues. "I was only tastin' it."

"That's what food is for." I snatch the thin cigar from Myrtle's fingers and take it and the ashtray to the kitchen.

"You weren't here for Myrt's tuna casserole," Frank calls out after me. "You woulda been smokin' *and* drinkin'."

The slap she lays on his arm is as loud as her threat. "Fine, you ungrateful mule. I'm gonna cream your corn at Thanksgiving."

"You ain't fixing Thanksgiving dinner," he retorts with a sly grin. "Haley is."

Her laugh is evil as the devil's own as she informs him, "I got me a coffee grinder and milk. It's only your serving I'll be creaming. Keep it up you ol' coot and I'll steal your dentures. You'll be eating tofu instead of turkey."

"Aw, Myrty," Stanley coos, taking her hand in his. "He's just teasing. Your tuna casserole was delicious. He ate three helpings."

"It was corned beef hash, you fools!" Myrtle hollers.

Frank snorts then chuckles. "Well, that would explain why it didn't taste like tuna casserole."

Both Stanley and Frank burst into laughter. "We're just pullin' on your leg, Myrty," Stanley tells her with a wink. "But that's only 'cuz you won't let us pull on your panties."

My eyes are closed as I lean on the counter, patiently waiting for them to finish tonight's geriatric banter. Thanksgiving dinner ought to be a real blast. When I found out they were going to the Senior Center for their meal – because they have no other place to go – the four of us immediately sat down together and planned a menu. I'm no master chef, but my skills with mac and cheese and a can of Spaghetti-Os have vastly improved over the past few months. I've even learned how to cut a sub sandwich without bleeding...profusely. How hard can it be to cook a turkey, peel potatoes, cut up veggies, and bake some pies?

Oh, how the mighty hath fallen.

Chapter 4

❄ Donner ❄

It's a three-story, brick building. Looks a little more like a former mansion converted into a multiplex, but with its own parking lot. Nice neighborhood. Tall palm trees, full shrubs, wrought iron fence around the perimeter, well kept, quiet.

Gator Springs is a tiny suburb north of The Villages and south of Summerfield in central Florida. The traffic inside the slice of paradise is minimal, not a heavily patrolled neighborhood. Two miles outside the tiny pocket tucked away in its own little world is where things get crazy. That's where we were on Monday.

I drove past her building twice yesterday and once again today while on a totally unnecessary patrol. The butt-ugly car sat in the lot; same parking space both days, seemingly unmoved from the last time she'd errantly parked. The right front wheel nearly touching the yellow line while the left rear wheel kissed the one on the other side. Seems Ms. Bainbridge could benefit from some lessons in parking. If it weren't a private lot, I'd wait for her to show up and threaten a ticket for illegal parking. At the very least, *sloppy* parking. It would be one way to interact with the spitfire once again.

Still in uniform and on my way home Wednesday evening, I decide to take one more trip past the apartment building at 165 Pelican Way. She apparently wasn't going away for the holiday; not with a trunk full of food. But her car hasn't moved since Monday.

A well-check. That's what I'll call it. The neighbors were concerned.

Taking the stairs to the second floor, I glance down a short hallway and find 2C easily. There are three doors on this floor, each with a paper turkey decoration hanging from it. Examining the decorations closer as I pass each one, I nearly laugh out loud. The first is a laid back turkey on a beach with a cigar hanging from its beak. The speech bubble reads, "I'd rather bake in the sun than roast in the oven". The next one is a grinning turkey with a cigarette hanging from his beak. The speech bubble reads: "I'd rather smoke than be smoked". The third one – the one at 2C – is a turkey wiping its brow with its wing, a bra tagged "minimizer" on the ground. The speech bubble reads: "Whew! I have a newfound respect for busty women everywhere. Safe for another year".

I knock on 2C and watch as shadows move under the threshold before hearing shuffling on the other side as well as hushed voices. Before too long, the door opens and on the other side stands a replica of what is commonly referred to as 'blue hairs' or 'snowbirds' here in Florida. AKA: little old ladies.

She's short, a slight pinkish tint in her hair, bright red lipstick, and an impish smile that reminds me of my grandmother. She slowly assesses me from my head to my toes and back up again. It's quite a stretch as she can't be more than a buck twenty and barely five feet tall.

"Oh my!" she breathes heavily, placing a hand to her chest and fingering the pearls around her neck. "Aren't you a tall drink of champagne, though I must admit I never did like the way the bubbles tickled my nose. My drink of choice is vodka tonics, but I wouldn't kick you to the curb. Christmas has come early to my house."

"Ma'am." I dip my chin, hiding my grin at her flirty greeting. "I'm looking for Myrtle Bainbridge. She drives the green Hyundai Sonata in the parking lot?"

Her gaze flits to the side momentarily as if she's distracted then back to me, tilts her head and grins cheekily. "Has she been naughty, officer?"

My chuckle is soft as I shake my head. "No, ma'am."

Her eyes twinkle with mischief as her brows rise. *Definitely reminds me of my grandmother.* "What would you do to her if you found her? Cuff her? Spank her? Strip her down and do a cavity check?"

Okay, maybe my grandmother after a bottle of gin.

An angry hissing sound followed by a thump draws her attention in the same direction her eyes flitted moments ago and she clears her throat. "That's the, uh...cat. Feisty little feline."

"I only want to speak with her, ma'am," I reassure her.

"That's all?" Her mouth twists in disappointment and she sighs. "What a shame. I was so hopeful. I'm Myrtle Bainbridge. Whaddaya want with me, copper?"

"You're Myrtle Bainbridge?"

My skepticism must be apparent because she tips her chin as if insulted and places her hands on her hips. "One and the same. Loud, proud, and still quite a looker. Just depends on who you ask."

"You'll get no argument from me." I grin in an attempt to stay on her good side and to get the new information I'm now seeking. "Would you happen to have a granddaughter?"

"Got a grandson," she answers stiffly as her eyes take in another drink from my head to my toes. "But he lives in California and I don't think he's your type."

"No ma'am," I reply with a chuckle. "Do you drive the green Sonata?"

Her eyes flit to the right again as if seeking answers from someone else in the room. "Occasionally. Why do you ask?"

Now, I can either piss Myrtle off or aim for the target that I suspect is listening to every bit of this conversation. Her driving skills were her Achilles heel on Monday. So defensive about who was in the right after giving me multiple opportunities.

"Have you considered a refresher driving course? Maybe even honing your parking skills? I couldn't help but notice the angle of the car in the space it's in. That could get you a ticket if it were in a public spot."

A gasp comes from inside followed by a low growl. She's here, hiding. She's not Myrtle Bainbridge, *thank God,* but at least I'll know where to find her.

"Does your cat always growl like that, Ms. Bainbridge?" The corner of my mouth tips in a smirk as my brows rise, and we exchange a mutual knowing glance.

She titters then glances to the right, grinning impishly. "It could be worse, officer. At least this one doesn't sit around licking herself."

Oh Myrtle, the thoughts that planted in my head.

Chapter 5

❄ Haley ❄

"If your bones weren't brittle, I would slap you!" I glare at a smirking Myrtle, who is totally unaffected by my words as she climbs off of her one-step booster after studying the nosey departing stalker through the peephole in her door.

Officer Friendly has finally left. Myrtle turns, hand on her hip, grinning like the Cheshire cat – one she doesn't happen to own by the way. She's allergic. Though at the present time I'm considering a visit to the local animal shelter. A big, fat, fuzzy feline should do well.

"You've got some explaining to do, missy," she says, pointing her arthritis-ridden finger at me. "Why on earth are you hiding from a stallion like that? Back in my day I would have ridden him like…"

"Yes, Myrtle, I know," I groan, having heard the well-depicted stories of the adventures of Myrtle and friends with benefits. Who knows if any of them are true, but she tells enticing stories. She was a nurse for 43 years and happily shares the innerworkings of the hospital she spent those years in, as well as the antics of her former coworkers. They make a daytime soap look like cartoon material. "And since when do you have a grandson?"

She shrugs. "I don't. I was simply investigating his sexual preferences. One can never be too sure. Look at Rock Hudson. I thought I had a real shot with Cary Grant, too."

We watched '*An Affair to Remember*' two weeks ago. Yes, I indulge them. Just don't tell them I'm a huge fan of old movies myself. Besides, he was old enough to be her dad. I crinkle my nose and huff, "Cary Grant was not gay."

She arches a brow and narrows her eyes. "Wasn't he?" She waves a hand from her head to her toes as if to display her own goods. "He turned this down."

I shoot her a wry look and roll my eyes. "Myrtle, that was Harry Brandt, and he was moving into a nursing home the day you offered."

She flips her hand in the air in dismissal. "Harry, Cary. What's the difference?"

Slow blink, deep breath. Small wonder she has never married. Her kitchen knife supply would have come up one short within two months of the vows.

I neglect to share after feeling Officer Friendly's semi against my ass on Monday, I can assure her his preferences are definitely of the female persuasion. Admittedly, it was partially my fault. I may have wiggled against him...more than once. But pulsing the pad of his thumb against the palm of my hand? You know, like he'd do if he were flicking my... Hey, buddy, two can play that game.

Her lips pursed, forehead wrinkled even more than usual, and her arms crossed over her chest, she demands, "So, what's wrong with him?"

"Just not my type," I lie with a casual shrug.

She cackles. "Sweetie, he's everybody's type. Did you see him walking away? I could bounce a quarter off that damn thing!"

I close my eyes and shake my head, ready to end this conversation. "I gotta go prep for dinner tomorrow."

"Did you buy Band-Aids?" She laughs. I don't.

"I bought a muzzle to put on you before and after we eat." I smile slyly. "And if you don't behave, I'll be putting Metamucil in your pumpkin pie."

She smirks. "Put enough vodka in my glass and I won't care."

"Goodnight, Myrtle."

"Love you, darling."

My phone lies on the counter as I chop veggies for the tray that will eventually go in the fridge, while one of my favorite people keeps me company.

"You're fixing Thanksgiving dinner?" my little sister Halston's voice shrieks through the speaker. "For your neighbors? Aren't they like old people?"

"They're getting up there in years, but they're fun. You'd like them."

"Haley, you don't know how to cook for yourself," she reminds me. "How do you cook for old people? Don't they require special diets? Things like chicken pot pie? Meatloaf? I don't know, maybe oatmeal?"

"It's Thanksgiving, Halston! You need turkey!" I pull my finger back from the paring knife I'm wielding a nanosecond before I slice through the tip of it. Maybe multitasking isn't a good idea. I have five videos to record for tomorrow and set on a timer to release throughout the day. Those are going to require three full face makeup applications and five outfit changes.

I'm baking the pies in the morning. I'll put the turkey in the oven at ten, peel the potatoes at noon and put them on to boil at one, rolls in the oven when the turkey comes out at two to rest, stuffing on the stove at two while the rolls bake. Sit down and eat between half past two and three o'clock. I've studied the menu and schedule so many times over the past week, I have it virtually memorized. Good thing my guests are flexible – figuratively.

"Halston, I have to go or I'm going to be rinsing my blood off the veggies."

"Wait!" she shrieks. "I almost forgot. Norton called yesterday. Wanted to know if he could get your number. He said he's been watching your videos and thinking about you."

"What?!"

Funny, he wasn't thinking about me while he was banging his secretary on his desk!

"Yup," she says with a pop. "I told him you'd been swept off your feet by a New York billionaire. You're living the high life in a high rise on the east side of Manhattan. Getting big dick on the regular that isn't being shared with the office staff."

"Halston," I breathe an exasperated sigh. "You could have simply said no."

"Hey!" she chastises. "If you'd heard his disappointment, you'd be thanking me. Nobody messes with my big sister."

"Thanks, Hals. I love you."

"Love you too, sis." She bursts into a fit of giggles. "Better brush up on the CPR skills before serving that dinner tomor…" I disconnect before she can finish. Leave it to Halston to put a smile on my face, laced with a touch of irritation. So…he's been watching my videos, huh? Oh, Norton. Will you never learn?

The veggie tray is finished and set in the fridge. All ten of my digits remain intact. I had turned on my music after the call with Halston. Didn't dance until I'd finished chopping, but once the knife was put down, my hips were swaying and the mood was flowing.

And here I am in my recording room. Circle lights are set, my mood is on point, makeup is perfecto, and the first outfit is ready to show. Lights, camera, action. My smile spreads from ear to ear. My eyes light with excitement. Tonight, it's not just for them, it's for me as well.

"Have I got some products for you! But before we get started, I'd like to share a secret I've come across lately. The new year is coming up soon and I've been cleaning out my closets. Sometimes, when you open a closet, you look inside and it's like 'what was I thinking?' They're wrinkled, ugly, too small..." My eyes flash a wicked gleam. "I call them Nortons. So, what do you say, ladies? Shall we make a pact to clean out all the ugly Nortons in our lives and replace them with *bigger,* better things between now and Christmas when they're on sale? Let's start with..."

I begin to model the outfit I'm wearing and show the multiple choice colors offered. I blast that video out of the water with a smile on my face, nearly dancing from beginning to the end. *Take that, you asshole!*

Finishing the first, I move on to the next, then the next, and so on. I proof the videos, set the release times, shut down the equipment, turn off the lights, blow a kiss via my middle finger in honor of Norton, and say goodnight before closing the door. My job here is done.

Closure. The final nail I hadn't given myself the opportunity to hammer into the coffin. At 28 years old, I needed it. Thank you, Halston.

I'd spent three years of my life with that man. Three years that I will never get back, including upending my life for a move to Seattle for his job. The first year wasn't all bad, the second one was okay, but by the third it was meh. He was doing his thing, I was supposed to wait until he was done doing his thing. Then I found out exactly what his thing was; his secretary. Bent over his desk, skirt up, moaning as if he were delivering the best thing since the creation of apple pie. Believe me, he wasn't. She was either a very good actress or extremely stupid.

I had walked in unannounced, and apparently unnoticed. I stood for a moment, taking it all in, shocked and hurt, but more numb than anything. Refusing to be humiliated, I chanted with a wave of my hand, "Excuse me for interrupting. Carry on." I turned fast to leave, pulling the door closed so hard it rattled.

I was at his secretary's desk by the time he screamed my name behind me. "Haley! Haley, wait!" He had said wait, hadn't he? It was right there, on the edge of her desk. Inspiration at its finest. Coincidence? I thought not. It was heavy, perfect actually. So I picked it up. Probably three pounds or so – maybe five. I threw it...hard; hitting him square in the middle of his forehead. Oh, the sight of my fiancé lying flat on the floor felt good. The tail of his dress shirt sticking out of the zipper opening of his pants versus the dick he had just had inside his secretary; his belt undone, blood now gushing from the wound on his forehead. Out cold. The paper "weight" lying on the floor next to him.

The secretary dropped to the floor onto her likely well-worn knees beside him. "Y-you killed him!"

"Only in my dreams," I deadpanned before pushing open the heavy glass door that led to the elevators.

It was the best and healthiest thing I could have done for myself.

That was the last time I saw Norton. Seven months ago. I went back to our condo, packed up as much as I could load into my car, drained my back account, and headed to Florida; the farthest point in the country from Seattle. During that drive, I found myself again. I can do my job from anywhere, and right here seems to fit me just fine. My parents live in Georgia, so we're not that far from each other. Halston lives in Destin, about two hours away. Looks like we'll be spending Christmas together this year.

Chapter 6

❄ Haley ❄

The alarm goes off at seven o'clock sharp, and I roll over long enough to lift it and swipe the screen for an extra five minutes of slumber. Then I rise with the next reminder as George Thorogood sings, "Move It On Over". *Don't judge!* If I can't have a sexy man to wake up next to, I want a sexy growly voice to wake me up.

The hot water does little to motivate me. Officer Friendly visited me last night. Not physically – unless of course you count the visit to Myrtle's – but in my dream. Did he really think my name was Myrtle? In my dream he was asking for my name again; close enough to brush my hair away from my face ever so gently, then tip my chin up and lean in to…

"No!" I scold myself out loud, slamming the faucet off. The goosebumps spread on my skin as if I've just stepped into a deep freeze as I shake off the last thoughts of that dream. "Get to work, Haley. You're fixing a feast for four today and you don't even know how to cook."

It's a tiny town we live in. Not like we can order out if I screw this up. We'll be driving an hour away to find a restaurant to feed us if my dinner comes out less than palatable. I'm worried about palatable? Let's work on edible, Haley. Safety first. Big Tom wasn't thawed after all when I got home on Monday. Barely had a squishy spot on him. The Cool Whip, ice cream and pies though? Those put Officer Friendly on my shit list. I had to replace them all.

Sliding into comfy clothes – AKA leggings and a T-shirt – I make my way to the kitchen. Pies in the oven first. Mix the veggie dip while they bake.

An hour and a half later, I'm removing two perfectly baked pies from my oven; one pumpkin, one apple.

"Ha!" the three people in the room – me, myself, and I – shout out loud. "Take that Martha Stewart. They even smell good, too!"

I pull Tom out of the fridge and begin to prepare him for the oven. Reading the directions again after cutting off his wrapper, I wrinkle my nose. "Salt and pepper the inside? Why? Who in the hell eats the inside of a turkey?" I question the instructions as I read further down. "Stuff it? With what? I bought Stove Top brand." Peering inside the gaping hole between his plump drumsticks, I see it's prefilled. Oh, that must be what they mean. I laugh out loud to myself. They did it for me. I'll have to write the Butterball company and thank them. I toss a little salt and pepper toward the opening and call it complete, then move on to the rest of the bird; massaging him with a stick of butter and meticulously sprinkling salt and pepper onto the skin evenly over the entire surface.

A quick glance at the clock indicates it is drumroll time. I look at the roasting pan in front of me that holds the main dish for the day. "Major Tom, you've given your all for the mouths of many. It will be my honor to have you on my table." I salute the fine featherless friend in the pan before hoisting him into the oven and closing the door. Maybe I should have done a prayer.

Scratch that. An entire litany.

I'm peeling potatoes over the colander in the sink when the phone rings at noon.

"Hey mom," I answer cheerily. "Happy Thanksgiving."

"Hi, sweetheart." She chuckles softly before adding, "Your sister tells me you're cooking today. How is your adventure in the culinary arts going so far?"

"Going great," I reply with a song in my voice, and my heart as it really is coming together quite well. "I've made a veggie tray with dip and baked two pies, and still have all my fingers and my thumbs and not a blister in sight. My apartment smells like a five star restaurant. Bobby Flay would be singing my praises if he were here right now."

"I'm very proud of you, Haley," she says with a laugh. "I hope those people you're cooking for appreciate you."

"I'm sure they do." I picture the four of us sitting at the table a couple hours from now and smile. If all goes well today, maybe mom will let me help cook for Christmas in her house. Other than setting the table and polishing the silver, dinner at mom's is pretty much a one-woman show.

"Well, I'll let you get back to it," she says. "Happy Thanksgiving, sweetheart. I love you. Daddy says him too. We'll see you at Christmas."

An hour and a half later, the potatoes are at a rolling boil on the stovetop when I detect an unpleasant rubbery odor. I glance around the kitchen, searching for anything that might be out of place; a towel too close to a burner, a spill on the stovetop, a spatula melting somewhere. A sudden long hiss followed by a loud pop from inside the oven below startles me, but it's the orange flame that bursts from behind the glass in the door that sends me into full panic mode. Smoke billows from inside the oven, making its way out of the vents in ugly shades of black and gray.

"What the hell!?!" I throw open the oven door so fast it rattles the pot of potatoes on top. The boiling water splatters over the surface and down onto the grease splattered on the inside of the door from the flaming turkey, intensifying not only the flames but increasing the amount of smoke tenfold. Smoke alarms sound throughout the apartment as the sprinklers begin to spray from the ceiling.

I snatch a hand towel off the counter and bat at the burning turkey to douse the flames. The towel catches on the handle of the roasting pan and is soon engulfed in flames as well.

"No!" I scream in horror, running for the cupboard under the sink to grab the fire extinguisher. On the way, my feet take a little side trip as I slip and slide on grease that has splattered out onto the floor, landing on my ass and elbows. The retched odor of the smoke and something else is overwhelming and burns my lungs.

Pounding on my door followed by Frank and Stanley's hollering is joined by the sound of sirens in the distance.

"Haley!" Stanley hollers. "Open up."

"Skeeter! We're comin' in!" Frank calls.

"Turn the knob, you idiots! Bust the door down if you have to!" Myrtle screeches. "Go save our girl!"

All hell breaks loose while I play slip and slide before finding my way to my knees. "Don't come over here! You'll fall and break a hip!" I choke through sputtered coughs before any of the geriatric trio can cross over onto the kitchen floor.

"Hank," a deep voice orders behind them. "Get them outta here. Folks, we got her. Don't worry."

Strong arms lift me off the floor while the intermittent spurts and blasts of fire extinguishers are being sprayed behind me as he carries me out the door.

"Kitchen fire," another voice says behind us. "Flames are out. Got a lot of smoke to deal with. Can you guys smell that? That don't smell like food to me."

"Tom," I sputter between coughs in the arms I haven't put a face to yet. "That's Tom burning."

The man that's holding me stops on the stairs mid step. "You got a cat in there we need to rescue?"

"No. I incinerated Tom," I whimper, dropping my head back on his strong arm, feeling dizzy and lightheaded. "He died in vain."

"Murphy!" he calls back up the steps. "You'd better call in some backup as well as forensics. Think she was burning more than dinner."

Spots dance in my vision as I stare up at the ceiling on our way down the stairs – the beefy arms holding me, bouncing with every step – before succumbing to darkness.

I've died. I must have. It's Karma. She's come to deliver her vengeance.

I should never have named my turkey!

Chapter 7

❄ *Donner* ❄

"All available units, report to 165 Pelican Way, Gator Springs. Fire has been contained. Suspect is being detained by fire officials." The dispatcher's voice interrupts my thoughts of blonde curls, a peach-shaped ass, and a smart mouth while I sit at a speed trap off Sterling and 12th.

Aw shit. Two hours left on my shift. It's a holiday for God's sake! A holiday preceding five days off for me. I've been eight days on, doing massive favors for guys with families so they can...

Wait a minute! Suspect? 165 Pelican Way? That's Myrtle's address.

I hit the lights and siren and head north as fast as the gas pedal and wheels allow. Two fire engines, the station truck, and one ambulance sit in front of the building that houses the spunky little old lady – who just so happens to be arguing with the fire chief about thirty feet away from the ambulance. Two elderly gentlemen stand beside her, hands in the air as if readying for battle.

"Donner!" Jizz calls out as I climb out of my car. "You're gonna love this one."

Lifting my hand in a quick wave, I head for the group of senior citizens and fire chief. I don't see the blonde spitfire anywhere.

"Ma'am," the flustered chief explains for what sounds like the hundredth time. "She's already admitted to committing a crime. She's not seriously injured. We're waiting for law enforcement. I cannot let you talk to her right now."

"What did she admit to?!" Myrtle demands. "Bad cooking skills?"

"I cannot disclose anything that was said," the chief tells them.

"The only crime Skeeter would commit is an act of kindness, you jackass!" one man yells. "Now let us see our girl."

Skeeter?

"Chief Anders," I greet him calmly as I approach. I nod to the others and acknowledge the squat fireball, "Ms. Bainbridge."

An angry Myrtle glares and tips her chin. "About time you showed up, Butt Cheeks. Now tell this butthead to let us go see our Haley. She coulda died up there!"

Haley. It's beautiful. Fits her.

The chief nods toward the rescue vehicles. "We'll talk over there."

As we reach the dedicated spot the chief has chosen, I glance toward the ambulance. It's her: the sound of sunshine when she laughs. Her hair is a disastrous mess of mussy blonde curls, skin pale with streaks of gray mixed with tears down her cheeks, an oxygen mask over her face, and a blanket around her shoulders. The pull to run to her, hold her in my arms and let her tell me her side of the story is strong, but I'm on duty. And a bit like Monday, duty outranks Donner, jr.

My eyes remain fixed on the blue-eyed wonder as I query, "Is she okay?"

"She'll be fine," the chief huffs.

"Let's hear it."

The chief sighs heavily, shaking his head. "She confessed to," he uses air quotes, "incinerating a guy."

My eyebrows lift in shock. "To what!?"

"We're waiting on forensics. We'll have what you need once they collect the evidence. Right now, EMTs are giving her oxygen for smoke inhalation and then you guys can take over." He looks back to her and furrows his brow. "Damndest thing I've ever heard. Using Thanksgiving as an opportunity to cook a guy in the oven."

Oh, Trouble, you didn't. Pinching the bridge of my nose, I can't be sure if I'm trying to hold my temper or temper my laughter. "Who did she confess to?"

"Everhart."

Figures. "Call him over."

Everhart struts toward us after being summoned and smiles cockily. "Got us a real nutcase today, Donner. It's always the hot ones, too. Damn shame."

I resist punching him though it takes effort. His highest point of pride isn't being a public servant; it's the calendar he poses for every year. Rumor has it he stuffs a sock in it, but I don't shower with him and quite frankly, I don't have two shits to give.

"What exactly did she say?"

"I was carrying her out of the building when she started whining and crying out for Tom. I thought maybe she had a cat, but she denied it. Then she confessed to incinerating Tom and that he died in vain. Murphy reported a funky smell." He shrugs casually and pastes on a smug grin. "Guess she figured she'd been caught."

Memories of Monday flash through my mind. *Tom.* Nineteen pounds, four ounces. That impish smile. My cuffs on her wrists. The feel of her back to my front. The scent of her hair.

I look to the chief. "The only thing forensics is going to find is a burnt turkey." Then I look to the smug moron standing next to him – pissed off at the thought of her in his arms – and roll my eyes. "By the name of Tom."

"Uh, guys." Murphy captures our attention as he saunters toward us from the door of her building then eyes us all one by one. "Any of you ever cook a turkey?"

Everhart laughs obnoxiously as if it's the most ridiculous thing he's ever heard. The chief chuckles, and I simply answer – tongue in cheek, "Still let my mom do the cooking at the holidays, Murphy. Why?"

"That shit they stuff inside when they pack 'em," he says, questioning, "you're supposed to take that out before you cook 'em, aren't you? I know my mom does. Calls 'em giblets."

"I think so," the chief tells him. "My wife stuffs ours with cornbread dressing."

"Well." Murphy crinkles his nose and nods toward the ambulance where Haley sits. "She didn't take it out. They wrap that shit in plastic lined paper. It stinks pretty bad. Kinda exploded. Giblets all over the place."

My eyes do a slow blink between glaring from one idiot to the next. "And you thought she murdered someone because of the odor?"

"No!" Murphy denies vehemently. "That's on Everhart. I only said something smelled funky."

Everhart throws his hands out to his sides and shrugs. "I took the lady at her word. She confessed to incinerating Tom."

Running a frustrated hand through my hair, I grip the back of my neck. "You owe her an apology."

Everhart huffs loudly. "What would you have thought if some chick confessed to burning a dude in her oven?"

Not willing to admit to having been played earlier in the week as well, I smirk. "I would have asked her if she planned on eating him after he was cooked."

Murphy laughs and slaps my shoulder. "You made your own Donner joke! Good on you."

Everhart crosses his arms over his chest, appreciatively studying the dejected, but still beautiful blonde in the back of the ambulance. He bobs his eyebrows and grins. "Think she'd go to dinner with me if I beg forgiveness?"

"Only one way to find out." I arch a brow and dip my chin, leaving no room for doubt. "But tell me, Everhart, how are you going to eat without any teeth?"

I leave two grinning firefighters and one slack-jawed idiot behind me as I make my way to the ambulance. Her shoulders are slumped and she sits cross-legged in the back of the ambulance as she stares at the ground. My shoes appear in her vision and she slowly looks up. Recognition flashes and tears pool.

"Hey, Trouble," I say softly, then smile as if I've won a prize and reach out, twirling a blonde curl with one finger. "So, Haley, huh?"

She tears off the oxygen mask, jumps to her feet like a professional gymnast, takes a dive off the back of the ambulance, and throws herself into my arms. "I swear to God, I didn't know turkeys were flammable!"

She feels good in my arms; perfect really. Her soft to my hard. Her chest pressed against mine. The way her chin fits into the crook of my neck with her arms wrapped around my shoulders feels like a second skin. Her legs wrapped around my waist so tightly...Oh shit! My gun! I slide my right hand quickly from her waist toward my hip, copping – maybe – a brush of her ass cheek and thigh as I reassure my firearm is holstered properly. It's there, her thigh locked around my waist above it. My hand follows the same path in reverse to wrap around her waist again, because – well, it felt too damn good the first time.

The two EMTs and Jizz, who stand close by, burst into laughter. I turn to shoot them a glare on her behalf when Myrtle appears, cane in hand, wielding it high in the air.

"Laugh at her again and you'll need that ambulance," she threatens Jizz. "Haley, climb off the stallion, honey. You can ride him later. Let me check you for injuries."

I chuckle lightly at the little old lady's spunk, but Haley begins to sob. "I burned their dinner. The Senior Center served at noon and now they have no place to go. They're going to starve."

Myrtle taps my leg with the cane and shoots me a stern glare. "Put her down, Butt Cheeks. You're enjoying this a bit too much."

Begrudgingly, I set Haley back in the ambulance and ensure she's seated safely on the edge. Myrtle and the two men she was with join her, each one taking turns delivering a hug and words of comfort.

Murphy appears at my side. "How's the apartment?" I ask him.

He grimaces and shakes his head. "Uninhabitable. Gonna need a cleanup service. Smoke damage is pretty extensive. Kitchen is the worst. We used foam to douse the flames. She had one room with a closed door but the sprinklers still went off. She's out for probably a couple weeks minimum." He glances in her direction then back at me, crinkles his nose and whispers, "Some, uh, odd stuff in there, Donner. Round lights, lots of clothes, bins of makeup, recording equipment."

Recording equipment? What the hell?

"What about the other tenants?"

"She rents the entire top floor," he replies. "No damage below. We used foam so there was no leakage. We got the sprinklers shut down right away and they only went off in her unit. Chief wants an inspection because of it. He thinks it should have set off the entire building's system."

My jaw nearly drops. These people can't be homeless. "So they're all out?"

"No. He simply wants an inspection."

"Officer Friendly?" The meek voice comes from behind us. No lace of teasing, no giggle that I long to hear. *Yup, sunshine definitely needs a sound.*

"Officer Friendly, huh?" Murphy grins then nudges my arm. "How many tickets has she talked you out of?"

"Go back to work, Murphy."

"Happy Thanksgiving, Donner." He slaps my shoulder. "Give her a good sleigh ride and maybe Santa will be extra nice this year." He turns to walk away and slashes his hand through the air, mimicking the sound of a whip. "On Dasher, on Dancer, on Donner…" He turns back once more and bobs his eyebrows. "Play your cards right, she will be."

"Shut up, asshole."

I don't correct his error. Donner is next to last on Santa's roll call. Just as well. I would have had to listen to more. Prancer, Vixen, Comet and

Cupid are before me. Blitzen is last. Lest we forget that little prick Rudolph who saves the night at the last minute.

Chapter 8

❄ Donner ❄

Recording equipment. The words roll over in my mind before I make my way back to her. She's not one of those nighttime entertainers that keep men company over the internet, is she? Dress promiscuously, talk dirty. No, Haley wouldn't do that. She's too sweet, too innocent. Too damn beautiful.

"Can I get into my apartment?" she asks as I approach the ambulance.

"You might be able to get in, but you're not going to be able to stay, Haley."

"It's okay, Skeeter," one of the men tells her. "We'll get your stuff out and you can still record. I'll let you use my living room if you want."

"You can use mine, too," the other says. "We can switch back and forth."

"You buffoons!" Myrtle scolds. "She can't use your places. What would her customers think? What's it gonna look like with a fish head on the wall behind her?"

One man winks. "It's a whole fish, Myrt. I caught it in Lake Michigan myself! Took me two hours to reel him in."

Myrtle glares until a vein in her forehead bulges. "Fish and females do not go together, you idiot! Haley's gotta show 'em her goods with a special background."

Lovely. Just my luck. Haley is an internet hooker.

Haley looks mortified as her eyes travel a path from one senior to another and finally land on me. The EMTs and Jizz take it all in with identical wide-eyed expressions, though they do have the decency to aim their gazes elsewhere – like each other...or skyward.

She stutters through a whisper, "It's – it's not what she makes it sound like."

There's something in her eyes that looks...vulnerable. I've seen her with these people out in public, taking care of their needs, treating them like friends instead of invalids. Her first concern was them not having a meal; not whether or not she had a home.

I take a seat next to her on the back of the ambulance. "Tell me what it is you do for a living, Haley."

"I'm an influencer," she says softly. "I represent different makeup and clothing companies on social media to sell their products. I record videos and demonstrate proper usage and instructions in application." She shrugs. "I model outfits, give makeup tips."

Shows them her goods.

Had this been my little sister, she would have throttled Myrtle. But instead, Haley tolerated the little old lady's questionable description and gave me a chance to not be an asshole.

Pulling my phone from my pocket, I tap the contact that never lets me down.

"Hey there," she says cheerily. "We're running really late. Diedre's flight got delayed. Tell me you're going to make it for dinner after all."

"You wouldn't have room for four extra faces at the table besides my ugly mug, would you?"

"There's always room!" she shouts giddily. "It might make for less leftovers for you. Tell me one of them is gorgeous and has captured your heart."

"10-4 on that."

"I can't wait." She giggles. "Is six o'clock okay?"

"Perfect," I tell her. "Thanks, mom."

I scan the faces of the people Haley obviously loves. "Thanksgiving is still on. I know a really good cook and she's looking forward to meeting every one of you."

Various elderly whoops of cheer reach my ears while Haley turns and stares from next to me where she sits. "B-but, I don't even know your name."

"Of course you do." I wink and smile. "It's Officer Friendly. Guess you needed me after all. I also have three bedrooms and two baths. So after dinner, I'm taking you home with me where you're going to stay until your apartment is livable again."

She gasps. "I can stay with Myrtle. She has a sofa."

"That won't work, honey," Myrtle is quick to object; a playful lilt in her voice and a grin aimed at me. "You know my cat doesn't like to share."

Haley whirls her head toward Myrtle, scowling. "You don't have…"

"Room," Myrtle interrupts before she can call her bluff. "Sorry, Haley. You know I would sleep on the floor for you if I thought it were best. But I think Butt Cheeks here might be on to something."

"I can stay in a hotel," Haley says with weak resolve.

"It's a holiday weekend." I tip her chin up with two fingers. "You couldn't find a room within fifty miles of here."

"But, I don't even know you," she protests once more.

"Only one way to fix that, Haley." I place my arm around her shoulder and help her down from the back of the ambulance. "Let's get some of your things from the apartment. We'll come back tomorrow and get everything you need to do your work. You can either get ready for dinner at Myrtle's or I can drop you at my place. I'll come back when I'm done with work and pick you all up to go to dinner. My shift ends in an hour."

"I'm going to smell like smoke," she whispers. "My clothes are going to stink."

"I'll loan you some of mine," Myrtle offers and Haley surreptitiously grimaces. The offer is heartfelt, I'm sure, but picturing Haley in geriatric Tinkerbell clothing is rather humorous.

"I'll bring you some sweats from the station. How's that?" I proffer.

She wrinkles her nose and her mouth does the funniest little twist that makes me want to straighten it with a kiss. She eyes me skeptically. "How big?"

I place my hands on her hips, my fingers itching to squeeze the softness on the backside of them. Leaning closer I bring my mouth to her ear and whisper, "A size small T-shirt and pants to fit this perfect peach that introduced itself to my crotch on Monday." I squeeze a little harder. "Sound good?"

If anticipation had a sound, it would be...Haley's whimper.

Myrtle easily tosses the cane to one of the men who catches it in one hand like a pro. "Thanks for the loan, Stan."

"You don't need that?" I question her.

She rolls her eyes and smirks. "Oh please. I only use it as a prop for sympathy. That thing gets me to the front of the line and through the grocery store faster than a palmetto bug on a feeding frenzy." She taps her temple with her index finger. "I'm as clever as I am sexy."

Definitely my grandmother – more with the gin than without.

We pack some clothing, shoes, and toiletries for Haley to bring to my house and drop them at Myrtle's one floor down. I wasn't sure she would agree to stay with me, but Myrtle was a phenomenal advocate on my behalf.

Haley sees me to the stairwell and stands on the landing as I start my descent. Her hair is a mass of tangled curls, her face smudged with gray, her eyes a bit red from crying. She is still the most beautiful thing I've ever seen.

"I'll be back as soon as I can to pick you up for dinner. I'll bring you a change of clothes." I look up to see her chewing her bottom lip and frowning.

"Sweats aren't very proper clothing to wear to Thanksgiving dinner."

"Clothes don't make the woman, Haley." I arch a stern brow. "And they're not going to care."

She nods and turns for the hall. "If you say so, Officer Friendly."

"Haley?" She glances back, brows lifted. "It's Finn."

She tilts her head as she studies my face. "Finn," she repeats softly. 34 years I've heard my name spoken, but never has it sounded the way it does when she says it. I want to hear her whisper it. Hell, I want to hear her scream it. She smiles mischievously. "I like it. But I kinda like Officer Friendly, too."

"See you soon, Trouble." I leave her giggling above me as I make my way out the door.

Yeah, sunshine definitely has a sound.

Chapter 9

❄ Haley ❄

I head down the hall toward Myrtle's apartment. Cat, my ass. She's simply grinning like the one that ate the canary as she peeks through the opening of her door.

"You!" I whisper shout, pointing a hard finger in her direction and charge past her into the apartment.

She tips her chin indignantly. "Yes, me. And when your wedding bells are ringing, you can thank me, young lady. I see the way he looks at you. Now, get in the shower and wash the grease off."

"Wedding bells," I grumble and snatch my essentials bag off the floor, heading for the bathroom. "The only aisle I plan on walking down is at the grocery store. No thanks."

"Haley Vixen!" she scolds, following at my heels like the puppy dog she also doesn't own. "Mark my words, young lady, this is your last Christmas being one of Santa's reindeer." I whirl around and glare. Her eyes light with mischief as she grins. "You can still be a sexy vixen. Maybe he'll call you his little minx."

My jaw clenches tightly and I huff, "Just for that, I'm not helping you with your makeup."

She points to her mouth and singsongs, "Already applied the Rambunctious Red. I left you a robe on the back of the door, sweetie." I slam the bathroom door behind me. Oh my God! The hem of this thing will barely reach the bottom of my ass cheeks.

And yes, you heard correctly. *Haley Vixen*. The little siren. Santa's sexy reindeer. All my life. Well, once I grew boobs anyway. Halston and I have both suffered the consequences of an inconvenient surname. We'd heard worse: Dr. Woodcock. Tom Hollopeter. Dick Wiener. Jennifer Wales (she really did). Probably shouldn't have had sex for the first time under the bleachers during halftime at the football game.

❄ ❄ ❄

Finn arrives an hour and a half later with a size small, cotton soft, Summerfield PD T-shirt and pair of sweats that hug my form a little too well. Perfect for lounging with an old movie, a pint of ice cream, and a bottle of wine – at home, all by yourself!

"Ready," I mutter reluctantly as I enter the living room to find a waiting Finn and Myrtle. My eyes nearly bulge out of their sockets as I take in a T-shirt and jeans-clad Finn. GQ really is missing a model, but I'm sure not returning him.

Finn reaches for my suitcase. "Where's your other bag?"

"Uh." I glance around the room as if searching for a lost shoe. I thought if I left something behind, I could come back after dinner and talk Myrtle into housing me until my apartment was habitable.

"Go get the rest of your things, Haley." He lifts an expectant brow then nods toward the hallway. "They're coming with you, to my place."

"I love a conscientious man, don't you?" Myrtle singsongs as she tucks her arm in his. "He wants to make sure you have everything you need. Hurry up, Haley. Let's not keep our hosts waiting."

"Where's the cat, Myrtle?" I grind through a clenched jaw.

She laughs evilly. "I let her out of the bag, dear. Now get moving."

As I make my way down the hall to the bathroom, Myrtle's not so subtle warning is unmistakable. "Hurt her, Butt Cheeks, and you will be fish food."

Frank and Stanley wait in the hallway and we all step onto the small elevator; seniors first, Finn and I following. The five of us together make for very cramped quarters, but it's doable.

"Did you give him the warning?" Stanley whispers behind us.

"You betcha," Myrtle replies.

"Did you tell him Groupers' favorite body part is the testicles?" Frank adds.

Finn's lips twitch as he feigns oblivion to their conversation.

I turn slowly and eye them one by one as the elevator doors open. "Are you quite finished?"

Myrtle nods sharply. "I believe I got my point across."

We exit onto the first floor and Finn steps off to the side so as to let the rest of us walk ahead of him. He gently reaches for my elbow to halt my footsteps, then slides his hand up my arm to the side of my neck. With his thumb under my chin, he tips it up so my gaze meets his.

"You can trust me, Haley. I promise."

In the parking lot sits a black Ford Expedition that elicits whistles from both Frank and Stanley. Finn loads my bags in the back while Frank climbs in the backseat on one side and Stanley opens the door on the other.

Myrtle's five foot stature places her at approximately *not gonna happen* level. She raises her arms in the air and calls out, "Need a lift, Butt Cheeks." Finn arrives immediately and gingerly lifts her by the waist with two large hands, and places her on the seat. "I think we need to do that again," she says breathlessly. "Just for practice."

"Myrtle." I shake my head and scold, "Slide your butt over to the middle and buckle up." *Little hussy.*

Twenty minutes later we pull into the long double driveway of a beautiful ranch style home in Summerfield. It's white with red shutters, and a tiled roof displaying Santa perched in a sleigh behind eight reindeer. A little early for Christmas decorations, but I suppose hung *now* versus *still* hung in July is preferred. Multicolor lights adorn every gutter and post as well as the trees and bushes in the yard.

Finn once again helps Myrtle as we exit the vehicle and offers his elbow to her and takes my hand in his on the walk toward the house.

"Oh look!" Myrtle shouts with a giggle, pointing up at the rooftop. "I recognize one of those. I believe it's the one in the second row and…"

"Myrtle," I warn. "Keep walking."

As we reach the front step, I look up and freeze. Oh, this is definitely Karma. Must not have gotten her fill for the day. Over the front door hangs a large decorative wooden sign. *"Welcome to the Donner Home"*

My voice is weak and my question comes out more of a squeak as I turn to Finn. "Your name is Donner?"

Myrtle cackles loudly beside us as the front door opens. "Oh, this is too good. We'll let you kids iron this one out." She calls up to whoever stands at the door, "You can greet them in a while. In the meantime, I'm Myrtle, this is Frank and Stanley. Why don't we go inside and have a drink?"

"Sounds good," the deep timbred voice replies with a laugh. The door closes a few moments later and we're left standing at the bottom of the steps.

"Yes, Trouble," Finn says on a drawn out groan. "My last name is Donner. Go ahead, get it out of your system."

"Like the reindeer?" My nose crinkles and I glance up at him warily. "Or the people eaters?"

"Depends." He reaches out and twirls a lock of my hair in his fingers, his blue eyes growing a shade darker as his lids lower in a heated gaze. "Do you like reindeer, and is it you I get to feast on?"

Now I know it's not the Florida heat warming body parts I've ignored for months. We stand frozen, our eyes locked, each one daring the other to look away first. As if it has a mind of its own, my tongue peeks out to moisten my lips, and I watch as his eyes follow its path.

"Oh, what the hell," he groans as if he can't help himself. His hands dive into my curls, pulling my face toward his. Our mouths crash together as if they're old lovers reunited after years apart – strangely familiar yet a deep need to reacquaint. He tilts my head so his mouth fits perfectly over mine. His facial hair is a blissful mix of bristly and soft; a teasing fantasy of how it would feel between...

"Damn," he whispers softly against my mouth when the kiss ends. "I usually have dessert after dinner."

He must hear, or feel, the unsurety in my shuddered breaths because he pulls back and studies my face. "Haley," he says reassuringly. "You set the pace here. I offered you my home because you need it. I want you, not gonna lie. But I want you to be comfortable, too. Okay?" He takes my hand in his and leads me up the stairs to the porch. "Let's go eat." He shoots me a wry look. "Food, not people."

"Would you explain to your mother it's best she keep me out of the kitchen? I'd probably burn that down too – or break all her China." A tear leaks onto my cheek as I recall the disaster of a day I've caused for everyone.

Finn pulls me into a one-armed hug before we reach the door. "Trouble, the only thing you're going to break is my heart." He lifts my chin with two fingers and swipes a tear with his thumb. "Because I can't stand to see you cry. They're just things, and they're replaceable. You're not."

We find Myrtle, Frank, and Stanley in the living room, seated comfortably on the sofa with drinks in hand, chatting with a man who looks to be an older version of Finn, and a woman who appears to be approximately Myrtle's age.

Before introductions can start, Myrtle eyes me and breaks into a fit of laughter. "You can't name the first one Rudolph. Already been done, honey."

As the low growl leaves my throat, Finn looks at me in question. "What is she talking…"

"Oh my God!" A loud shriek comes from my left before I'm suddenly pulled away from Finn into arms that squeeze my neck so tightly I forget how to breathe – rather can't breathe – as the body attached to them jumps up and down. "You're Haley Vixen! I follow you on Tik Tok! And you're in my house! With my brother! Can I get a picture?"

Finn reaches out trying to calm the bouncy ball with appendages attempting to strangle me – out of excitement, I'm sure, but just the same. "Dee," he chastises, gently removing me from her grasp. "Now is not the time. She's had a shitty day. Let her breathe, have a drink, eat dinner."

The young lady gives me a concentrated look as her brows pinch. "But you just cleaned out all your Nortons. Did it not work?"

Curious eyes throughout the room are fixed on us. That was the first video to run this morning and she must have seen it. I did clean out Norton. Hell, I disposed of him long ago. But I still can't seem to hit my ass with both hands and I literally upended three lives today because I can't even cook a turkey.

I look to Finn and burst into tears. "Can I use your bathroom?"

"Come here," he whispers, as he once again takes me in his comforting arms and starts to lead me out of the room.

"I got this, Butt Cheeks." Myrtle slides her bony hands under his arm and over my shoulders in a firm, but loving grip from behind me. "Grab her purse and hand it to me. Point us in the right direction. Save this conversation for another day. I gotta fix her makeup so we can eat, drink, and be merry. Better uncork two bottles for her." She mutters from six inches below my ears, "I'm going to hunt him down and cut his Tweedle-dee dick off."

Chapter 10

❄ Donner ❄

If heartbreak had a sound, it would be...Haley's sobs.

"What did I do?" Diedre asks, her eyes wide as she looks down the hall where Myrtle led Haley to the bathroom. "Dee" is my little sister. Senior in college at NYU. Apparently an ardent fan of ...wait a minute! Haley *Vixen*? Oh, the irony.

"How do you know Haley?" I ask her.

"The same way 3.5 million other people do." She grins puckishly. "Tell me, bro, how do you know Haley? And what's with Butt Cheeks?"

3.5 million people? Some evangelical preachers would kill for that number; consequences be damned.

I'll bet none of those people have kissed her, tasted her. I know how she feels against me; front and back. Hell, I know how her legs feel wrapped around me. And I have every intention of feeling and tasting her again...and again ad infinitum.

Myrtle and Haley return from their retreat; Haley looking a little more refreshed, though apologetic. That will not do. She has suffered enough today and there is absolutely nothing to apologize for. I place an arm around her shoulder and prepare to introduce her to the room when my mom enters. It's love at first sight as she takes in the woman next to me. The gleam in her eyes and the smile on her face is a dead giveaway. Then I realize, that gleam and that smile are a reflection of my own.

"You haven't answered yet," Dee reminds me. "How do you guys know each other?"

I respond to my sister's question as I look at Haley and wink, "A mutual friend by the name of Tom." She sniffles before her face lights with a smile and a burst of laughter escapes. It's dark outside, but I swear the room just filled with sunshine.

❄ ❄ ❄

If Myrtle and her cohorts sing one more verse of "99 Bottles of Cheer on the Wall", I may pull a stop and drop. They've sung their own version of "Jingle Balls", changed the lyrics of others to include "best nuts roasting on an open fire" – to which Frank and Stanley argued over whose were – and "later on we'll perspire as we screw by the fire, to face unafraid the kid we just made, rompin' in our winter underwear". And now the words are stuck in my head. Never again will I eat a roasted chestnut nor walk in a winter wonderland without recalling this evening. I've already sent up silent apologies to Nat King Cole and Elvis.

The back of my SUV has leftovers packed in three individual containers – one each for Myrtle, Stanley, and Frank. Probably enough to feed them for the next couple days. My parents may have hosted, but these three provided the entertainment. My grandmother found a new bridge partner and my dad gained two new fishing companions. Diedre swore secrecy to Haley's location, took only a few selfies with her, and begged to have lunch and a girls night out, to include makeup tips, the next time she's in town.

"Are you sure it's safe to leave them alone?" I whisper to Haley who sits next to me in the front seat. As much as I look forward to quiet time with her, the public servant in me feels responsible for the senior citizens in my backseat.

She waves a hand in dismissal. "They're not drunk." She turns in her seat to scan the offenders in the back and scowls. "They're just...obnoxious." She reaches over the console and places her hand on my arm. "Thank you for today. I don't know what we would have done without you."

Taking the opportunity to hold that hand while it's within reach, I bring it to my mouth and kiss her knuckles. "Best Thanksgiving I've ever had."

We drop the three seniors at the apartment building, escorting them to the second floor, carrying their leftovers.

"Need a word, Butt Cheeks," Myrtle says as she rolls her index finger, indicating I'm to follow her.

"Myrtle," Haley huffs in warning behind me. "You're out of words. You haven't shut up all day."

"I've got a few left in me," she retorts, turning the key in her lock. She looks to Haley. "You wait here, let him bring my leftovers in."

I step inside as Haley is calling out, "Myrt...", and the door closes before she can cross the threshold.

"Set the bag on the table," Myrtle orders. "This won't take long." I do as she says and turn to see a hard-set face with narrowed eyes. "I realize rut season has two weeks to go. Reindeer or not, Donner won't be on Vixen. You earn her. Got it?"

She's sharp, spunky, and how in the hell she knows when, or what, rut season is, I have no idea. But she loves Haley. Of that, I have no doubt.

"You have my word," I promise her and head for the door, opening it to a fuming Haley.

Myrtle chimes behind me, "Thanks for the quickie, Butt Cheeks." Then finishes with a hard slap on my ass and, "Until next time."

Haley smirks and rolls her eyes. "Myrtle, you'd be more convincing if I didn't already know it takes you ten minutes to get your support hose off. Go to bed."

Once out in the parking lot, Haley looks at the row of garages at the back. "I need to get my car."

"You have a car but you drive Myrtle's?"

"Myrtle likes hers driven once in a while so it doesn't sit for weeks at a time," she explains. "Besides, mine doesn't have a lot of trunk space. Hence, the reason you saw me in hers on Monday."

"We can pick it up tomorrow." I take her hand and pull her toward my SUV. "You don't know the way to my house and we have to come back to get more of your things anyway."

She pulls her hand from mine and stares up at me. "Don't you have to work?"

"Got the next five days off." I spread my arms wide, flashing my sexiest grin, and wink. "Officer Friendly at your service."

Her nose crinkles before she buries her teeth in her bottom lip. "Well, if you plan on sharing cooking duties, I hope you like Spaghetti-Os."

I nearly cringe before pulling her into my side. "Come on, Trouble. Maybe I'll show you how to fix real spaghetti."

"You'd let me cook in your kitchen after today's disaster?"

"Best if only one of us is homeless at a time, Haley." I open the door to my SUV and spin to pick her up by the waist, lifting her onto the seat. I tap her on the nose and grin. "I said show you."

Chapter 11

❄ Haley ❄

Five days under the same roof 24/7! I knew we'd be crossing paths; maybe a few hours in the evening, but it would be easy to make myself scarce and work during those hours. Maybe they can expedite my claim and get me back home in a couple days.

Dinner with his family was incredible. The only reason I agreed to it was so Myrtle, Frank and Stanley wouldn't go hungry. But once there, I almost forgot I was amongst strangers. His mom made up for the hug I didn't get from my own, his sister filled in for Halston – other than the initial greeting – and his dad even hugged me goodbye. It felt like home away from home.

Now back to reality. So many phone calls to make tomorrow; i.e. landlord, insurance, cleaning company, etc. Oh God, the day after Thanksgiving. Are these people even going to be available to take my call?

Finn pulls in the drive of a beautiful ranch style home on the rural edge of Summerfield and parks in the garage. He unloads my suitcase and bag from the back, despite my protests that I'm capable, and opens the door that leads to a mudroom containing the washer and dryer.

He sets the suitcase down in front of the washer. "Shall we get these in now so you have clean clothes in the morning…" he dips his chin and grins "…that don't smell like Tom?"

A snort-laugh escapes my throat but soon turns into the same sad sobs of earlier today. How I wish I could go back in time and either make better choices or been more successful with the ones I chose. Not just today's, but many others too.

"Haley, what can I do?" Finn's whisper is more a plea than a question.

"I-I c-could use a h-hug."

He spreads his arms wide, palms up. "You're in luck. Got an unlimited supply."

I fall into the embrace easily. His arms are so strong and comforting, I think I could stay here for hours. I've never been held like this. It's like a warm blanket that keeps the cold, cruel world out and the cozy, fuzzy feelings in. He runs one gentle hand up and down my back in soothing motions while the other tucks in my hair, holding my head to his chest. His warm breath is like a whisper against the top of my head before he drops a kiss to it. My arms wrap around his torso, feeling the solid muscle beneath. His heart beats strong in my ear as my own beats in time with his. My palms flatten as I begin to explore the defined ridges of muscle. His heart rate increases and his grip in my hair tightens as I continue my exploration. His muscles grow taut under my fingernails that graze slowly across his rib cage. Norton was fit, but nothing to write home about. Finn is novel material. God, it's been so long.

"Haley." His whisper is a combination of warning and restraint.

I pull back from his grip in my hair and look up into eyes a few shades darker than I've ever seen them. "Kiss me."

He hesitates – a war within raging behind that darkened blue gaze – before he delivers a lip lock that feels like sex with my oral cavity. The kiss by the porch was enticing, wanton, maybe even a touch playful. But this? This is downright decadent. There's tongue, there's teeth, nips, tugs. I'm moaning so loud, my vocal cords vibrate. I'm singing from the inside out, and I can't even carry a tune in a basket. Apparently my lady parts like the ditty too, because they're dancing. Finn Donner knows how to kiss. However, as fast as it started, it is over.

"Haley," he breathes hard, taking my cheeks in his hands; forehead to mine. "Not like this."

My shoulders deflate, as does my ego, and I take a step back. "I thought you said you wanted me."

He tips my chin up, his face stern, but his eyes sincere. "I do." His eyebrows pinch and he sighs. "Damn, I do. I've never met anyone like you, Haley Vixen. I'll admit, your beauty and your ass were my first attraction." He reaches for a curl and twirls it in his finger as he studies my face. "But you had me fooled. So smart, funny, kind. The day I pulled you over was quite intentional. The couple times I'd seen you before, I couldn't get close enough to get the plate number because it was a temporary tag..." he shrugs "...and I wasn't on duty. Monday was my luckiest day ever."

My jaw hangs agape. He'd seen me before? Wait a minute. Not so fast, Officer Too Friendly. "Do you always pulse your thumb on the inside of a lady's palm like you're flickin' her..."

"No," he snaps defensively before I finish the question. "I'd never done that before and would never consider it again." He runs a fast hand through his hair in frustration. "You brought out something I didn't know I had in me." He arches a brow, narrows his eyes, and dips his chin. "You rubbing your ass against my crotch didn't help."

Glancing at said crotch and back to him, I smirk. "You enjoyed it."

He chuckles. "Not gonna lie."

"Did you really think I had a body in the trunk?"

He lifts one shoulder in a shrug. "Job first, Trouble."

"Have you been stalking me?"

"No, Haley. I simply wanted to ask you for a date."

I eye him skeptically, tipping my chin. "Did you put an explosive in Tom so you could come to my rescue today?"

The tic in his jaw and flare of his nostrils indicate I may have poked the bear. He suddenly reaches under my ass cheeks, lifts me off my feet and carries me into the kitchen where he plops me on the counter. Standing between my thighs, he leans in close, bracing his hands on either side of my hips. His voice is near scolding as he narrows his eyes. "You left the explosive inside Tom before you put him in the oven, love. They're called giblets. You're supposed to remove them. The bag exploded." I open my mouth to speak but he places a finger over it. "How in the hell you managed to set your kitchen on fire is beyond me, but I find you are multitalented in many areas, Haley. Cooking apparently is not one of them. I would have jumped through hoops to find you, figured out a way to wear you down, and fuck you senseless eventually. Starting a fire in your apartment is not one of them."

He grasps the nape of my neck, his fingers tight in my curls as he pulls me to him. The kiss is harsher this time – demanding – the dance with my tongue being gifted to me once again. I melt into his touch, savoring the kind of kiss most women only dream of.

"I thought it was stuffing," I whisper against his mouth once the air returns to my lungs.

His chuckle is devilish yet the sexiest thing I've ever heard. "Still gonna fuck you senseless, Haley." He places a fingertip on the left side of my chest and traces the pattern of an X and whispers, "But only after I get this. I want the whole vixen."

Chapter 12

❄ Donner ❄

I have never seen my home decorated so nicely as it is when Haley appears from the guest bedroom in my T-shirt. Her hair is a mass of disheveled curls that I want to tangle my fingers in. I had given her a shirt to sleep in last night as her clothes needed to be washed before wearing. Damn! I thought my shower remedy half an hour ago might tame the beast, but apparently it was only symptomatic treatment.

"You look good in my shirt," I utter, turning to retrieve a cup. "Coffee?"

"Black, please."

My home is an open concept design; living room, dining room and kitchen all visible from one to the other. Pain in the ass if you don't feel like cleaning immediately after a meal, but living alone and eight years in the military can make for a lifetime of habits – some good, some bad. Cleanliness is one of my good ones. Walking around fully dressed in my own home is not. Hence, my gray sweats and shirtless state at the present time.

I pour her coffee and set it on the counter. She remains at the edge of the hall, forehead creased, mouth puckered as she eyes my bare torso. "Did I steal your only T-shirt?"

My mouth twitches in amusement. "If I say yes, are you going to give it back?"

She tugs at the hem, her thighs squeezing slightly. "When I get my clothes back."

I pick up her cup and walk to where she stands, handing it to her. "They're in my bedroom in a basket, folded. I didn't want to wake you."

She looks shellshocked as she stares up at me. You'd think I'd just gifted her with a new car. "You folded my laundry?"

Bending slightly to kiss her forehead, I whisper against her skin, "Even your delicate unmentionables. Can't wait for the day I get to take them off you." I turn her toward the hall. "Come on, Trouble. Let's get your clothes. I'll fix us breakfast." My hand drops low on her hip as I guide her down the hall. *Oh no she did not!* There is no resistance as the soft cotton slides against her ass cheek. She's bare under my T-shirt! No panties! Oh wait! I feel a strap under my thumb. It's a thong. *Even worse.* I bite down on my lip so hard I draw blood; the metallic taste filling my mouth as I fight for composure. I rush for the basket that sits on my bed and hold it in front of me, shielding the beast that begs for release.

"I'll drop these off in your room," I mutter, squeezing past her in the hall. "I'm going to grab a shower and then I'll fix breakfast."

She scrunches her nose. "I thought you already got one. Your hair's still wet."

Unloading the items onto her bed as fast as possible, I retain my shield in the form of the empty basket and head back to my room. "Think I missed a spot."

❄ ❄ ❄

Three hours later, we've loaded up as much as is salvageable from Haley's apartment in order for her to work. The water damage from the sprinklers is extensive. The clothes on the racks are soaked, some of the makeup cases are ruined. The computer and lights still questionable until we get them tested back at my place.

She studies what look to be baby monitors in the room and bursts into tears. "I forgot all about them. Who's going to hear them if they need help in the night?"

Baby monitors? What the hell am I missing?

Myrtle, Frank and Stanley make their way in the door without knocking as she sobs in my arms.

"We got 'em!" Myrtle yells as she holds out a lanyard hanging from her neck. Frank and Stanley mimic her actions, proudly displaying identical lanyards of their own. "I wanted to test it to see how beefy the EMTs are, but you weren't around to do my makeup. Think you can fix that, Haley?"

Haley stares, speechless, at the three grinning seniors. I now note, attached to each of those lanyards is a medical alert button. There's a tap on the open door before a man steps in, looking a bit uncomfortable as he clears his throat.

"Ms. Vixen." He nods at Haley then scans the room scrupulously.

"Mr. Merrell," Haley acknowledges softly. "I'm – I'm sorry about all this."

He continues to nod as he eyes the damage. "I'm sure you are. But we have a bigger problem, Haley. Your lease was up three weeks ago."

"Wh-what?" she stammers. "I'm paid up. I've never missed! It was open-ended."

He jingles the change in his pocket – irritating as hell – and nods once again. "I'm aware. But you didn't renew it, and as of now your lease is no longer available. Since you don't have furniture to move, I'll give you one week to be out, so the cleaning crew can come in and get this mess cleaned up."

"You can't do that!" she shrieks. "You have to give me 30 days' notice!"

"According to what?" He smirks. "An expired lease?"

My blood boils before I reach for my wallet and pull out a card, handing it to him. "Sergeant Donner, Summerfield PD. We have authority in Gator Springs. Having witnessed this interaction, I feel it my duty to remind you of renter protection laws. If this is your method of evading return of Ms. Vixen's deposit, you're looking at some stiff fines. Maybe even jail time." I smile smugly. "Because that would be fraud. She'll be out by tomorrow at noon, and you'll be here with her security deposit in hand."

Looking to a heartbroken Haley, I ask, "How much was it?"

"$2500.00," she sniffles.

I scowl at a wide-eyed landlord. "Double it and we didn't have this conversation. The banks are open. Certified check will be fine. Understood?"

I've never used my position of power but never have I been so grateful for it. I believe the fire chief might want to take his time to perform an extensive inspection after all. At least he will after we have a chat. I'll find the three seniors a hotel for a month. Maybe my parents would like the extra company. The landlord will be paying their room and board anyway. The first floor occupants aren't my concern, but they will be his.

He's pissed, but he's not stupid. Double her deposit is a lot less than recourse for his violations...for now. He'll get the bill for displacement of the residents after Haley gets her money.

"Done," he grunts before storming out the door.

"I have no place to go," Haley mutters through her tears.

"Yes you do." I wrap her in my arms and whisper, "Let's go home."

Myrtle pinches my ass on our way out. "So far so good, Butt Cheeks."

Once out in the parking lot, Haley turns toward the garages. "I need to get my car."

I redirect her toward my loaded SUV. "We'll get it tomorrow. You're too upset to drive." I don't add I'm not about to risk her taking off. "What garage is it in?"

"Number six," she sniffles. "I have to get the spare fob from Myrtle tomorrow too. Don't let me forget."

Sending a text to two recipients, I call in a favor; one of many. At seven o'clock in the evening there's a fast knock on the front door. Hot Rod storms in, red-faced and fuming – a laughing Jizz behind him.

"First of all," Hot Rod rants, "there isn't enough leg room in that thing for a fucking midget. Second of all, a heads-up about the ball-grabbing granny from hell would have been nice!" He slams the fob into my hand. "All favors paid, asshole. Where's my beer?"

I frown at Jizz. "You didn't warn him?"

He belly laughs. "Hell no. It was too much fun watching him squirm."

In my driveway sits a shiny red Cabriolet convertible. It suits her perfectly. Haley appears from the third bedroom where she's been arranging her *goods*.

"Well, hello there," Hot Rod drawls. Recognition flashes in his eyes as he recalls our conversation in the bar – *under my surveillance, slippery.* He turns to me, arching a playful, questioning brow. "House arrest or are your grip skills improving?"

We order pizza, explain what happened today – Jizz already aware of the fire – and lay out our plan for tomorrow.

"So what time should we be here?" Hot Rod asks, stuffing the last bite of pizza in his mouth. I know why he's asking. They both drive pickup trucks.

"For what?" Haley's inquisitive gaze only makes her more beautiful.

"To get you moved," Jizz replies easily. "Three cops oughta have that landlord shaking in his shoes. In, out, you get your money, done."

"B-but you don't even know me," Haley whispers in amazement.

"We know Donner." Jizz's eyes flit to mine and back to Haley's. "He's family, which makes you the same. Eight o'clock good?"

Hot Rod groans. "Can you keep the old lady from humpin' my leg?"

For the first time today the sun actually shines, because Haley giggles.

Chapter 13

❄ Haley ❄

For weeks we've spent every evening together. Finn cooks, we both clean. I did make cold sub sandwiches with chips on the side one night. Fingers still intact, thank you very much – Finn sliced the subs. I work while he does. We do daily checks on Myrtle, Frank and Stanley, who are currently residing at the Waterfront in the Villages while the building is under inspection for fire code violations. They're actually considering a permanent move there – something about black loofahs. I'll have to investigate that later. We've done gift shopping together. We watch movies, take long walks, talk into the wee hours of the morning, unaware how much time has passed. He makes me laugh until my cheeks hurt. And yet, both bedrooms remain occupied at night. Myrtle has had more ass play with the man than I have! We've come close. I actually have – literally – a couple of times just by straddling him, but don't tell him that. Truthfully, I think he knows. The twinkle in his eyes outdid Santa's in any pictures I've ever seen.

❄ ❄ ❄

My red gown dips low in the back, sparkly silver shoes, makeup spot on, hair pulled back on one side. I feel like a princess. The policeman's ball, and I'm Finn's date. Christmas in Summerfield. Almost. It's only two days away.

We sway on the dancefloor to Don Henley's "Please Come Home for Christmas". I used to change the station every time this song came on because once again I wasn't going home. I was stuck in Seattle. But tonight? I realize I am home. Home isn't a place, it's the people... or the person. I'll be with my family soon, and the thought already has me missing him.

"You ready to go?" I ask. We've been here for three hours. I want him to myself.

"Anytime you are." *So accommodating.*

The door closes behind us as we pass through the kitchen. I know he half expects me to go to my own room – it's my usual – but tonight I take his hand and pull him behind me as we make our way to his room.

Once inside, he closes the door with his foot and spins me around to face him. He takes one step closer so we're mere inches apart. He lifts a fingertip to the edge of my breast where he traces the figure of an X.

"Do I have this, Haley?"

"Yeah, Finn, you do."

His voice is low as he shrugs his tux jacket off and throws it toward the chair. "Still have time to change your mind, Trouble."

"Do I have yours?"

He chuckles as he reaches for a pin in my hair. "Baby, you've had mine since you jumped off the back of that ambulance into my arms."

"Are you going to fuck me senseless now?" I ask playfully.

"Not the first time," he whispers, sliding another pin from my hair and watching the tresses fall over my shoulder. "I want to make love to you, show you what you mean to me." Reaching behind me, he leisurely lowers the single zipper that holds the material snugly in place. His fingertips slide slowly up my arms, leaving goosebumps in their wake, until his thumbs rest on the shoulder straps. He peels them off my shoulders while holding my gaze until the dress falls to my feet, leaving me in a red silk thong. His eyes drop to my bare chest and a breathy moan escapes his lips, "Spectacular."

He coaxes me toward the bed, mouth on mine in a deep, slow, demanding kiss; hands on my hips to steady my backward steps, and places me on the edge. He kneels before me to remove my sandals and looks up and winks. "We'll save these for another time."

Watching Finn strip off a bow tie, shirt, and pants puts Magic Mike in *"meh"* territory. It's hard not to stare; enjoy the show. The tie goes one way, the shirt another, the pants drop to the floor. In one fell swoop, he pulls me to my feet then lays me back on the bed, climbing in over me, burdening his weight on his elbows. He drops a kiss to the corner of my mouth, my jaw, my throat, and finally the inner part of my left breast.

"I want you, Haley," he murmurs, "every inch of you. But I want what's under here." He takes a nipple in his mouth, nipping it gently, then soothing it with his tongue. "The whole package."

I'm speechless at the moment because he doesn't stop there. No, those kisses continue a path to a red silk thong that he removes with his teeth initially; his thumbs finishing the job until it's off my ankles and thrown across the room. Who needs Magic Mike when you've got a magic tongue between your legs?

Chapter 14

❄ Donner ❄

If ecstasy had a sound, it would be Haley whispering my name. Or Haley's moans.

Her thighs quiver in the aftermath as I kiss the inside of each before making my way back to her, shedding my jerseys on the journey. She's breathless, flushed, and beautifully dazed.

"That was…" she breathes hard.

"Just a prelude," I whisper over her mouth before rising to reach for the nightstand to pull out a strip of condoms. God, I bet she'd feel good bare. Not that I've ever; it was never worth the risk. But it is now on the top of my list of things to do…with Haley. Sheathing myself, I take my position once more.

"Is it mine, Haley?" I brush the side of her nose with mine and whisper, "Are you going to let me keep it?"

She runs her fingers through my scruff, her eyes squeezed closed as if preparing a memory she may have to tuck away for a rainy day. "Promise you won't throw it back when you're tired of it?"

When I find who hurt her, I just might kill him.

"Look at me." She slowly opens her eyes; vulnerability and pain stealing the sparkle in the sapphire blue I live for. "How would mine beat without yours?"

Tears rim her eyes, but before they have a chance to escape, I take her mouth in a kiss she won't soon forget – because it's the very moment I slide in slowly, to a tightness and warmth that envelops me like a second skin. I…am…home.

She breathes deep and moans with the action, then delivers music to my ears when she whispers, "Finn." She runs her hands through my hair, lightly scraping her nails over my scalp.

"Gotta move, baby," I groan in near agony, "or this party's over before it gets started. You feel too damn good."

She wraps her legs around my hips and squeezes my dick in a vise-like grip with well-toned pelvic floor muscles, causing a pleasure so deep it's nearly painful and makes me moan so loud I feel it in my bones.

Her voice is light as she teases, "I'm sorry, officer. Is the cuff too tight?"

I have met my match. Haley Vixen has ruined me. Never in my life has anything felt so good or so right. I grind my teeth as I try to stave off an orgasm that is screaming for release. "That borders cruel."

Her eyes flare with mischief as she bobs her eyebrows and squeezes once more. "The benefits of yoga."

I narrow my eyes. "Think it's time we test your flexibility skills, Trouble."

Is it possible to be euphoric and exhausted at the same time? Because two hours later that is exactly what I am. Next to Haley, spooning.

"I have to get up early," she says with a yawn.

"Why?"

"I'm meeting an agent to see two apartments in the morning."

My chest burns and my stomach rolls. She's moving? She doesn't need to move. I thought she was happy here.

"Why are you moving?"

"Finn, this has always been temporary," she says as if nothing's changed. "Something finally opened up. I don't want to be in your way."

"You're not in my way," I snap. "Why would you think that?"

"I need my independence."

"Independence," I repeat bitterly. "Do I smother you?"

"No!" she protests. "You've been wonderful. But you won't even accept rent!"

I throw the sheets off and climb out of bed, pulling my jerseys on. Standing at the door, I look back. "Why did you wait until now to tell me?" She sits up, her mouth twisted, and shrugs. "I really must have fucked you senseless." I shake my head and sigh. "Because you really don't get it, do you?" I pull the door open. "Dinner with my folks tomorrow for an early

Christmas before you leave for Georgia. I'll be home from work by six to pick you up. You promised my family. Please don't let them down."

"I wouldn't..." I close the door before she can finish and before I lose it.

Temporary?

Chapter 15

❄ Haley ❄

It was supposed to be temporary! I didn't mean *we* were temporary. I've taken up two bedrooms, a bathroom, and live in his general space day and night. He won't accept rent money, share grocery expenses, utility bills. But damnit, my goal was to prove I could make it on my own! I didn't need *Norton* to survive, despite his efforts to convince me otherwise.

Five o'clock this morning I heard him in the kitchen and then heard him leave. He didn't come into the bedroom to get his uniform and shower. I know he can shower and change at work. He must have slept on the sofa or in my room. At least one of us slept. *I think.*

I met the agent at ten; hated both apartments. Not because they were bad, they just felt…wrong. Now I wait for Finn to arrive home. It's the day before Christmas Eve and I leave early tomorrow to spend the next three days with my family in Georgia.

He walks in the door at six sharp, dressed in street clothes. As he locks his gun in the safe he keeps his back to me. "You ready?"

"Can we talk first?" I ask timidly.

"No time," he replies abruptly. "They're waiting."

"Finn…"

"Let's go, Haley."

The drive is agonizingly silent; Finn gripping the wheel, me staring out the window. I'll explain later – if he'll listen.

The front door to the Donner home opens and we're met with cheerful greetings from the usual occupants as we carry gifts inside. Myrtle, Stanley and Frank sit on the sofa, drinks in hand.

I scowl at Myrtle. "Black loofahs? Are you nuts?"

I Googled it. Kinda wish I hadn't.

She titters and tips her chin. "You haven't met Sam."

"Or Ella," Frank and Stanley chime in unison.

My eyebrows skyrocket. "Sam and Ella?" *Huh. Guess I didn't need Amazon after all.*

Three bodies round the doorway from the kitchen, bright smiles on their faces.

"Mom? Dad?" I burst into tears as I run toward their open arms. I haven't seen them in seven months.

My dad lifts me off my feet with his hug. "How's my baby girl?"

Mom and I share a long squeeze and cheek kisses before Halston grabs me in a tight hug and whispers, "Tell me that man has a brother. Hot damn, Haley."

"How-how did you..." I stammer.

Mom smiles. "Finn thought it would be nice if we got to know the people in your life down here, so we came to spend Christmas with you. He set it up last week."

I make my way back across the room to where Finn stands. "You did this for me?"

"I'd do anything for you, Haley," he says softly, brushing a knuckle across my cheek. "And I didn't want to spend Christmas without you."

"You're not working?"

"Nope," he says. "First time I've ever had real reason to take a holiday."

"I didn't take the apartment. It would never be home without you."

He wraps his hand in my hair and pulls me close to whisper in my ear, "I knew I didn't fuck you that senseless. Merry Christmas, baby."

"I love you, Finn."

"I love you more, Haley." His mouth crushes mine in a kiss that claims a heart that didn't want to be owned. But it's his; there's no denying it. His lips brush mine and he chuckles. "Still not allowed to cook, Trouble. We don't want to be homeless."

The End

Merry Christmas To All and To All A Good Night

About Annie Mick

Annie Mick is a diehard laughaholic who has learned to take everything with a grain of salt followed by a good dose of sarcasm.

If you can wiggle while you giggle, it's added exercise and spares you ten minutes on the treadmill.

If you can laugh while you cry, the tears are saltier, and it makes the margaritas taste better.
Life is too short to not get lost in a fantasy; if only for a day, if only in a book, one page at a time.

Books By Annie Mick

Available Now

<u>The Crew Series</u>
Run To Me
Wicked Lemonade
Find Another Hero

<u>The Attorney Series</u>
Tell Me Why, Jannie
The Fresh French Connection

<u>Standalone</u>
Old Farts and Pop Tarts
Saari Not Sorry
The Chauffeur: Phoenix Rising
Manipulation 101: Code Of Ethics

Social Media Links

Follow me on:

Instagram
@anniemick_author

Tik Tok
@anniemick_author

Website
www.anniemick.com

'Tis The Homecoming

by Kayla Baker

Blurb

I've been in love with him my whole life. I never hid how I felt about him. He just never saw it. At least that's what I've been telling myself since I packed my bags and ran to Nashville to follow my dreams.

When tragedy strikes, I find myself on the first flight back home. Of course, the first person I see is the sinful hot cop I've tried to forget.

Axel Parker.

Christmas is my favorite time of year, but the last thing I want to do is spend my favorite holiday fighting the pull our souls have to one another. The choice isn't mine, though. It belongs in the hands of Fate herself, and the second Axel wraps his arms around me again, I know she's won.

But being with Axel, my home, comes with a price... One I'm not sure I can pay.

Chapter 1

❄ Daisy ❄

Rockfield, Alabama.

My home.

My life.

At least, once upon a time, it was. That all changed five years ago when I decided it was time to move on in my life. I wanted to start my career and move to a new place. I wanted to make my way in this life. And I did. I became more successful than I ever imagined.

But it never felt right.

I never felt whole.

Being alone in a new city like Nashville makes a person miss their roots. I wanted to end my dreams the moment they started because much like anyone else from a small town, I missed my mom and dad. There were even times I missed my boneheaded brothers, they are twins, Colt and Huck. My best friends, Lee and Nathan. But none of that compared to the way I missed him.

Axel.

I've never told anyone how I feel about him. How can I? He isn't just any guy. He's my brother's best friend; my best friend's older brother. I never understood why he always hung around us so much, but I always thought it's because of Lee's then-boyfriend, Nathan.

Nathan and Lee were my best friends since childhood, but as we grew older, they started to view each other as a bit more. When we were in the sixth grade, Nathan asked her to be his girlfriend, and that was the beginning of their story. They're still together to this day. They were the reason I delayed my Nashville plans, to begin with.

You see, after I landed the deal with Juniper Records, Nathan proposed to Lee underneath the big willow tree in her parent's backyard. It was so beautiful. Nathan waited until the snow began to fall all because he knew how much she loves the snow. He knew she could never say no or turn him away because he made sure to involve everything and everyone she loves.

Lee, of course, did say yes, but she immediately started to panic. She thought I was going to leave without watching her walk down that aisle. As if I could let my best friend stand in front of him by herself.

I called the record company and explained the situation to them. Originally, my manager was furious with me asking if I could have just a bit more time until Lee can figure out when she wants to get married. But as soon as Axel started to see me break down from the thought of missing her wedding after all, he took matters into his own hands.

Axel called my manager. I still have no clue what he said or what he did, but whatever it was, it worked. My manager not only pushed back my arrival by nearly a month, but also started sending a moving crew over once a week to take bits and pieces of my life here to my new home. Nashville.

I haven't been home in a long time, but the frantic call I received only an hour ago from Colt has me rushing back home faster than I can think. I didn't hear all the details of what happened because my ears and heart were shattering around me. My parents were in an accident on the farm. Mainly, my dad.

Colt told me that Mom was feeding and watering the horses in the pasture when she heard a loud bang. She ran back to the barn where she found my dad. They don't know the full story of what happened, but my mom swears she has all the answers she needs.

My dad was having a really good year with his crops and his livestock. A couple of the neighboring farms and ranches were claiming he must have cheated the system somehow. One even went as far as to say my father stole half of their livestock when he saw they were better than his.

Anyone who knows my dad at all knows just how much of a lie that is. My father is one of the kindest, most gentle, loving souls to ever step foot on this earth. I know the allegations are ridiculous, but I still can't help wondering why someone would go this far to try and prove he did anything wrong. My family keeps to themselves.

Huck is a police officer for Rockfield Police Department. I was speechless the day he called to tell me he graduated from the Police Academy while Colt was finishing up his Firefighter training. I honestly never saw them growing into the men they are, but I'm so glad they did.

Axel and I didn't stay in touch as much as I thought we would. That might have been on my part, but he didn't make the time either. I heard that Axel was in a relationship after I left. I'm not sure how it ended or why, but I know it changed him somehow. He's stayed pretty silent for the past five years now. Maybe they worked things out, and she told him he wasn't allowed to talk to me. I'm sure she knows I'm like a sister to him, but what if she can sense my feelings for him? I've never met her, but what if?

As my plane starts to land, I feel my heart beating faster than a cheetah's after a run. My hands are sweaty from the nerves taking course throughout my body. I didn't tell anyone I was coming home right this second, but I can only imagine how upset they'll all be when they see me running through the hospital. Which is exactly what I plan to do.

I make my way through the crowded airport until I see the car rental station. I may not have had any time to pack a suitcase full of clothes, but I made sure to call my manager and tell him to book me a car. He didn't hesitate. He would have five years ago. Since the day Axel said something to him, he's been an easygoing man. Anything I've ever wanted, needed, or asked for has been given to me without a second thought. It's always made me curious about what Axel told him.

The little girl at the rental car counter notices my rushed movements and hurries along with the car. She hands over a set of keys to me as I swipe my card. I don't care how much it costs. I'll use my entire checking and savings account if that's what I need to do.

The traffic in Rockfield has never been crazy like Nashville's can be. We don't have freeways or three-lane highways. Most of the time, we're lucky when we find a backroad that fits more than one car at a time on it. I don't know how many accidents I've seen around the curve by Old

Man Holliday's house. When I was younger, my dad told me about the time someone wasn't paying attention and went directly through the guardrail nearly dumping them into his pond. Thankfully, his car missed it by half a foot, and the guy was able to see his wife and kids again.

The snow on the ground right now, though, is another situation altogether. It's making it a bit more difficult to navigate through town. Everyone is moving so slowly, as if I have all the time in the world while I'm trying to get to the hospital. Maybe I'm overreacting about the situation. Maybe it was my excuse to finally find a reason to come home. I know I've never needed an excuse. I just needed to be sure I wasn't coming home to see him again.

As I finally make my way inside the hospital, my eyes land on the man wearing the police uniform before me. My throat constricts, making it impossible for me to breathe. His neatly shaven face stares down at the clipboard, paying no attention to me.

Axel.

I'd heard he also joined the force, but I didn't expect to see him so quickly. So, I slip behind him, hoping he doesn't see me, and whisper to the nurse at the station as best as I can. "Excuse me, I'm looking for Roger Macknight."

Her nails begin typing away on her keyboard, clicking with each little tap. "Down the hall, fourth door on the right, room two-eighteen." She points down the hall before dropping her eyes back to the screen in front of her. I spin around quickly, still pleading with whoever is listening for him not to see me, and hurry down the hall as he's still talking to another officer and the doctor standing with him.

I'm not entirely sure how I got away from him seeing me, but I'm grateful that it worked out so easily. I quickly enter my dad's room. My mom's head snaps toward me with wide eyes. A single tear slides down her cheek.

"Daisy," she whispers as the tears start flowing even more. I look down at my dad lying in the bed. His forehead has a deep cut, both of his eyes black and blue. He looks so peaceful, yet he feels so far away. I didn't even ask Colt for any details.

"Mama," I whisper as the tears start pouring down my face. "I-I'm s-sorry," I choke out. "I'm so sorry, mama." I close my eyes, letting the emotions take over.

I feel her arms wrap around me tightly, her soft lips pressing against the top of my head. "It's going to be okay, sweetheart. He's going to be okay."

I nod my head, praying that she's telling the truth.

Chapter 2

❄ Axel ❄

I have to be dreaming. There's no way possible she's here. That she was so close to me only to disappear all over again. I shouldn't be so surprised seeing I just left her parent's house where her Dad was assaulted. I haven't had a chance to talk to her mom yet, but all the evidence is leading us to believe this wasn't an accident. Someone hurt him on purpose, and now more than ever, I need to find out why.

But my mind is now stuck on the hurricane of a woman that just walked back into my life with ease. Only now, I'm more confused than ever. Daisy had to have noticed I was the one standing beside her. Why didn't she ask me to be with her like she used to?

Has our five years created such a distance between us that she can't even say hello anymore?

I can't blame anyone but myself for this. I was the reason she left. I know I was. She made her feelings obvious all our lives, but my damn respect for her brothers overpowered my feelings for her. She's always been the most gorgeous girl in any room, but now. Now, she's the most stunning woman in this entire world.

I quickly finish my conversation with the doctor currently in charge of her father's care. She needs me. I don't care if she didn't say the words herself. I'm fully aware of how she feels. It's almost like I can still feel the full charge of energy between us.

I rush down the hall to where I know she'll be with her parents. I might not be visibly shaking with the nerves in my body, but my soul sure is.

The day she left, I stood there and listened to her confess her feelings for me. She never said I was the one she was talking about, but I knew. I always knew it was me. Stupidly, I told her the guy wasn't worth the hassle. I told her to follow her dreams instead of the guy in her story. I saw the way she broke inside when the words left my mouth. I saw the small tears that formed in her eyes, even though she never let them fall. I felt her shattered heart more than I felt my own.

All eyes in the hospital seem to lock on me. It's not unusual to see a police officer here, but for them to be running as fast as I am, it's sure to raise a few eyebrows. Especially as all the holiday decorations in the hall whip around from the velocity of my speed. The bells jingle. The tinsel sways.

Christmas always was her favorite time of the year. She would drink hot cocoa until she was comatose. She would hang the mistletoe in every doorway of her house. The presents she bought for each of us were so thought out and perfect, I would think she was inside our minds. We all volunteered with her one year to donate funds to several charities and ensure kids around the world got something for their own Christmas. It's one of my fondest memories.

But when I open the door to her father's room, I no longer see the girl I once knew. Instead, I'm met with the ghost of who she used to be. She's still the same woman with her same soft red hair and stormy gray eyes, but tears are running down her cheeks when she dares look up at me. She's completely devastated. I can tell. I can't say I blame her. Her first time home in five years is all because her father, her best friend, was assaulted on his own property. Her childhood home. I would be a damn mess just like she is.

"Axel." I watch as her lips move with my name slipping free between the velvety red skin. Daisy wipes the tears from her cheeks, hiding her pain from the one person she used to always allow to see it.

"Daisy," I whisper as I take a slow step closer to her. Her breathing shudders as goosebumps begin to rise across her silky smooth skin.

Her mom places her hand on my shoulder, stopping me from moving any closer to Daisy. I turn my head to meet her tear-filled eyes.

Janice always has felt like a second mom to me. Growing up, Janice and my Mom, Rebecca, were best friends. They planned their pregnancies so they could have kids close in age that would be best friends as well. It's cheesy in its own way, but it worked for them. My mom was blessed with me at the same time Janice was blessed with the twins, Colt and Huck. The next time around, they were both greeted with girls, Lee, my baby sister, and Daisy.

From the moment Daisy was born, I became her protector. I made sure no one hurt her. I made sure every guy who so much as looked at her knew I was surely going to kill them if they made a move on her.

"I'm here, momma," I say as I wrap my arms around Janice's shoulders. She tucks her head into my chest as the tears start to fall all over again.

I can't imagine this is easy for her. Janice has always been a devoted, faithful, and loyal woman to her husband. She was a singer, like Daisy, when they met one another. The moment she met Billy, though, she gave up on her dreams and moved to Rockfield, Alabama, to be with him. My mom followed right behind her and gave up her dream of being a musician's manager. She met my father soon after, and the rest is history. Truthfully, none of that means anything. Janice is just as much my mom as my own mother is.

"Do you have any leads? Does Huck? Please tell me you found whoever did this to him," she cries out. I run my hand down her back soothingly until I find the words I need to say. It's only been a few hours since the attack, but I should have more than I do. I should have the man behind bars. I should be proving to Daisy that I've changed and become a better man.

"No, I don't. Huck is digging as deep as he can, but there was no evidence left at the scene. Whoever did this had the whole thing planned out ahead of time. I promise you, we'll find this asshole, and justice will be served."

Daisy scoffs, causing my eyes to move back to where she's shaking her head with her shoulders shaking as if she's laughing. "I'm sure you'll find him. I'm sure you can find anyone you want to. Isn't that right, Officer," she says in a condescending tone. Her sarcasm isn't very subtle. I'm well aware of where she's going with her statement.

"It's pretty easy to find someone, Daisy." I let go of Janice, turning to face Daisy. "Sometimes, it's more fitting to let someone find themselves first, though."

Daisy throws her head back, laughing harder than before. "And what if that person already knows who they are? Do you just let them go on with life?"

I open my mouth to speak when my phone starts ringing. I lift my head, pausing the conversation as I answer without looking, expecting Huck or another officer to be on the other line. But I'm met with the tiny voice of a beautiful little girl instead. My girl. "Daddy," she coughs out. "I feel icky. Home?" I listen to her stuffy little voice as she coughs again.

"I'll be there soon, sweetheart. Can you give me five minutes to finish with work? I promise when I get home, we can cuddle up in bed and watch whatever movie you want to watch. How does that sound?" I ask her with a small amount of hope that she understands.

"Snacks?" she sniffles while asking.

"Of course! What kind of monster do you think I am?"

She laughs as loud as she can before she starts coughing again. "Five and home," she demands. In my mind, all I can see is the way her tiny little arms cross over her little body with her foot tapping the floor. If I had to guess, she has her teddy and blankie tucked into her chest with her fists.

"Five and home, Pickles," I state.

"Otay, Daddy. Oof you!" she yells as loud as she can.

"Love you, too, Pickles. See you soon." I hang up the phone before running my hand down my face. Of course I need to be at work and home at the same time. I'll have to call Huck before I head out. He's not supposed to be working this case, but I knew I couldn't stop him. I might be his Lieutenant, but not even I can stand in his way when it comes to protecting his family. I don't have the heart. I'd do the same thing anyway.

"Is everything okay, honey? Is something wrong with Natalie?" Janice asks in a quiet voice.

"She's sick. I'm going to head home. I'll notify Huck and have him keep me updated. I'm sorry. I have to go."

I give Janice one final hug before turning back to Daisy. The way she's looking at me feels like pure pain pouring from her soul into mine.

"Should've known you'd find someone one day, right?" She shrugs her shoulders before wiping away a single tear. "Better get home then, huh?"

I open my mouth to protest, but I know it's no use. Daisy won't listen to me when she's upset. She never has. Instead, I walk over to her, pressing my lips to her forehead, and whisper against her silky skin. "We'll catch up later."

"Yeah," she says quietly.

As much as I want to stay where she is, I know I have other duties that need my attention. Another little girl who needs my attention. I turn away and walk through the door leading me out of her father's room. My mind is one jumbled mess, but the one thing I can pick out through all the haze is the tears in Daisy's eyes.

Chapter 3

❄ Daisy ❄

I've been home for a week. It's strange to say that, since I consider Nashville my home now, but Rockfield will always be my true home. This is where I grew up. Where I learned who I was. It's where I found my love for music. More importantly, it's where Axel is.

I haven't spoken to him since the day at the hospital. I've chosen to avoid him at all costs, actually. What do I say to the man I've always loved and cherished when I know he has a family at home? A family that doesn't involve me. How do I keep moving forward when my life feels like it's grinding to an immediate halt?

Huck and Colt have been by my side every day. When they saw me the first night, I was sure they would both need to go to the emergency room themselves. I'm still not sure how neither one of them passed out from lack of oxygen after holding their breath for so long. It's been entirely too long since I've been home to see my brothers or parents, but I had to stay as far away as I could. I couldn't take the chance of seeing Axel again after so long; having my heart ripped out of my chest all over again.

"What's on your mind, Dais?" Colt asks, dragging me back to the moment.

I blink my eyes a few times as we stare at the feast in front of us. "Why are we having Thanksgiving dinner when it's already December?" I ask as I push the food on my plate in a circle with my fork.

Colt sits back, his eyes pinning me to the chair. "Because you never come home, Daisy. Dad just got home last night, but all he and Mom could think about was spending as many holidays with you as they could. I mean, it's been five years. Don't you think they've missed you around your favorite holidays?"

I look away from him. I hate how right he is, but at the same time, he doesn't understand why I had to stay away. None of them do. "I was working, Colt."

Huck is the next one to bark out with laughter. "We work, too, Daisy. Doesn't seem like we're too busy for our family, though."

His words cut into the aching muscle that is my weak heart. He's right. I could've simply come home around the holidays and seen them. I could've told my manager that the holidays were off-limits, and he would have listened. But I chose not to. I wanted to stay busy and away from Axel so badly that I forgot my family needs me just as much as I need them.

My mom claps her hands, cutting the three of us off from the argument that is bound to happen. "It doesn't matter now, sweetheart. You're home for the time being, and that's all we care about. Isn't that right, boys?" Her eyes narrow as she glares at the two of them.

In unison, they both chirp out a defeated, "Yes, Ma'am," before bowing their heads.

The fact that these two are twenty-eight now and still fear our mother makes me giggle. Colt is a good six-foot-three. He towers over our mom's five-foot-nothing height, but he also knows that woman won't bat an eye twice at busting his ass if he doesn't listen to her. Colt's always been a momma's boy.

Huck, on the other hand, has given our mom a run for her money over the years. He's the same height as Colt, but he's definitely more independent. She could tell him not to do something until she was completely blue in the face, and he would still do it about fourteen times before our mom would find him and drag him from wherever he happened to be by the tip of his ear. I've seen her put him in his place so many times. But it's so funny to witness it all over again now they're adults.

"Daddy," I say innocently with a soft voice. "How are you feeling?" My mom told me that someone broke into the barn and hit my dad over the head with something. Axel wasn't able to find the weapon, though.

My dad reaches over, cupping the back of my hand with his palm. His eyes shine with happiness as he watches me curiously. "Better than I could've ever imagined, Peanut." He gives me a weak smile before letting go of my hand.

I look around the table for a moment when I finally notice the two empty chairs at the other end. "What are the chairs for?" I point with my thumb as their heads turn.

"Oh!" my mom almost shouts. "Those are for Axel and Pickles. He had to work for a bit today but said they would be stopping by as soon as he got off work." She looks down at the ancient watch on her wrist. "Hm, that's strange. They should've been here by now."

Huck pulls out his phone, I assume to call Axel. When the doorbell chimes, I watch my excited mother jump up from her chair and practically skip to the front door. My heart feels like it's shattering all over again. Not only do I have to see Axel, but I also have to watch him with another woman. Can this get any worse?

"Where's Pickles?" I hear my mom ask him as they move closer to the room.

"Lee took her to the movies tonight. Apparently, they had this planned weeks ago and never told me." The sound of Axel's voice has me practically panting. How can he sound so fucking sexy without being anywhere near me?

"You good?" Huck asks, snapping me out of my Axel trance yet again.

"Yeah, I'm not feeling the greatest," I lie. They wouldn't understand the turmoil slipping through my head if I even tried to explain it.

"Why don't you go lie down, sweetheart? It's been a long week for all of us. I don't think we even considered how tired you might be. You've barely slept since you got here," my dad announces.

But as soon as I try to admit the truth to him, Axel walks into the room wearing that god-forsaken uniform. Drool slowly starts to fill my mouth. I should listen to my dad and go lie down, but how can I when the most handsome man I've ever known is standing in front of me staring at me as though he might devour me whole?

"I'll be okay," I whisper. "I just need to run to the restroom really quick. I think I'm just a bit overwhelmed by everything."

Nobody says anything as I stand from the chair and quickly exit the room. My feet move as fast as lightning until I'm finally inside the hallway bathroom. I place my hands on the edge of the sink as I stare into the mirror. I see the person staring at me, but she isn't me. Not anymore. I changed who I was because all those memories remind me of him. Every breath I take is for him. So, why should he get to have every memory when he looks at me as well? That's why I changed; why my hair and makeup are different.

I try to calm my racing heart, but nothing seems to help. My palms are growing sweatier by the minute, and my face is slowly starting to pale. My stomach feels like it's flipping around until it's tied into one big knot. I try to even out my breathing as much as possible, but it's not helping. Nothing is helping.

I stand in front of the mirror for what feels like an eternity before the door bursts open. I scream out in horror, but the sound is muffled so quickly that it sounds more like a squeak. Arms wrap around my waist and pull me against a rock hard chest. I clench my eyes together tightly, terror filling every part of my body. This would be my fucking luck. I come home because something terrible happens just for something even worse to happen to me.

I fight the onslaught of tears as I begin begging my captor to let me go. I don't know if he can hear behind his hand, but I hope he can. Instead, his arms tighten around me as a growl breaks through his throat. "Quit wiggling!" The familiar voice booms low in my ear. "It's just me, D. It's just me, *my Little Blossom.*"

My eyes snap open, forcing me to look into the mirror once again. "A-Axel," I manage to stutter. "W-Why are you i-in here?"

His arms tighten even more, crushing my body bit by little bit into his. It might just be my fucked up imagination, but I swear I can feel his cock hardening against my ass with every wiggle I make.

"Because you were gone for far too long, and I was worried." His voice skates across the shell of my ear, eliciting a silent moan only I hear to break free. "So, tell me, *Blossom.* Why did you lock yourself inside a bathroom? Is it that horrible to be in my presence?"

No!

God, no!

All I've ever wanted was to be the center of his attention. To be the girl, or woman, he fantasizes about, but I'm not. The hard truth of the matter slaps me in the face, breaking the haze he wrapped around me.

"Please, Axel, just let me go." I close my eyes again, holding back the tears for the life I dreamt of since I was a child. "I can't do this again. I can't go down that rabbit hole for a second time and make it out alive."

"What are you talking about, Blossom?" His arms loosen just a tad. "What can't you do again?"

I hold back the tears as much as I can as I squeeze my eyes tighter. I can't risk looking at him. The onslaught of emotions would throw me directly over the edge into my own heartbreaking abyss. Feeling his body against mine as his strong arms hold me in place, I feel the abyss getting closer to my broken heart.

"Please, Axel," I beg. "Just let me go."

"Fine," he clips as he releases me. "But I'm not letting *this* go. We're talking about it later. Is that understood?" I nod my head because the serious tone of his voice tells me he isn't going to drop this.

Once his arms slip free from my body, I notice the missing heat from his. The bulge I thought I felt suddenly disappears as I hear him walk through the door, closing it behind him. My heart beats wildly until I can find some semblance of self-respect to not walk out of this bathroom and leap into his lap in front of my whole family.

I shake my head, reminding myself Axel isn't mine. He never will be. I'm sure the girl Lee is toting around with her today wouldn't appreciate the thoughts I seem to keep having for *her man*. Lee would probably smack me in the back of my head and tell me to get my shit together because he isn't available. Maybe it's my childhood crush coming back around to stun me one final time before breaking free from my soul.

Chapter 4

❄ Axel ❄

I knew I made a mistake that night as soon as I followed her to the bathroom after she had been gone for so damn long. But the thoughts filling my head forced me to see it all in a different light. She could have been long gone all over again with the amount of time she spent in there. I could have lost my entire future if she would have disappeared.

Daisy isn't aware of it yet, but she's mine. Completely mine. This time I don't have any plans of letting her run away before I make my feelings clear. I have a plan, but I need help getting it pushed through. Christmas is only two weeks away, and I'll be damned if I don't make it her best yet.

Over the past few days, I've been thinking about the way her body felt pressed against mine. It took everything I had inside my soul to keep from kissing her plump lips and taking her the way I should have done all those years ago.

She was always my endgame, but I showed her the worst side of me. I would take home girl after girl just to keep her away before I was mature enough to realize all I did was break her. Something in my head always told me she would notice me more if she saw the attention I was getting, but that was a terrible idea. I saw the pain in her eyes every time one of those girls would latch onto me like a leach. Slowly, the happiness in her eyes faded away when she looked at me, and they filled with a burning hatred.

By the time I realized how badly I had screwed it all up, she was gone. The tears that fell down her cheeks that night nearly shattered my soul. I drank myself into a drunken stupor until a busty blonde woman sidled into the stool beside me. We didn't talk very much, but her hand was on my cock the whole time. She was so much different from Daisy. So fake in comparison. But in my head, all I could see was her light brown hair, hazel eyes, and puffy pink lips. Her innocent glances were enough to lock in the drunk dream.

I let that woman lead me to her hotel room where I closed my eyes, and with each thrust inside her, I thought of Daisy. My mind was reeling as the imaginary feelings took over. The woman thought I was crazy over her, but the truth is, I would never fuck Daisy doggy-style unless she asked for it because I want to see every bit of pleasure as I push us over the edge. I want to see the love in her eyes as she screams my name in complete ecstasy, over and over, again and again.

That night, I broke my own rule. The number one thing I promised myself I would never do. I fucked that blonde bimbo without a condom. Nine months later, I saw the woman when she showed up at the hospital with a very pregnant stomach. I was checking on the victim of my latest case at the time. Blondie's eyes were wide when they locked on me, but something in her expression was almost grateful.

The doctors rushed her pain-stricken face into a room. I heard shouts for hours on end. Something told me I shouldn't leave the hospital until I checked on her and the baby. So, I did. I sat in the hospital waiting room for what seemed like days but was really only close to twelve hours. The ear-piercing screams of a new baby broke the yelling from the woman before my feet took their own course to her room.

When I opened her door, my eyes landed on the newborn baby girl in the light pink blanket with a tiny little pink hat on her head. I was instantly pulled to the baby girl. She was absolute perfection. The woman's eyes were watching me with fear, but also appreciation. The doctors informed both of us that they needed to take the baby for some tests, and while I wasn't sure at the time why they were so calm about my presence, I soon learned.

To this day, I still don't know her name. I never wanted to. She was nothing to me or my little girl anymore after that day.

When she told me the truth about not only her daughter, but my daughter, I was furious. She wanted to give the baby up for adoption after she saw her. She wasn't sure if she could do it on her own, and when she saw my instant connection with her, she knew she wasn't the mother type. I told her I wasn't going to let that happen, and I would fight her to hell and back if I had to.

As if luck was on my side, she immediately signed over all her rights and granted me full custody of my daughter the second a DNA test proved the little girl was mine. Something we both already knew. It's been nearly five years now since we saw that woman, but I wouldn't care if I ever saw her again. She's nothing more than an egg donor in my eyes. She didn't even wait for the day my daughter was released to say one final goodbye. She never hugged her. I know for a fact that she never told her that she loves her either. How could any woman be that cruel?

I know Daisy has no idea about any of that. She doesn't know about my little girl. She doesn't know just how important she is to me, or what I would have done to make sure she never had to go into the system in any way. I know she would be proud of me for growing the way I did, but will she accept my daughter as her own when I admit everything to her?

Of course, she will. Daisy isn't like my little girl's egg donor. She wouldn't walk through the door without the intention of coming back at some point. But something deep inside my head is screaming that my risky choices and behaviors as a teenager and young adult will be the screeching halt to our lifelong pull to one another.

As I walk into the precinct, I make my way to Huck's desk. I need him to help me with this, but I also need to make sure he and Colt aren't going to kill me first for falling in love with their sister and never telling them. Surely they'll be pissed off at me, but I can handle it. I can handle anything to make this all right with her in the end. I don't have another choice. This is my last chance, and I refuse to screw it up.

"Who died?" Huck asks when his eyes lock onto my frantic motions.

I sigh as I drop into the chair on the other side of his desk. "We need to talk in my office. Do you have some time now?"

He tilts his head questioningly, doubt surely filling his head. "Not really," he admits with a shaky voice followed by a hard swallow. "Is everything okay? Wait, is Pickles okay? Who has her? Where is she?" Huck starts to grab everything he would need if something were really wrong with my little girl. It makes my heart both grow and break apart. Will he ever forgive me for what I need to tell him?

"Calm down," I say. He pauses all his movements. "Pickles is fine. I just need to talk to you and Colt about something."

"Did you get a lead on Dad's case?" Hope fills his words. "Should I call Mom and Daisy as well?"

"No!" I shout a bit too loudly as I damn near launch myself over his desk, placing my hand over his phone as he's reaching for it. "I just need to talk to you and Colt. It has nothing to do with anyone else. Well, not entirely. I just need your advice on something."

He scrubs his chin with his hand furiously. Inner turmoil fills his head, but he doesn't let his emotions show on the outside. Huck has always been the more sensitive and emotional one between him and Colt. He worries more than Colt but isn't afraid to go into battle to defend their honor. He's truly one of the best friends I could ever imagine having.

"I can have Colt here in an hour. I should be done with my paperwork by then, and we can go to your office." He slowly reaches for his phone again as I let go of it and sit back down in the chair across his desk.

"That works for me," I reply. "What are you working on anyway that has you so on edge?"

He takes a deep breath as he hits send on the message he was no doubt typing as I was talking to him. "Well, Cap got wind that I was working on my Pops' case without my superior's permission. I had to turn everything I found over to him so he can go through it with a fine tooth comb. I know none of it is admissible in court since he got his hands on it, he'll make sure of that, but I didn't really have anything good to begin with. Everything I had was everything my mom already told him. He didn't suspend me or put me on desk duty, which shocks me, but he did give me a new case that has my head spinning on end."

I groan loudly. The one thing I told him to do was not get fucking caught. I wasn't going to let him work the case, but I also knew I wouldn't be able to stop him either. Huck is one of those guys that when he has his mind set to something, he won't back down from it until he knows the complete truth.

"So, you're telling me I should be expecting a call from Cap today," I state the obvious. It's one of the major downfalls of being your best friend's lieutenant, especially at such a young age. Cap is always looking for things I've done wrong or things my officers do wrong. "That's fucking fantastic."

"Sorry, man. I thought I was staying pretty low on my investigation."

"It's not your fault, Huck. Cap has a serious boner for trying to rip apart my department to figure out why I have more respect than he does. I'm almost positive the asshole finds enjoyment in ruining my day." I throw my head back and look up at the ceiling. "What's the new case? Why didn't he put it on my desk with the details?"

"It's strange," he answers with a scrunched face. "This guy was in witness protection for years, but was suddenly released. The original case wasn't even closed yet. The guy should have stayed in witness protection, but they deemed it unnecessary. Cap told me something didn't feel right and said it was my job to find out why. But the thing is, I can't see why he gave me the case. He just got mad that I was investigating my dad's incident, then hands me a huge case? What the fuck is he playing at?"

I feel the gears turning in my head. None of this makes a bit of fucking sense. There is absolutely no reason for Cap to skip my desk when handing out cases. There's also no reason for Huck to turn over his evidence when it's all useless now. It might not be explicitly wrong for him to investigate, but Cap will find a reason to invalidate anything Huck found.

What the fuck is going on?

I start to shake my head as the thoughts begin pouring in. "Where's the guy you're looking for?"

"No fucking clue. It's like he just disappeared into thin air. His birth name hasn't been used since he was placed in the system, and the identity he was given hasn't been used since the day he was released from witness protection." He looks up at me with the most confused face I've ever seen. "But something about him and his case feels familiar. I swear I've seen this before. I've seen *him* before. I can't place my finger on why, but I'm going to figure it out if it's the last thing I do."

His eyes snap back down to his computer where his fingers begin to fly across the keys in anger. Something inside Huck is starting to snap. He's upset over whatever is happening right now. I'll have to get more out of him later. For now, though, I need to leave it where it is or he won't be able to concentrate at all.

I stand from the chair, slowly walking away from his desk and over to my office. I'm dreading the phone call I'm sure I'll have to face today, but I can handle it. Cap doesn't scare me. I'm not sure he scares anyone. Everybody in our house knows how this crooked fucker got his job, and what he has done to keep it. One day, though, his house of cards will come crumbling down. When it happens, I hope that I'm on the side with the wrecking ball destroying his life.

Chapter 5

❄ Axel ❄

Tick...
Tock...
Tick...
Tock...

The fucking clock in my office is seriously starting to piss me off. Everything is starting to piss me off. After I got into my office, Cap called me. I didn't even have the chance to brace myself for the impact this time.

He gave me the same speech that he always does. "You're letting Huck get away with way too much. Did you know he was looking into his father's case? How could you be so blind and stupid to not see it?" Really, the list of shit he rambled off is endless, but he didn't reprimand me or Huck. Why? He had all the ammo to shoot his shot at me, but he didn't. Why?

The door to my office slams open, bouncing off the wall behind it. Colt marches inside with Huck hot on his tail. The quiet sound of Christmas music in the office plays as the door closes. My thoughts instantly swirl back to why they're here. Why I called them in here.

Daisy.

They both take their seats, anger settling inside their eyes and bodies. Something isn't right with these two. Maybe I shouldn't bring her up right now. But if I don't do it now, will I ever have the chance, or balls, to do it again? No. The answer is simply, no. I need to do this now or I may never do it.

"You guys good?" I ask as they narrow their eyes on me.

"That depends on why you called both of us into your office. I don't even fucking work here, Axel. I shouldn't be getting called into the principal's office when it's not my school, bro," Colt snaps.

I hold my hands up in surrender, not willing to make this worse than it might already be. "First off, who pissed in your fucking Cheerios? Secondly, this is a friendly call, asshole. If you can't keep your dickhead ways under control, then you can find your way out of the door. I'm not coddling you because you're in some kind of fucking mood, Colt."

"Fuck off," he groans as he rolls his neck, cracking it. "What did you need?"

I take a deep breath, closing my eyes to calm myself as much as possible. "I need both of your help with something. It's not for Pickles, but it is for a woman. I need to prove myself to her. I need to show her I'm not the person I used to be. The person she knew and hated. She needs to know the truth, but I don't know how to fix the damage I caused."

I watch as they both turn their heads to stare at one another before they turn back to me. Both of them smile as if they have it all figured out before I even admit my feelings for Daisy to them. "How dumb do you think we are, exactly?" Huck asks with quiet laughter in his tone.

I narrow my gaze on him. "What the fuck is that supposed to mean?"

Huck throws his head back as he claps his hand down on Colt's shoulder. "It means you're talking about Daisy. Do you think we haven't noticed all the looks you give her whenever you do see her? Or do you not notice that your eyes are practically jumping out of your head to find her in any room?"

Well, this isn't what I was expecting. "What?" I say before I can stop the word from slipping from my lips. Of course I knew what my eyes were doing. I just didn't think they noticed it.

"Just fucking tell us what you need from us, Axel," Colt grunts. I really want to know what has his panties twisted in a bunch, but now isn't the time.

Taking a deep breath, I let it all out. "I've fucked up more times than I care to admit when it comes to Daisy. I always thought you would be upset with me, and pushed it all aside out of respect for the both of you. I always felt the way she looked at me. I know how she feels, or at least, how she used to feel about me." I run my hand over my face. "Christmas is coming up, and I want to do something special for her. I want to make sure she understands that she's the only person that matters to me in this world."

"And what about Pickles? Are you going to tell Daisy about her?" Huck asks with a raised brow.

I sigh, my shoulders slumping. "I wasn't hiding Pickles from her," I admit sheepishly. "How do I explain her to Daisy, though? I assumed you guys had told her about Pickles when I found out about her, even though I said I wanted to because I wanted to be the one to say it."

"Not our story to tell," Huck states with a shrug of his shoulders. "Daisy asked about you nearly every damn day, but we never told her anything more than you were doing good. We were trying to get the two of you to talk to each other, but that didn't work. We've always known the two of you had something. We just wanted you guys to finally say something to one another."

"Yeah, what he said," Colt groans. "You know Daisy as well as we do. She hasn't changed much over the years. Well, besides the fact she won't date anybody." Huck and I both snap our attention to Colt. "Oh, come on. It's not like it's some huge secret. Daisy isn't one for dating. She doesn't want to get close to someone to have her heart ripped out and shit on all over again. It took her months to even leave her apartment in Nashville after she moved there because she didn't have you with her. That's all she's ever wanted, Axel, but when you let her walk away without so much as a 'goodbye' she shut herself off from the world. That's where you need to start. Show her how you feel before it's too late. Women like Daisy are one in a million."

Before either of us have a chance to comment on what he said, he pushes the chair back and stands up. As he walks to the door of my office, he starts talking over his shoulder. "I need to go back to work. If you need me, come find me. I'm not stepping back in this station unless I absolutely have to." With that, he leaves my office, successfully confusing both Huck and I to new levels.

"Well, that was interesting," Huck announces.

"I was thinking more along the lines of confusing, but whatever floats your boat, I guess." I shrug my shoulders, locking all of my attention on Huck. "Do you think he's right, though?"

"Colt might be an ass, but he's rarely ever wrong. Maybe you should take his advice into consideration. I know I would." He pushes the chair back before slapping one of his hands onto the top of my desk. "Call her. Ask if you can take her out for lunch. Nothing else will happen before the two of you talk. It has to start somewhere, right?"

How am I supposed to answer that? Does he want me to answer that? My head is a spinning mess of chaos as he walks out of the office, closing the door quietly behind him. Alone with my thoughts, I think about everything they've said. I hate to admit that they're both right, but that's why I called them here. I need their help.

I pick up my phone, scroll down to her name that's always been stored in my phone with her beautiful face that takes over my whole screen. I press the call button and wait. My heart hammers in my chest as each ring goes unanswered. And just as I'm about to hang up, I hear the faint sound of her soft voice on the other end.

"Axel," she whispers. Sweat beads in the palm of my hand. My voice suddenly catches in my throat. "Axel, are you there?"

I close my eyes hoping that she'll agree once I have the chance to spit it out. I have to do this. We need to move forward. Both of us need to grow, and this time, we won't be alone. This time I plan on holding her hand as we find our path back to one another.

"Lunch?" I rush out. "Can I take you to lunch?"

Silence meets my ears. When I'm positive she's hung up on me for being a truly idiotic man and start to feel all my hope dwindle away, she answers. "Yeah, we can get lunch. Where do you want me to meet you?"

My heart leaps from my chest. This isn't happening. It can't be, right? God, I feel like such a little kid when I think about her. She was the first and only crush I've ever had. Maybe if I wouldn't have been such a boneheaded idiot, we could have been together this entire time.

"I'll pick you up at noon."

"I'll be outside waiting." Her statement lingers for a beat before we both hang up the phone.

Finally, I can start working on fixing the two of us and get to know her again. This time, I'll make sure she knows she's mine. That she's always been mine.

Chapter 6

❆ Daisy ❆

Checking my phone, I notice the time. I have five minutes to finish putting myself together before Axel comes to get me for lunch. What do I make of this? I haven't the slightest clue, but knowing he wants to spend time with me alone is enough to keep me from questioning him.

It's not as if we've never been alone before. We've just never been alone as two adults. Will my obsession for him come leaking through my soul until I'm completely embarrassed? I mean, he has someone at home waiting for him. Is it really right for us to be going to lunch without her?

My heart leaps from my chest as I walk out of the front door of my parent's home. Axel starts to get out of his truck. He walks around the side until he's standing at the passenger door. I swallow the thick goo filling my throat and walk to him, my hands shaking; legs trembling. How am I supposed to be able to go to lunch with him if I can't even get to his truck?

"Are you alright, Dais?" Axel tilts his head to the side curiously.

I quicken my pace until I'm nearly brushing my body against his to get into the truck. "Yeah, just a bit off today is all," I lie. How can I explain that I'm not okay because I'm simply in his presence?

He offers me a panty-melting smile before closing the passenger door, patting it before he circles back around to the driver's seat of the truck. I start fidgeting my hands nervously as he takes the seat behind the wheel. His large hands gripping the wheel so tight his knuckles start to turn white.

"Are you sure you're okay?" he asks, his voice gravelly. .

"Axel, I said I was fine. I'm just a little in my head about some things, but I'll be okay. Promise." I hold my shaking pinky in the air for him to wrap his around.

He lets out a low chuckle, relaxing his tight hold a bit. "Still all about those pinky promises, I see."

I start to laugh lightly. "Nobody can break a pinky promise. If they do, I don't need them in my life." I shrug my shoulder nonchalantly as he takes my pinky. I'm not sure if he believes me or not, but that's besides the point.

We drive down the road for a few miles until we're parked out front of Hippy Diner. This place has been around for ages. It's actually one of the oldest standing homestyle restaurants in town. The best part about it, I get to see how much it's changed since Lee and Nathan took it over almost four years ago.

The diner had been passed down for generations in Nathan's family. His grandfather opened it back in the seventies alongside Nathan's grandmother. They ran it successfully for over twenty years before passing down the torch to Nathan's mother. His parents kept the old-style theme and original menu during their time. Lee and Nathan had other plans, though. They didn't want to change the atmosphere of the place because that's what made it Hippies, but they did want to update a lot of other things. The menu was the first to see the changes. Lee went to culinary school just to perfect the menu. They've put everything they have into the diner, and from what Colt and Huck have told me, it's paid off tenfold. The diner is thriving more than it ever has.

But knowing this was Axel's first choice for a friendly lunch, I feel my chest slowly caving in. *He has someone at home, Daisy. This was nothing more than two friends catching up,* the voice in my head starts pointing out the facts.

"I know it's just Hippies to you, but I promise it's so much more than that now. Do you remember all the times we sat here for hours after everyone else already left?" Axel asks.

I look at the building, allowing all of our memories to come flooding back into my head. "Chocolate milkshake, cheeseburger, two orders of fries, and a piece of strawberry rhubarb pie." I groan as the taste of Hippie's famous Strawberry Rhubarb pie fills my mouth.

Axel laughs again, nodding his head with the world's biggest smile filling his face. "The fact that you still remember our late-night order surprises me."

I cock my head to the side, spinning in the truck seat to face him. "What's that supposed to mean?"

"It means, I can't let you go another second without tasting it for yourself." He launches himself out of the truck, runs to my side, and opens the door as he offers me his hand to help me down.

"Thanks." I take his help as I climb out of the truck. My hands are sweating, and I'm sure it didn't go unnoticed by him. Axel is just nice enough not to ask me why.

He leads me into the diner, his hand still holding onto mine. My mind starts to swirl with accusations of what this could mean to him. What I could mean to him. Surely, he wouldn't be holding my hand if it didn't mean more, right?

But once the hostess greets us, all of those thoughts dwindle away. Axel lets go of my hand and offers her the smile I've always only ever seen for me. It's when she starts batting her eyes at him like a horny little bitch that I find myself ready to claw her eyes out.

Shaking my head, I push away all of the crazy scenes playing in my head. Maybe I should just run away now before anyone can see my embarrassment.

The hostess leads us to our old corner booth that seats at least eight people and sets down our menus. Axel thanks the blonde barbie as she rolls her eyes at me. Honestly, it's taking everything I have to not get up and run after her. I used to be a brawler in school. Well, that's what my brothers always called it. I was so sweet to everyone, but I only gave them one chance. Anything after that was fair game. Maybe that's why I always kept my inner circle so small. Even back in Nashville, I only have a select amount of friends, but they don't come close to the ones back home.

"So, how's the music coming along, Superstar?" Axel asks with a teasing tone.

"I'm not a superstar. I'm a country star," I correct him with a small smile. "And it's going pretty great. I have a tour set up to start after the beginning of the year, and I have a new album that will be released in

February. My manager has become one of my best friends now that he understands I won't bow down to every demand he makes. The other artists are so nice. It's pretty close to the life I've always dreamed of."

"Close?" he questions. "Daisy, that sounds like the dream you've always told me you wanted. What's missing? Is there anything I can do to help make all your dreams come true?"

Yes. God, yes. I almost shout with glee as he anxiously leans against the table. "That part of my dream sailed years ago. I've come to realize that it was just a fairytale stuck inside my head. I'm over it now. But maybe if you tell me what you said to my manager over the phone five years ago, I can think of new dreams?" I shrug my shoulders as the waitress comes by.

Axel chuckles under his breath. He knows I'm joking because my dreams are what I live for. I would never just replace one with something so silly. "I told him that if he ever tried to control you again, I'd pay him a personal visit and arrest his ass on some mundane charge. You should have heard the way he swallowed a large lump down his throat. He might have even pissed himself."

Much like the hostess, she gives all her attention to Axel as she takes our drink orders. He gives her the same smile, making me want to scream and cry all at the same time. Am I being ridiculous? Yes. Do I care? No. Axel asked me to lunch, yet he gives them *my* smile. So, when the waitress turns to me, takes my drink order, and rolls her eyes as she walks away, I growl in anger.

"She's a pain in the ass sometimes," he states as he throws his head back against the booth seat. "You'd think she'd take a hint by now that I'm not interested in her."

"What?" I ask, completely taken aback.

He slides around the curve of the table in the booth until he's sidled right next to me. "The waitress. She's been trying to get me to ask her out on a date for a few years now. It started after she moved here. At first, it was nice to have someone flirting with me again, she wasn't the one I wanted. I never had some insane urge to drop my life and settle down with her. She just can't seem to get that picture in her head." He drapes one arm over my shoulder as I process his words.

"Well, I'm sure your girlfriend is very proud that you can keep it in your pants." I grab hold of his hand, freeing my shoulders from his arm.

He turns in the seat, facing me, and places his hands on each side of my face, trapping it between them so I can't look away.

"I don't have a girlfriend, Daisy. It's just me and Pickles," he admits.

Before I have a chance to think better of it, I ask him the question burning in my head since I first heard the name, Pickles. "Who's Pickles?"

The look in his eyes almost rips me apart. He's terrified to tell me more about the person he keeps talking about. "My daughter," he states with a shaky voice. "Pickles is my little girl. Before you start picking everything apart in that head of yours, I'll answer some questions before they're even asked. Her mom and I were never together, relationship-wise that is. I was really drunk one night and slept with her. I never knew her name. I still don't. I happened to see her at the hospital while I was at work, and she happened to come in because of her water breaking. That was the day I found out about my daughter. She didn't want her, but I did. I wanted my little girl more than the air I breathed. She gave birth to a beautiful, seven-pounds, six-ounces, and twenty-one inches long, baby girl. She never held her after she was born, and we haven't seen her since that day in the hospital. It's been Pickles and I since then."

The waitress drops off our drinks, takes our orders, and leaves quickly after she notices that Axel moved to sit next to me instead. "I-I don't know what to say," I stumble through the words. "You have a daughter." I let my own words soak in my head. "You never told me. Nobody ever told me." I pull away from him, looking down at the table where my drink sits. "Did you guys forget about me that much? None of you could even tell me about her?" I feel the tears burning the corners of my eyes, but I refuse to let them fall.

"I told them not to tell you. I wanted to be the one who explained everything to you." I feel his eyes burning into my broken soul. "I'm sorry if I hurt you by not telling you sooner. I just thought it would be better said in person."

"But why?" I turn to look at him, a single tear breaking loose with a sniffle. "Why couldn't you have just called me, Axel? You shut me out of your life for five years. You had this whole world in front of you, and you never told me. Did I do something to upset you? To hurt you?" My voice breaks as my emotions begin to slowly take over.

Axel wraps his arms around me, pulling me into his chest. I want to fight and protest against it, but he's my safe place. He always has been. "I've been broken a few times over the years, but one thing broke me more than the rest. One person. I have a lot to fix, Daisy, but I promise you I'll fix it all." He gives me a soft kiss on the top of my head. My mind starts reeling about what he could possibly mean by all of this. It doesn't make sense. Who hurt him so badly? And what does he need to fix?

I look up at him with curious eyes but find him staring down at me with nothing but love filling his. Am I going crazy? Am I imagining the way he's looking at me because that's how I want him to?

Yep, I've become certifiably insane.

Chapter 7

❄ Axel ❄

I can't miss the way the falling snow highlights her face. She's absolutely perfect in my eyes. I'm sure she thinks I've gone mad since I haven't spoken a word to her for close to five minutes. Instead, I'm staring at her as if she'll disappear at any given moment.

Maybe I'm dreaming? Maybe she told me no and this date is nothing more than a figment of my imagination. But as I blink my eyes furiously like a madman, I find myself fully awake, Daisy staring at me with one brow hitched on her forehead curiously.

"How old is your daughter?" she asks.

I shake my head, trying to collect myself before this conversation. I take a sip of my drink before clearing my throat. "She's four now. It's crazy how fast she went from this tiny little baby that I could hold in my arms for hours on end, to a little girl that only wants my cuddles when it's convenient for her." I roll my eyes dramatically.

"Oh, come on, you can't fool me with that," she teases with a laugh. "What kind of girl wouldn't want to cuddle with you at any time of the day?" She smacks her hand over her mouth, and I watch as her eyes triple in size.

"What was that? Don't be shy now, Little Blossom." I wink, noticing the way she shifts the lower portion of her body.

She clears her throat as best as she can before straightening her shoulders. "You heard what I said, Axel," she growls through gritted teeth. "Doesn't seem logical for me to repeat myself when you know what I said."

I laugh as I throw one of my arms back around her shoulder, leaning in closer until I feel heat radiating off her body. "Maybe I just want to know if you're one of those women. Would you cuddle with me at any time of the day, Blossom?"

Her eyes shift from left to right as she stares into mine for any truth in my assumption. But I can also see the broken woman inside crying for me to see. Daisy might have changed over the years, but I can still see the way she reacts to me. Her heart is racing, thumping louder and louder for me to hear. I won't lie and say I'm completely calm, though, because I'm dying over here. Daisy's in my arms, staring at me, and all I want to do is kiss her soft lips. I want to make her mine.

"Stop, Axel," she pleads. "Don't do this to me."

Trying to even out my breathing, I lean in closer to her, stealing the gap that was between us. "Tell me, Blossom," I pause as I lick my bottom lip. "Would you cuddle with me?"

Her body trembles in my arms as she melts into the booth. "Yes," she whispers. "You don't even have to ask, Axel." She drops her gaze from me, hiding the way she feels. I lift her face by her chin and force her to look into my eyes.

"Prove it, Daisy." Her eyes widen. "I want you to prove it to me."

"What? H-how?" she stutters while her wild eyes dart over every feature on my face.

"The same way I plan on proving everything to you." My control snaps. Crashing my lips to Daisy's, I feel her give in to me immediately. I don't care that we're in a busy restaurant. Why should I give a shit that they see me kissing the only woman I've ever cared about?

She moans into my mouth, breaking the small thread of control I had tucked away, and I devour her. My tongue breaks through her lips, and I taste everything inside. Just as I imagined, she tastes like heaven. Her soft purrs of ecstasy go straight to my cock. What I wouldn't give to rip those tight jeans off her body and slam myself inside of her. I'm positive I can hear her screams as I pull away from her lips.

We both sit there, staring at each other as we try to catch our breaths. The look of hope in her eyes brightens my day, but when the waitress comes by and drops off our food, I can see the pain and hurt as she turns away from me. I have a lot of work to do.

❄ ❄ ❄

Dropping Daisy off at her parent's makes me feel more alone now than I ever have in my life. I always knew she was the one who was destined to walk through this life with me. We were always meant to be with one another, but life decided to throw us some curveballs. It's my job to make her see this is where she belongs.

With Christmas around the corner, I need to step up my game. I have to make her see my arms are the ones meant to hold her each and every night. With Colt and Huck on my side, I have more hope than I've ever had in my life.

Going back to the precinct, all I can think about is Daisy. How was I so stupid for so long? I knew that she was my forever when we were little kids. I can still remember it all like yesterday.

(Flashback to Axel: Age 7)

Cute little curls. Big, blue, puppy dog eyes. Small little arms crossed over her chest. Daisy is such a perfect little thing. She's younger than me, but she's still so cute.

I shouldn't feel the way I do at such a young age, but who can blame me when I get to see her every day? But on Christmas Day, she's always the happiest. It has nothing to do with the presents she's currently pouting over, She loves it because of her family. They've made each and every one of her holidays the best ever. She loves that Christmas means a whole day with her family, and mine, where all we do is spend time with one another.

I'm her protector, though. Her brothers told me earlier this year when we started to all form these little crushes on girls that Daisy was and always will be off limits. If I feel anything toward her, I'm to ignore it and find someone else. Is that how it works? Can I just simply like someone else because I can't like her?

But when she's handed that first present, and her eyes light up as bright as the lights on the tree, I know I'll never be able to find another girl as pretty as her. Even if I force myself to like someone else, I'll never be able to. I'm young now, but one day, I'll be a strong man, and Daisy is the only girl I'll ever let in my life.

Thinking back on the day it all started to hit me, I see just how badly I fucked everything up. From denying my feelings to pushing her away even though she's the only one I've ever wanted. Even though I knew she wanted me, too. All because I didn't want to ruin what I had with her or her brothers.

Maybe if I prove myself to her enough, she'll forgive me enough to let me into her life.

Chapter 8

❋ Daisy ❋

What the actual fuck was that?

When I went to lunch with Axel, the last thing I was expecting was for him to kiss me the way he did. I can honestly say it was the best kiss I've ever had in my life. Maybe it was because I've dreamt of it my whole life, but does that explain the sparks I felt? And what was he meaning by he will fix it all? What is there to fix? I don't dare hope he's talking about us.

My mind continues to swirl in circles as he drops me back off at my parent's house. I offered to get an Uber so he could go home and see his daughter, but he refused. I would be lying if I said it didn't make me the happiest girl on earth to know that this one time I had his attention.

But when I walked into the house, I felt alone. For the first time in my life, I wanted to stay here. Just not in this house. Yes, this is my home, but it's not where my heart has always been. My mom told me when I was a little girl that our home isn't four walls, floors, and windows. Our homes are where our hearts reside. Her example was my father. She picked up her entire life just for him and moved across four states just to be with him. She hasn't regretted the day since. Is that what I have to do in order to prove to Axel that I'm the one he belongs with?

My career, though, will that be the end? Will my label drop me as soon as I tell them I want to go back home for good? Surely they wouldn't do that to me, but I know it's always a possibility. And for the first time in my music career life, I don't care. The lights, fame, money, none of it compares to the whole heart I feel around Axel. If he isn't willing to admit his feelings after that kiss, then I'll pry them out of him.

With a new mission in mind, I run up the stairs until I reach my parent's room. I remember when I was little and it was this close to Christmas, we weren't allowed to disturb our parents. They always told us they had a secret door so they could go see Santa and talk to him about our behavior and what we wanted for Christmas. Truth be told, they were wrapping our presents the whole time. Looking back at it now, I love the way they handled it. If I have kids one day, that's going to be my Christmas trick.

I swing open the door to my parents' room to find them following holiday tradition. Presents are wrapped and stacked all around the room. My dad is lying in the bed with their comforter tucked around him. My mom is cutting paper and placing pieces of tape where she needs as she wraps it.

Shutting the door behind me, I make my way to them before taking a seat on the edge of the bed. I let out a long, dramatic sigh that gains their attention. My dad leans forward as much as he can without pain radiating through his body. He isn't back to one hundred percent yet, but I know he won't let that stop him.

"What's wrong, Daisy?"

Turning to face him while keeping my mom in view from the corner of my eye, I let out a deep breath. "I want to move home," I admit.

"Sweetheart, you're always welcome back home. You already know this. But what about your music? Your career? Won't you be giving up everything you've worked so hard for, for so long? I'm not saying I don't want you to move back home, but I want to see you happy." My dad leans forward a bit more, hissing in pain as he takes one of my hands in his.

"Dad, I'm not talking about this house." I look down, suddenly embarrassed for the small confession.

"Oh, honey," my mom coos as she sets down the wrapping paper, presents, and tape. She leans forward, taking my other hand in hers. "I told you that one day the time would be right. I'm going to guess that you've

111

both finally talked to each other. How does he feel about all of this? Have you two finally given up on this little fight between you?"

My dad's head snaps to my mom at the same time as mine. Both of us, in unison, say the only word we need to. "What?" My heart rate spikes to higher levels than ever before. My dad, on the other hand, sounds completely lost and confused.

She throws her head back with bellowing laughter following closely behind. "I was your age once, little girl. Do you think I never saw the way you both looked at each other?" She narrows her eyes at me intimidatingly. "You both are so obvious that I'm not sure how this whole town never knew."

"I-" I pause as I try to collect myself before going on. "I don't know what you're talking about, Mom."

She tsks before standing up from the bed. She lets go of my hand, but waves for me to follow her. "Come on. I have a lot to show you, honey."

She walks away without waiting to see if I'm going to follow her. I look at my dad who has his head tilted to the side curiously. "You better follow her and tell me everything." He laughs, causing me to laugh along with him. He knows I'll always tell him what's going on.

I jump up from the bed and follow the path I saw my mom take. Walking through the door of their room, I look left and right. Noticing the door at the end of the hall standing wide open, my heart leaps into my throat. There's one room in this house that I've never walked into. I'm actually not sure if anyone other than my mom has actually ever walked into the room before.

But as my feet follow the path, I find myself suddenly worried about what stands behind that usually closed door. I walk through the entryway and look around at the room with light gray walls, white trim, and little pink elephants lining the center of the walls as a border. I see one lone rocking chair sitting off to the side with a small, twin-size bed on one wall, and a crib on another. I feel tears burning my eyes because my mind instantly thinks the worst thing possible. Why else would she keep this a big secret from our entire family?

"Mom," I choke out. "What's going on?"

She keeps staring out of the window for what feels like an eternity before she spins on her heels to face me. "What do you think this room is for?"

I take a shaky step forward to try and feel the comfort of my mom. "A nursery." I stop about a foot in front of her, but she doesn't move or step closer. Odd. "I just don't understand why you brought me in here. I'm not pregnant, Mom."

She laughs wholeheartedly, breaking away some of the tension between us. "I'm sure you're thinking the worst right now, but don't. This nursery was never meant for any of my children, honey." She looks around the room with a wide smile and tears glistening in her eyes. "I started working on this room when you were close to six-years-old. It was the first time I saw Axel look at you. Really look at you. I knew from that day on that you both were meant to be together. You're both just too damn stubborn to admit it." She rolls her eyes in annoyance. "I've only ever let one other soul into this room. Did you know that?"

"No," I whisper my admission.

"Mhm." She nods her head before walking across the room. She starts riffling through a drawer until she pulls out a small box. "Pickles may not be our blood, but she's still one of ours. I remember the day Axel brought her home from the hospital. He was so clueless about what he needed to do. He was sure that he would be such an unfit father. I couldn't let him think that way. He stayed with us for close to a month, just until he was able to figure some things out. He put his life together because of that little girl. Within a month, he had a house for them, not an apartment, but a house with a large backyard. Every night for a month, I tucked Pickles into that crib and slept in that tiny little bed. From the moment I held her in my arms, I knew she was our family. I want you to sit in that rocking chair and look through this box. It may leave you with more questions, but it may give you some peace of mind and closure."

I open my mouth to speak, but she pushes the box into my hands. "You wouldn't have thought about moving back unless he told you about her, honey. As I said before, I was your age once." She leans forward, pressing a tender kiss to my forehead before pointing to the rocking chair. I walk to the chair and sit down. She nods her head with a big grin on her face, and walks out of the door, closing it softly behind her.

Looking down at the box, I start to feel the sweat coating my body. I open the box to find pictures, a letter, and small, little trinkets. I take out the pictures first, flipping through each and every one. A small, little girl who looks just like Axel takes my breath away. In every picture, she's smiling as though the world has no evil inside it. As if her mother never abandoned her without a care in the world. Blonde curls wrap around her small little face. Is it crazy that I can already hear her sweet laughter?

Wiping away the tear that slid down my cheek, I put the picture down on the window sill by the chair and move on to the trinkets locked inside. The first thing I pick up is a small locket necklace. I open the silver circle to find a picture of me on one side and Axel with his daughter on the other. More tears start to fall down my cheeks. My mom never should have had to make her own family picture of us.

The next thing I pull out is a tiny, hospital wristband. Natalie Parker. With Axel's last name, I can only assume this is Pickles' wristband. It's so small. More tears start to slide down my face. I should have been here for him. For her. I should have been with them through all the hard times.

The last trinket in the box is a small lock of hair with a ribbon tied around it. Curiosity fills me with why there's hair inside, but I can't figure it out. I set all three items with the pictures on the window sill.

I reach into the box one last time and pull out the letter inside. Setting the box on the sill with the other items, I sit back in the chair and open the first letter. Heartbreak attacks me as I see Axel's handwriting.

My dearest Little Blossom,

I'm not sure you'll ever see this letter. I'm actually not even sure you'll want to read it if you have the chance. I have so many things I need to tell you, but a letter isn't the way.

If you found this letter and just so happen to be reading it, I just want to say I'm sorry for everything. I wanted to stop you the day you told me you were leaving. I wanted to beg you to stay with me. But I couldn't be that selfish. I couldn't be the reason you gave up on your dreams.

One day, I hope you will forgive me for everything. Young boys make stupid decisions for the future man they are trying to become. My greatest regret was letting you walk out of my life.

The pictures in the box are all the ones I took to show you one day. Pickles was never meant to be kept a secret from you. You just deserved to be told in person. That's another thing I need to apologize for. I wanted to be the one who told you, but I always assumed when I didn't, someone else did.

She's such a perfect little baby who turned into a beautiful little girl. I hope you can see that in her pictures. I wanted to document everything for you, so that one day, when I held you in my arms again, you would know everything there is to know about her.

The little trinkets were another of my ideas. The locket was something I got soon after she was born. I wanted us to be a family. You should have been her mother, and I'm incredibly sorry that you weren't. I hope that one day you can love her as if she's your own.

The hospital band is to make sure you know I was thinking about you the whole time. Even if you weren't the one lying in that bed. I knew you were with me every step of the way, Blossom. I could feel you holding me. You're the only reason I made it through any of this.

Last but not least, the small bundle of hair was from her first haircut. She was so scared, but do you know what I told her? I told her that I know the most beautiful girl in the world, next to her, and how brave she always was. I showed her your picture, and I swear I saw the light shine in her eyes all over again. She sat there like such a big girl while the hairdresser cut off some of her curly locks. You got her through that without even knowing her or being with us. She knows who you are, Daisy. I made sure.

This letter is my way of telling you how much I care about you. How much I love you. It always should have been us against this world, but I fucked that up. If I could go back and change the hands of time, I would in a heartbeat. I'd find a way to keep both you and Pickles. You two are my only reason for living,

Blossom. I truly hope that one day you can see how much I love you.

Until you're in my arms again, Blossom.
Love, Axel.

P.S. You'll always be mine, just as I will always be yours.

Time seems to stand still as I fall apart from my seams. This is everything I needed to hear and more. I don't have any questions like my mom thought I would. Instead, I have all the answers I need. Axel may think he's the only one who made mistakes, but he's not. We both have.

With a plan in mind, I call one of the only people I know I can trust. When she answers on the first ring, I feel like the world will finally stop spinning so fast, and I'll have the life I always dreamed of.

"Lee, we have things we need to do. Christmas is soon, and I have a man to make mine."

Chapter 9

❄ Daisy ❄

With it being Christmas day, I'm so excited for everything I have planned. Axel and I have been talking all day every day. I had the chance to meet Pickles a few days ago when Lee and I were out buying Christmas gifts, and just like I suspected, she's perfect. Axel was right when he said I'd love her. But for him to think I couldn't love her the way I already do, blows my mind. How can anyone willingly give away that sweet little girl?

I start placing my gifts under the tree as Colt and Huck both walk in. The minute they see, though, they freeze in place. Their eyes widen as they stare at me. I tilt my head to the side, examining them. "What's your guy's deal today?"

"Nothing!" Huck shouts before bolting out of the room. I roll my eyes at him, narrowing my gaze solely on Colt.

"Out with it." I cross my arms over my chest, tapping my foot on the floor.

He holds his hands up in surrender as he steps back from the room. "Nope. Not my pig, not my farm, little sister." I shake my head as I follow his steps. "Daisy, I'm serious. I'm not telling you anything. It's not my place." We both stop walking.

"Then don't look at me like I'm doing something wrong by putting presents under the tree. Keep it up, and I'll take all of yours back to the damn store where they should have stayed." I lock my eyes on him as he drops his shoulders.

"D, you know I'd tell you if I could, okay?" He sighs. "You're not doing anything wrong. It's actually really nice to see you back home for Christmas this year. I do have to ask, though. How long until we see you for another one?"

I feel the crack in my heart spreading wider than ever before. Colt isn't usually the one to express his feelings and emotions, but now…, now he's letting them run wild in the living room where only he and I stand.

"Well, if my plans work out the way I want them to, I shouldn't miss another one ever again."

The smile I've grown up seeing from him and loving about him spreads across his face before his arms wrap around me in a tight hold. He lifts me from the ground and starts to spin us in circles. We both laugh out loudly until I hear a throat clear in the entryway of the house. Colt sits me back down, and we both turn to see Axel standing, leaning against the wall next to him. Little Pickles pokes her head around him, screaming when she sees me. She takes off full sprint, leaping into my arms as I squat down for her.

"Daddy! Look who's here!" Her little arms wrap tightly around my neck as the excitement bubbles inside her.

"Why don't we let Daisy breathe, Pickles? I'm sure Nana needs help in the kitchen. Why don't you go see what she has set up for you?" Pickles lets go of my neck before pressing a sweet little kiss to my cheek. I let her go, and she takes off running toward the kitchen. I smile as I watch her little blonde curls bounce with each step she takes.

"She's perfect, you know?" I turn my attention back to Axel as I see Pickles enter the kitchen where I know my mom and Axel's are in there cooking for our Christmas lunch.

His eyes lock onto mine the minute I stop turning. "She's not the only perfect one, Blossom."

My mouth goes dry as I take in his statement mixed with the way he's staring at me. Colt excuses himself from the room completely and nearly sprints to the kitchen with everyone else. "W-where's Lee and Nathan?" I stutter.

He takes a large step closer to me. "They'll be here soon. Promise." He reaches out one of his large hands, caressing my cheek. Heat burns through my body from his touch. Since the kiss we shared at lunch, he hasn't made another move. Thankfully, I read that letter when I needed to the most. "Can we talk for a bit? I need to say some things before everyone else gets here."

"Yeah, of course. Let's go talk in my room. You already know that nobody ever bothers me there." I laugh.

"You've also never taken a man upstairs with you. I have a feeling Huck and Colt will bust down your door." He laughs with me.

I tap my finger to my chin, thinking for a moment. The idea that hits me seems so traitorous, yet so right. My mom always told me to follow my heart, and I think it's time I start listening. I take Axel's hand in mine and lead him to the most private room I know of.

Opening the door to the secret nursery, I look around, much like I did the day my mom took me in here. This time, the air feels thin. I know the truth. I have the answers I need. This room wasn't made for anyone other than mine and Axel's future. It only seems fitting for us to talk here when we need to speak privately.

"So, this is where she always takes Pickles to. I always thought that if I walked into this room, your mom would kill me," he admits with a slight chuckle. "I should have known she'd do this the moment I came to her with Pickles in my arms. It looks great in here."

Looking over to the window, I see the box, pictures, trinkets, and the letter sitting the way I left them. I thought my mom already put them away. She told me she would take care of it when I told her I was crying too hard to see everything and make sure it was back in the box. I'm sure it was intentional to leave it there.

Axel's eyes follow mine until they land on the box as well. He walks over to it, picks up the letter in his hands, and turns back to me. "You read the letter," he says instead of asking. Axel has always figured things out faster than anyone else I've ever known. It's no wonder he got as far as he did in his career.

"I did. Is that okay?" I take a step closer to him as he sets the letter back down. He takes a seat in the rocking chair and picks up the locket next. His eyes shine with unshed tears as he opens it. "I loved the locket. It felt like I was part of your family somehow."

"You always have been, Blossom. You already know that." He looks up at me with so much hope it kills me.

I walk the rest of the way to him. Taking the locket out of his hands, I set it back on the sill next to the box and on top of the pictures. The one on top is a picture of him and Pickles on her first birthday. I didn't even notice before, but in that picture, Axel is wearing the locket around his neck.

I pick up the picture, studying it closer than I had before. "You were wearing it? Why did you take it off and put it in the box?"

"I didn't take it off until the day you came back. Even if it was for a really shitty thing happening to your family, I had to make something to show you everything. I wasn't even sure you'd ever see any of this. I know it's not the same as the memories I have with her, but it's something, right?" I notice the small tear forming in the corner of his eye.

"It is," I admit. "It's everything, Axel. Thank you. These are all things I'm going to cherish for the rest of my life because it's about you and Pickles." I take in a deep breath to push away all the nerves. But when Axel notices my shaking body, he pulls me down to straddle his lap. Just being in his arms calms me more than anything else ever has or can.

"I'm sorry that I was such an idiot." He presses his head to mine. "I'm sorry I took away so much of our time."

I place one of my hands on his cheek, causing him to look into my eyes again. "You were never an idiot, Ax. You've always been the smartest man I know. You weren't the reason we were apart. I took a job that pulled me away from you. From everyone. I never knew how you felt, but that's not your fault. My mom told me the other day that it was plain as day how we felt, but we're both stubborn. Thinking back on it now, she was right. You never hid how you felt about me, and neither did I for you." I press my lips to his.

"At the risk of sounding completely and utterly selfish, I want to say how much I don't want you to leave again. But I know it won't be the end of our story this time, Blossom. This time, I'm following you anywhere you go. If you choose Nashville, then so do Pickles and I. She already told me on the way over here that I'm not allowed to lose you. I think she loves you more than she loves me already." We both laugh as he wipes away an unruly tear that slides down my cheek.

"I don't want Nashville, Axel. I want my home," I state. My eyes dart back and forth, staring into his with every bit of hope I have left in my body.

He leans back slightly to see me better than before. "And where is your home, Blossom?"

I close my eyes for a brief second as I collect myself. Opening my eyes, I dive into his. "Wherever you and Pickles are. That's my home. You are my home, Ax. You and Pickles are my forever. That's if you want me."

"Fuck yes, I want you. We want you. You've always been my home. Always will be. Pickles loves you, and after her statement, I'm going to say you're her home as well." Love blooms inside his eyes.

"I already spoke to my manager a few days ago," I lean back slightly as he tightens his hold to ensure I don't fall. "I had a chance to live out my dream, and I did it. But now it's time for me to follow my real dreams. I gave it all up. I didn't even hear what they had to offer. My contract was up anyway, and the moment I saw you, I knew I wouldn't be signing it for more years of traveling farther away from you."

"Daisy," he growls. "You're not giving up your career for us. I'm telling you right now to call him back and sign the contract. I'm following you this time. I'm not letting you lose everything."

I smile as I kiss his lips again. "I'm not losing anything this way, Ax. I'm gaining everything."

He stares at me for a moment, testing the legitimacy in my words. When he smiles and nods his head, I know he understands what I'm telling him. "Where are you going to live?"

"With you and Pickles. I'm not really asking either. You'll just have to move some of your shit to the side and make room for me," I tease him as we both break out in laughter.

"Darlin', you've always had a place in our home." I melt as he calls his home 'ours'. He swats my ass lightly, making me jump a bit in his lap. "That was a bad idea on my part," he groans as I feel his cock hardening beneath me. I lick my lips as I lean forward to kiss him again. I don't think I'll ever get enough of him.

"Axel, I need more. I need to feel something just to make sure this isn't some big dream. It wouldn't be the first time I've dreamt about us, but I need to know this is really us this time. I can't be broken apart by another empty dream."

He wraps one of his large hands around the back of my neck as he pulls me closer. "Then let me show you what it's like to feel alive again."

His lips crash onto mine in fiery passion. I moan into his mouth as his tongue slips inside. He groans in ecstasy as he lifts his hips to meet mine.

I pull back slightly as I look around the room. My mom knew this room was meant for Axel and I somehow. She knew this was where we would begin our lives. "I love you, Axel Parker. I always have and always will."

"I love you, Daisy Parker. Always have and always will." Parker may not be my last name, but damn does it sound good.

Axel's hands move to the bottom of my shirt and he raises it above my head. My breasts bounce in the little-to-nothing bra I have on, earning another groan to slide from his throat. He unsnaps the hooks in the back, freeing my chest for him. He licks his lips like a starving man before latching onto my nipple and feasting like it's his only meal.

Writhing in his lap, I try to press his cock against my clit for any kind of friction. He grips my hips to hold me steady as he lets my nipple slip free with a pop. "I want to take this slow. I want us to learn who we are all over again. But I also have this feral animal inside telling me to make you mine. To take you and show you just how much I fucking love you, Daisy."

"Then take me, Axel. Make me yours the only way you can." I grind my wet pussy against him, feeling the fabric from my wet panties rubbing against my sensitive clit. I moan as the feeling swarms inside. "Fuck me the way you've always dreamt of."

He nearly growls as his fingers dig into my skin. Before I have a chance to even breathe, Axel has me lifted from his lap and throws me down onto the small bed. Like a man on a mission, he rips my jeans clean from my body. He wastes no time even seeing the panties he destroys next. He runs one finger through my soaked lips as he presses another deep inside. I arch my back as moans fly from my mouth.

"So fucking wet for me. So fucking perfect. My little Blossom." He leans forward, stealing my lips from me. "I can't wait, Daisy. I fucking can't. I need you as much as I need air. You're my fucking oxygen." His chest heaves as he slides another finger inside. "Look at my tight little pussy swallowing my fingers. That's it, baby. Let my pussy take what she wants from me. You'll never have to touch her again." He continues thrusting his fingers inside me.

"Axel, please," I beg. I can't explain why, but hearing him call what is actually my pussy his spurs on my desire for him. "Please, give me what I need. Give me you."

"Hold on tight, Blossom," He warns before sliding his fingers out of me. "I don't plan on being gentle."

He doesn't give me any warning or a chance to speak before he has all of his clothes off. His cock springs up before he takes it into his hands. Stroking his cock, he smiles down at me. This is our moment. Our chance to finally become whole.

"Make me yours, baby," I whisper.

Without hesitation, Axel moves until his body is right above mine. He lines his cock up with my entrance, and in one long, hard thrust, he pushes inside. I scream out as he starts thrusting in and out. My words come out as mumbles of pure nonsense. He kisses me with everything he has as he keeps up his punishing pace. I push my body down further, meeting him thrust for thrust.

"That's it, little Blossom. Open up my pussy for me. Let me inside." I spread my legs wider as he pushes in deeper. "Fuck," he hisses. "So fucking tight." He keeps thrusting as my eyes start to cross.

"Axel," I moan breathlessly. "Yes!" He slams inside of me as I scream.

"Mine. All. Fucking. Mine," he growls into my ear as he nips my neck. "Daisy, fuck." I feel the tension in his body. I can tell he's getting closer to the edge just like I am.

"Axel, I'm close. Fuck! Yes!" I yell out for anyone and everyone to hear.

I don't care that our families are here. I don't care about anything other than me and him. And neither does he as he grips my thighs and lifts my legs over his shoulders. He holds on to me as tight as he can as he slams inside of me.

My legs begin to shake as my orgasm draws closer. "I'm-" He slams inside of me again, pausing any thoughts I had. "Fuck, Axel!" I throw my head back as he keeps thrusting inside. "I'm coming!"

He pulls out of me completely as I scream out. Just as I'm about to force him back inside, he gives me a brutal stab with his cock. Everything around me starts to go fuzzy as he growls, "Look at me, Blossom. Look at me while my pussy comes all over my cock." My eyes snap open as wave after wave of pleasure rolls through my body. "That's it, baby. Such a good fucking girl." His movements become faster. "My good fucking girl." I feel his throbbing cock inside of me ready to burst.

"Come for me, Axel. Fill your pussy until it's dripping. I want to leak you." I groan as he roars out his own release, filling me completely.

He stays inside of me as he drops my legs from his shoulders. Leaning forward, he presses his lips to mine. "I'm never letting you go again, Daisy. Not in a million fucking years."

"I think I like the sound of that, Lieutenant." I kiss his lips once again, fueling the fire burning between the two of us.

Axel slowly pulls out of me before rushing to the bathroom. Returning with a wet washcloth, he cleans me thoroughly with gentle hands. My heart swells to the size of Texas as he helps me stand from the bed. I look down at my shredded clothes, causing us both to laugh as he helps me back to my room. Thankfully, everyone is still downstairs, which means we won't be caught yet.

I have to say, this might be my best Christmas gift yet.

Epilogue

❄ Daisy ❄

It's been one year since Axel and I finally admitted our feelings to one another. One full year of being with him and Pickles. We've had our fair share of ups and downs in the past year, but we stayed strong through it all. We never gave up on one another.

A week after our last Christmas, Axel and Huck finally found the person responsible for my dad's accident. Huck took great pleasure in slapping the cuffs on the guy as he manhandled him into the back of a cruiser. It was justice well served after what he did. I can't say that my father was surprised either. It turns out his lifelong friend was affected by the livestock turnover in town. He became so jealous of my father's success that the rage blinded him.

Colt has been a bit off recently, but that's nothing new with him. What surprises me the most is that he won't talk to Huck about anything happening. It's all been a bit strange around here, but that's nothing that we can't handle. Colt will talk when he's ready.

Pickles accepted me into her life immediately. She even asked Axel if they could keep me because she loves me so much. I'm pretty sure I melted into myself that day. But nothing will ever move me as much as the day she called me Mom. I'm pretty sure I cried with joy for days after.

I can't say I ever saw our lives turning out this way, but they did. I love my little family with everything I have, and I know that no matter what gets tossed our way, we will conquer and overcome. We're stronger now than we ever have been. I refuse to lose either of them ever.

This year, we're taking over Christmas dinner at our house. It's time for our parents to sit back and enjoy their holidays with us, finally. I know my mom will bug me to let her help out, but Pickles has strict instructions to keep them all occupied.

I kept singing, but only in a local bar as their Friday and Saturday night headliner. It's not the glitz and glamor I'm used to, but I think that's making it easier for me. I hated all of that stuff.

Looking back in time, I think I always knew my running off to Nashville was my way of escaping the feelings I had in my heart. I was pushing myself away from Axel because I was scared of rejection. I'm not saying my dreams were a lie. I just see that I was forcing them more than I thought.

One thing I know for a fact is that I'll never have another lonely holiday. I'm finally where I belong.

Home.

The End

About Kayla Baker

Wife, dog mom, and mother of two. Reading has always been a favorite hobby of mine, and when the opportunity came to me a while back, I created my first book. After that book, I wanted to give up, but with great support comes excellent strength from within. I have many more books to go and many more to think of in the future. I hope you all enjoy the stories as much as I enjoyed creating them.

Books By Kayla Baker

Available Now

The Shining Series
My Shining Stepbrother
My Shining Bad Boy

The Shining Series
The House Of Blood's Point

Social Media Links

Follow me on:

Instagram
@kaylabakerauthor

Tik Tok
@kaylabakerauthor

Website
www.kaylabakerauthor.com

Snowed In For Christmas

by Melony Ann

Blurb

He hates me. I hate him.

Nico Jasper will always be the one who broke me but kept my heart after he threw me away. I did all I could to hide it. I threw myself into my job and worked my way up to a casino host at one of the hottest hotels in Las Vegas.

Now, two years later, I'm still trying to navigate my way through the shattered pieces. I refuse to allow his stupidity to keep me away from celebrating the wedding of one of our mutual friends.

I'll just make sure I stay far away from him.

I guess Santa has other plans. After a multitude of disasters, I find myself stuck with him.

On Christmas.

It's my favorite holiday, and I won't let him ruin another Christmas for me.I just don't know if I can keep him from destroying me…

Chapter 1

❄ Nico ❄

"Who the fuck has a wedding on Christmas day?" I ask, glaring at the road in front of me.

"People who really love Christmas," the woman driving the car we're in says without even missing a beat. I'd smile at her for being so quick, but she's the last woman I want to be in this vehicle with.

Noelle Snow.

She's beautiful. Her strawberry-blond hair looks like it was kissed by the sun. Her gray eyes are as bright and as beautiful as her. She's a small woman. Petite, but she has curves in all the right places. I should know. I know her body very intimately. Her ivory skin tone has just enough color for people to know she's not a vampire.

I'm not convinced she's not, though. She's evil enough to be one. I'm sure people think she's the sweetest person to ever walk the face of this Earth, but I know what's underneath. She's crazy. Vindictive. The type of woman who makes a man want to jump off a fucking building and pray for the most painful death imaginable because it would be better than being in her presence for another second.

I glare at her. "Do you even know where you're going?"

She sighs. Loudly. Just the sound of her breathing makes me want to jump out of the car and get hit by a log truck, but it's her dead silence after that sigh that really makes my blood boil. She only does it when she believes whatever I just said is the stupidest thing possible.

I wouldn't even be in this car with her if I had any choice at all. If things had gone my way, I'd be happily stretched out in the first class section of a Delta flight on my way to Denver, Colorado, for my best friend's wedding. I'd be sipping on a beer listening to anything other than the fucking Christmas music floating through the speakers of this silver Ford Fusion piece of shit.

But nope. My flight was canceled to Denver because of a snowstorm. I couldn't even get a flight into any other airport in Colorado and rent a car to drive the rest of the way. Because apparently, the storm is blanketing the entire state. Yeah. My ass. I doubt that very seriously, but again. My life is being controlled by the Government. This time, though, it's not the United States Marine Corp. It's the damn FAA.

"Really, Noelle. Do you know where you're going?" I ask again. I'm getting extremely nervous with the amount of snow coming down right now.

According to my weather app, it's not snowing in Denver. It's underneath Denver. By fucking miles. Which means it should be underneath where we are right now if she's even going the right direction. I shouldn't have handed over the wheel. I shouldn't have fallen asleep. I should've toughed it out and drove straight through.

Noelle lets out an exasperated sigh. "Nico, I'm on the Interstate. Interstate 70 literally drives right into Denver. I know where I'm going. I'm trying to be nice and give you a break from driving. Maybe you should give me one and let me drive. Stop being an ass."

"I'm not trying to be an ass, sweetheart. It's just fucking really snowy right now. The snow is supposed to be below us. That's all."

"First of all. Don't call me sweetheart. You lost that privilege two years ago when you broke up with me. And second. I just passed a sign. It said Interstate 70. So, I'm going by the sign instead of your stupid weather map."

"App."

"Nico! Please shut up!" She takes one hand off the steering wheel to wipe her eyes before she quickly puts it back. I feel the car slow quite a bit. She's white-knuckling the steering wheel. Her attention is focused on the road. As it should be, but I can see how scared she is.

The snow is getting heavier and heavier as the miles go by. Finally, after a few minutes of nothing but the Christmas music, I give in. "Pull over," I say calmly and soothingly. She doesn't need my mood right now.

"I'll be fine. I just need to focus," she says quietly.

"Noelle. I'm not asking. Pull over. Let me take over. You're fucking nervous. I'm a better driver in the snow."

She sniffles. "We live in Las Vegas. We don't get snow there."

"Did you forget that I was born in Vail and lived there most of my life?" I wouldn't put it past her to have forgotten that.

Noelle isn't my biggest fan, but truthfully, I'm not hers either. We were engaged to be married a couple of years ago. We dated for almost two years before I popped the question. During the engagement, I was sent out on my last deployment before my contract with the Marines ended. I didn't plan to re-enlist. I'd already given them almost twenty years of my life. I wanted to settle down. I wanted to turn my part-time job as a police officer with the Las Vegas Police Department to a full-time one.

But mostly, I wanted Noelle. I didn't want her to worry about me being off running missions in countries thousands of miles away. It was enough for her dealing with me being on patrol on the streets of the city. I wanted to ease her fears. She never tried to get me to quit either. That was something she'd never do. It was something I wanted to do for her, though.

When I got home after my deployment, I didn't tell her I was going to be there. I wanted it to be a surprise. I'd even enlisted my brother's help. His only job was to keep her out of the house until I texted him and told him to bring her home.

I was going to make her favorite food, barbecue chicken on the grill with grilled corn on the cob. I even grabbed her favorite fruits, watermelon and cantaloupe, as well as white chocolate covered strawberries drizzled with milk chocolate that had been given a red color. I bought her flowers, a gorgeous Spring bouquet, and stopped off at the jewelry store to grab the necklace she wanted but wouldn't buy for herself, no matter how many times I told her to. It was on a silver chain and had a hummingbird charm.

When I pulled into the driveway, I expected to see her car parked there. I didn't expect to see Christian's, my brother's. It was at that very moment my stomach sank. My feet carried me into the house. It was dead silent. I put all of the groceries and flowers on the counter before making my way through the house.

That's when I saw it. My beautiful fiancè in our bedroom wrapped in nothing but a fluffy, white towel sitting on our bed.

And my fucking brother with his head between her thighs.

I lost it. Noelle didn't even have the decency to get up and say anything for herself. It was my brother who stood up. My brother who told me it wasn't what it looked like. My brother who said she'd sprained her ankle. My brother who said I was early. That he hadn't gotten a chance to take her out yet.

Those words took on a whole new meaning then.

It took everything in me not to choke him out. Not to pummel him until he was nothing more than a bloody pile of steaming dog shit. Instead, I turned around and walked out. I texted her and told her to leave. She did as she was told, but not before both her and Christian texted me and called me a thousand times. I never answered either of them and blocked them both after she was gone. Christian tried again and again to talk to me, but I refused.

It's been a little more than two years since that day. I almost said fuck it and re-enlisted. I chose not to and stuck with my original plan. I became a full time cop with LVPD, and I love it. I don't need her. I don't need Christian. I'm good.

I feel Noelle start sliding and quickly reach over to help her before she starts spinning. She screams and lets go of the wheel at the same time she takes her foot off the gas and curls into herself like she's bracing herself for a crash.

"Hands on the wheel!" I snap. She immediately puts her hands on the wheel, but she's still screaming. "Stop, Noelle! Hands on the wheel!" I realize the mistake of my words far too late.

Noelle grips the wheel like I told her to, but she also stomps on the brakes. I had us out of the spin, but she put us right back into one. Before I know what's happening, we're spinning in circles. Noelle is screeching and crying. My heart starts racing, but before I can tell her to take her foot off the brake, I see a wall of white coming right at us...

Chapter 2

❄ Noelle ❄

I could've already been safe in my hotel room. Instead, the FAA grounded my flight. I don't even know why I accepted the invite to this wedding. I shouldn't have bothered. I knew Nico would be there. Aaron, the groom, is Nico's best friend. Nico is supposed to be his best man. If I'd listened to myself and chosen the better option of skipping this, I'd be home warm in my bed instead of buried in a giant snowbank with the one person in this world that I truly despise.

I refuse to burst into tears like I want to. I wipe my eyes and look around. The airbags have deployed. I'm thankful for that. My chest hurts, but I'm sure the airbags cushioned us from the hard crash.

Other than the airbags, I see nothing around us but piles of white with a dark backdrop. The snow falling makes everything look gray. The last time I remember looking at the time, it was 1:37 in the morning. The snow is coming down like sheets of rain. It's quickly blanketing us. Thankfully, the car is still running. That means we won't freeze. Right?

The windshield wipers are still going.

The lights are still on, though the front end is smashed to hell. I guess it's lucky the headlights work at all.

Suddenly, the airbag deflates with a soft pop. I jump a little, then see Nico stabbing his own with his pocket knife. His expression is dark and even more angry than it was when he got it in his stupid mind that I was cheating on him. With his brother of all people. I blink the tears away and turn so I'm not looking at him. I have to figure out how to survive this disaster.

I take a breath and search for my cellphone. It's on the floor at my feet. I unbuckle my seatbelt and reach down to pick it up. I quickly open my internet and wait for it to load.

And wait…

And wait…

And wait…

"You think you're getting reception out here?" Nico asks, his voice low and gravelly. I hate him. I hate what his asshole voice does to me.

I refuse to allow my body to shiver, but it doesn't stop my bitch of a pussy from becoming a traitorous jerk.

I ignore him and keep trying as he looks at me both amused and furious. Unfortunately, he's right. I'm not getting any reception at all. I can't even send a text or make a call. I bite my lip when emergency calls won't even go through.

Okay. Stay calm. It's okay. You have heat. You have warm clothing in the back. The snow should stop soon. We can get out and make a call then. I've always been told to stay in the car in bad weather. If I get too wet or cold, I could get hypothermia and die.

I nod resolutely to myself and start climbing into the backseat.

"What are you doing?" Nico asks, exasperated.

I ignore him and keep going. "If I can get to the clothing, we can layer up and stay warm. The back seats have a safety feature in case you get stuck in the trunk. We have to stay warm. We might be here for a little while until the snow stops. We can get help then."

He wraps one of his muscular arms around my waist and stops me in my tracks. "Do you really not keep up with anything? This storm is supposed to be the storm of the century, Noelle! We stay in the fucking car, we're going to get buried alive. Just sit down and let me fucking figure out where the hell we are." He nearly shoves me back into my seat, then reaches into the back for his backpack. He takes out something that looks like a phone, but it's thicker and Army green.

I huff. "No reception. Remember?" I cross my arms over my chest and chew my lip as I glare out the window.

"Satellite. I'm a fucking Marine. Remember?" His tone is just as cocky as it is mocking and condescending. I stay quiet. "We're a couple of miles out of Genesee Park. There's a cabin near here. It's mine. About a mile in from the Interstate. We're about a hundred feet from the access road." He pauses and gives me a jerk of a grin along with his stupid glare. "Nice place to crash, Ace."

"Asshole," I grumble.

He shrugs. "I've been called worse. Let's go." He pulls the handle to open his door, but it doesn't budge.

"I'm not going anywhere."

He pushes the lock button and tries again. "Motherfucker." He tries again, slamming his entire, beautiful body into the door. Nico Jasper, everyone. He thinks he can get anything he wants through brute force.

I sigh. That's not fair. He's never been an abusive person. Nico isn't like that. He can be scary. He's almost six feet four. He's solid muscle. Titanium. Impenetrable. The hair on his head and stubble on his jaw is as dark as his nearly coal colored eyes. He has a few tattoos on his arms, but it's the wings on his back that have always made my mouth water. It's because he had always been my angel. He's an angel to everyone he loves.

That all ended for us long ago. Maybe it's because I'm too young. I'm not trustworthy yet or something. He's thirty-seven. I'm barely twenty-six. I have a good job as a casino host. I worked my way up to that position from a hotel receptionist. I graduated at the top of my class in high school and college.

Nico was in the military when I was still in high school. He got a part-time police officer position with Las Vegas PD. He wanted it that way because he never quite knew when he'd get deployed. I met him when he showed up on a call at the casino. We hit it off. We were together for almost three years before he decided it would be fun to destroy my life. I was only twenty-four then. Since he broke up with me, I've thrown myself into work. I became the best employee I could be and moved up quickly.

He has no idea how badly he tore me and Christian, his brother, up. He doesn't care anyway. He blocked us both from his life just as easily as he did from his phone. He didn't care to know what really happened. We both know how it looked, but the fact that he refused to listen to either of us is what hurt the most. It still does.

I jerk my head to him when I feel cold air hit me. My eyes widen. "Oh my God! What are you doing?" I screech.

He pauses and looks at me. "I'm getting the fuck out of here before your gas is gone and we end up freezing to death. Come if you want. Or don't. I don't give a fuck."

"Nico! You're going to freeze out there!" I nearly squeak as he pulls himself out of the window he opened.

He pauses when his feet hit the ground and looks back in at me. He shrugs so nonchalantly that it infuriates me. I nearly scream. "Guess that's my problem. Put the window up and pop the trunk so I can get my stuff."

I don't hold back the scream. I push the button so the window goes up and push the button for the trunk. "Fine! If you want to die, it's not my problem!" I scream again just because of how frustrated, angry, and upset I am. Screaming keeps me from crying.

I close my eyes and do all I can to regulate my breathing. I don't need to start panicking. It's not going to help me. I need to be calm and rational. That's what's gotten me through most of my life.

That goes out the window the second my headlights go out. The car starts to sputter. My eyes drop in horror to my gas gauge. It's close to empty.

"No... No! No! No!"

I jump nearly a mile when Nico slams the trunk closed. It's all it takes for the car to die.

My heart shoots into my brain and fights to escape through my head.

My lungs stop inflating.

I gasp for air. I feel the oxygen going into my mouth and down my throat, but it doesn't seem to be doing anything more. I don't even know if my heart is pumping.

I quickly try to open the door, but like Nico's door, mine doesn't budge no matter how many times I throw myself into it. It hurts my chest even more because of the airbag deploy, but I don't care. I have to get out.

The window! He climbed out the window!

I quickly hit the button. Even if the key is turned but it's not running, it should go down.

As soon as I hit it, though, I realize just how wrong I am. I can't see the front of the car anymore, but I can see there's smoke coming from under the hood.

"Oh my God! Nico!" I scream. The wiring. It has to be on fire! Is that why the car shut down?

I start pounding on the window, praying it'll break.

It's then I see the silver glint of something next to me and snow flying, but I can't figure out what's happening. My mind is solely on the fact that I'm stuck in a car that's going to blow up at any given moment.

Unable to stop them, the tears I was fighting burst from my eyes. I start frantically searching for anything that will break the window. Nico has to be long gone right now. He's not going to help me.

He'd probably leave me in the car to die.

He hates me that much...

Chapter 3

❄ Nico ❄

I shake my head and keep shoveling snow away from Noelle's door. There's no point in trying to calm her down. She's thrown herself into a panic. It took me a few moments to realize what the fuck she was screaming about. Then I noticed steam coming off her hood. She probably thinks there's a fire. What actually happened is her battery shorted out. I don't think she was quite out of gas, though she was nearing empty.

She's lucky I'm too fucking nice to leave her ass here. I'd never be able to live with myself, though. The snow is heavy. It's already almost up to the window on her side. It's not stopping anytime soon either. This storm was supposed to hit tomorrow afternoon. Not today. It was one of the reasons I was so pissed off they canceled the flight. I saw nothing anywhere that said it was snowing right then in Denver. Even the news they had on in the airport said it hadn't started.

I almost called my buddy and told him I'm not making it, but Noelle is some kind of angel. I didn't know she was at the damn airport, let alone the same flight as me. While I was arguing and trying to force my way onto any other flight flying into Colorado, Noelle was smartly booking a rental. It's only about a twelve hour drive from Las Vegas to Denver.

I started out driving but started to get tired a few hours ago. I haven't been sleeping too well lately. Sometimes, some of the shit I saw overseas hits me hard. The past few days, I guess it's just that time. Maybe it's because one of our friends didn't make it home.

I shovel a little more vigorously as Noelle cries. Maybe the reason I haven't been sleeping is because we lost him on this day two years ago. Aaron and I were home three weeks later, both having made the decision not to reenlist. Who knew my fucking life would just keep unraveling before my very eyes?

Of course, Aaron has been on Noelle's side this whole time. He's never shoved it down my throat, but I knew he continued to talk to her. He told me as much. He'd even told me I should talk to her a few times, but I refused.

I should be grateful to Noelle for getting me this far. I won't miss Aaron's wedding. It's been the most awkward fucking drive, though. Neither of us have said more than a few words to each other. The most we've spoken was at the airport when she said she got the last car rental. If my truck wasn't in the shop, I wouldn't have taken her up on the offer. I even made her wait until after I tried booking a private flight.

No dice.

And now here we are. Her rental is going to be buried within the hour. The temps are dropping fast. I pulled her stuff out with mine when I went into the trunk. I've never been more grateful that I bought this shovel from the gas station we stopped at when I turned the wheel over to her. She rolled her eyes, but I never ignore instincts. The storm was underneath us and stalled, but I'm always prepared. It's what Marines do.

After I get the snow shoveled enough for her to get out. I yank open the door. She screams, and I almost fall backwards. I guess I didn't realize she was in full panic mode until right now. Maybe I should have tried to comfort her.

"Noelle, it's okay. I -" I'm cut off by her leaping out of the car. I have to step back to balance us both before I land on my ass in the snow with her on top of me.

"It's going to blow!"

"What?" I shake my head. "It's just steam, Noelle. From the melted snow and the warm hood. You probably didn't notice it until the battery shorted and the car shut down." I hug her closer and tighter as she gasps and sobs, trying to help herself come down. I want to shove her away, but not even I'm that big of an asshole.

"I'm sorry," she chokes out as she lets go after a few moments. She sniffles. "I… didn't mean to do that."

I drop my arms from her body and ignore my reaction to her. I hate that she's the only woman who has ever set my body ablaze like this. One look, and she has my dick trying to escape my jeans, but the second I feel her against me, it's all over. There's no hiding the erection. If he could stand at full attention and salute, he would do it just as if she was the fucking General.

I clear my throat and move her out of the way. "Don't be." I lean in the car and grab our stuff from the back.

We both have coats on the seat as well as what we would have carried onto the plane, boots included. She was smart. She knew she was flying into a city that was likely to have snow. Her tennis shoes wouldn't cut it. I put the bags on top of the luggage.

"How are we going to carry all of that? Where are we even going?"

"I have a cabin around here. I told you that already. I planned to stay there. It's only about twenty minutes from the city. I have a buddy check on it from time to time for me when I'm not there, but I go there when I need a break from Vegas or life. It's a peaceful retreat. I knew I'd be getting in late so I texted him after we left and asked him if he could stock me up with food and stuff, then sent money via Venmo. I didn't know if I'd be able to get fully stocked up before the storm hit. I told him I'd be there really early in the morning. He texted me a couple of hours later and told me I was all set. If we can get there before you freeze, we'll be good."

She shakes her head. "Because I'm incapable of a hike, right? Nothing but an airhead city girl."

I sigh as I turn to her. "I didn't say that, Noelle. You're fucking five feet nothing on a good day. You've lost a lot of weight since…" I trail off and shake my head. "Fuck it. Sure. I meant you're an airhead city girl. Sit down and put your boots on."

Her lip trembles, but she wisely doesn't say a damn word. I already changed into my boots, but I throw my coat on and hold out hers when she's done changing into the boots. I put her shoes into my backpack while she puts her coat on.

"So, how are we getting to your cabin? There's no way we can hike out of here. The snow is up to my waist," she says quietly, defeated almost. It might break my heart if I weren't already fed up with her.

I point to the road. "We cross it. We walk down the access road. Viola." She nods and starts grabbing her bag. I shake my head. "I'll take it."

"I can take my own stuff. I don't want to put you out more. I already almost killed you by my own stupid driving and panic." She gestures to the totaled car.

I sigh and pinch the bridge of my nose. "Stop, Noelle. You hit ice. You're not used to this. I should've made you pull over sooner. Let's go."

I'm grateful she packed a duffel bag instead of a suitcase. It's easier for me to carry. I put my backpack on, then put her bag and mine over my shoulders, one on each side, before helping her with her own carry on. It's a smaller duffel bag, but I'm impressed that she packed so efficiently.

I turn and lead her up to the road. For a busy Interstate, I haven't seen any vehicles. I'm pretty sure that's because a travel ban was put in place. If I could get some kind of internet signal for my phone, I'd know.

We hike in silence for a while. To her credit, Noelle says nothing. I've taken quick glances back at her, and even with the snow piling up quickly, she's trudging through like a trooper. I can't help but notice that she's shivering pretty uncontrollably, though.

We're only about half way, and I'm starting to question if she'll make it before she freezes. The snow is lashing down like sleet at us. Despite the hood on her head, she's soaked. The coat is waterproof. So are the boots. Her jeans, though, aren't, and she's a lot shorter than me.

I glance behind her when I hear what I'm hoping is a plow. It will make things a fuck of a lot easier for her if it is. I quickly grab the flashlight I put in my pocket before we left the car. I turn it on and stop. Noelle nearly runs into me since she's hunkered into her coat with her head down.

I steady her from falling as I shine the flashlight at the vehicle and start moving it back and forth on the road. I want to warn the driver that we're here so he doesn't hit us, but mostly, I want him to stop. Noelle isn't going to make it, and I'm actually starting to feel like shit about it. Fuck my heart and morals.

"W-w-what's h-h-hap-p-pening?" she says between chattering teeth. She tries to glance around her but coughs instead.

"I'm hoping this is a plow, and he can drive us the rest of the way."

"I c-c-can m-m-make it."

I chuckle at her tenacity, but I know she's just trying to be brave and prove me wrong. I let out a relieved breath when the plow slows down.

The person in the passenger seat pops his head out the window with a grin. "What the hell are you doing out here, Marine? Need a new challenge?"

I bark out a laugh. "No, asshole. We spun out on I-70. Our rental is probably buried right now."

Jim, the older man in the passenger seat who also owns a general store in town, nods. "East or West?"

"West. We were just heading into town. Hit some ice. Spun out and got buried in the snow in the ditch. When we got out, the car was half buried already."

"I'll send one of my guys out in the morning when this shit lets up. We're gonna get hit again, hard, but we'll have about an hour window," the driver, Ted, says. He owns a small auto shop in town. He and his team are the only drivers.

"Appreciate it, man. Thanks," I say with a nod. "Think you can get us to the cabin? She's pretty cold." I tilt my head towards Noelle. As if on cue, she hugs herself even tighter than she already was and shivers violently.

"Absolutely," Jim says. "Hop on in. Not a lot of room, though. She'll have to sit on your lap." He waggles his eyebrows, but my stomach sinks. I just nod as he opens the door.

I start handing him our stuff so he can put it in the small space behind the seats. He slides over. I climb into the cab and reach out a hand for Noelle. She looks at it for a moment before gauging how hard it'll be for her to get into the truck on her own. Finally, she takes my hand and lets me pull her into my lap. If she weren't shivering so violently, she might choose Jim's over mine. Fuck, the option ain't off the table. I'd happily let her.

Instead, I close the door and keep my arms to myself. It's enough that every shiver makes her ass press against my dick. Sometimes, she jerks. When Ted hits a bump, it's even worse. I have to fight myself to keep the groan tamped down. My cock sure as hell isn't cooperating with my commands to tone it the fuck down.

Her being this close to me is torture, but having her in the same house as me as we ride out this storm is going to be pure hell.

Chapter 4

❄ Noelle ❄

We've been at Nico's cabin for a couple of hours. The sun is just starting to rise. I'm so tired, but I can't fall asleep because I'm still so cold. He was nice enough to make us hot chocolate. He even started a fire in his fireplace. Whoever his friend is, he was nice enough to not only stock up his fridge and cabinets with food, but he also brought him enough wood for the fireplace to last weeks.

Even though I've been as close to the fireplace as I can possibly be without being inside it, I can't get warm. Nico even gave me the thickest blanket he has, which was the comforter off his own bed. It's no use.

"I'm actually starting to worry about you," Nico mumbles from the longer couch across from me. The one I'm on is a loveseat that he's moved closer to the fire.

I shiver. "C-can't s-stop." I close my eyes and sniffle.

Nico stretches as he shifts onto his side. "Come here."

My eyes widen at him. "I'm f-f-fine."

"You know if you don't do what I tell you, I'm just going to make you."

I shake my head and snuggle more under the comforter. "It's r-really f-fine."

"Noelle. Come on. Seriously. You're cold. Everything I've tried so far isn't helping. Including giving you a pair of my sweats and my sweatshirt that I warmed up in the dryer. I've given you hot chocolate. I've made sure that fire is roaring. Get over here. I can't get you to the hospital, and you're nearing hypothermia stages at this point. Your lips are blue, and I know it ain't lipstick because you hate makeup. Let me use my body heat to help warm you up. It's not like you haven't been in my arms before."

"Th-that w-was before you f-fucked up."

"Before I fucked up?" He barks out a laugh that's filled with such an intense level of anger and hurt that I briefly forget about how cold I am. His reaction takes me aback. "Just get over here, Noelle. Trust me. I don't want to be anywhere near you. I hate you as much as you hate me, but I can't handle watching you die when I know I can help. Just do it, or I'll just walk over there, pick you up, and bring you over here myself."

I just stare at him in open-mouthed shock, but I do what he says because I don't want to shiver anymore. I know how serious hypothermia can be. So, I take a breath and throw the comforter off me. I stomp the few steps to the couch and lay next to him with my back to him as I throw the comforter over us both.

Almost instantly, and much to my dismay, I feel warmer. His body heat against mine feels way too familiar. Too comforting. I close my eyes as he adjusts the comforter. He wraps his arms around me and pulls me as close to his body as he can. He locks his arms around me, forcing me to relax as he wraps around me.

We say nothing for I don't know how long, but he never moves. His steady breathing, as it always has, lulls me into a state of comfort I haven't felt for a long time. For the millionth time over the past two years, I think to myself how there is nothing in this world that can compete with him and the way he makes me feel. The thought, as it normally does, makes me tear up. Nico was supposed to be my ride or die. Why did some stupid misunderstanding have to ruin all of that?

I force the thoughts away and close my eyes. I let my imagination wander. For a few moments, or even hours, I fall asleep thinking of him as mine again.

When I wake up, I'm not sure how long I've been asleep, the fire is nothing but embers. It takes me a few seconds to reorient myself, but when I do, I can't help melting into Nico. I'm not meant to be with anyone else. Nico is it for me. I have to convince him of that. I can't live without him. Being with him like this has made me realize it. Everything he's done since we left the airport has been nothing but selfless.

Purely Nico Jasper.

My Marine.

The thoughts being in his arms elicits quickly fade. He's not mine anymore. He hates everything about me. He's too stubborn to listen to reason. He's the one who broke me in a million tiny pieces. So many that I still haven't managed to put myself together again. I'm like Humpty Dumpty. Nothing can fix me, and if I really think I'm going to do whatever it takes to prove to him that I'm not who he thinks I am, well, I'm sure the rejection will shatter me more.

The question really becomes if I'm willing to risk it all again. I'm already fragile. I still haven't healed. My love for Nico was hotter than the hottest fire. I thought that's how he felt for me, too. I guess I was wrong.

Feeling more like myself, warm on the outside, dead on the inside, I shift against him just enough so I can sit up. What I don't expect is his face to bury itself deeper in my hair. I certainly don't expect his solid as the hardest diamond cock to push closer to my ass. But it's when his arms and legs tighten around me that I gasp.

"Nico," I whisper.

He groans. "Just give me a minute. You owe me that."

My eyes widen on their own. My heart beats faster. I can't lay here like this with him. It's too dangerous. My body isn't on the same page as my head. I try to get up, but my body obeys his raspy-voiced command and sinks into him even more. It takes the full minute he asked for before my body catches up with the conclusion my brain has already reached.

I push myself up, ignoring the sudden chill of not being in his arms. "I *owe* you that?"

Nico growls and turns his head into his arm before glaring up at me. "I don't know. For saving your life? Keeping you warm? Keeping you from being buried in snow? Oh! How about this one? For fucking my brother while I was deployed." His coal eyes manage to darken impossibly more, but his voice is as smooth as the finest butter.

Which does nothing more than get on my last nerve. I should scream. I should haul off and slap him with every ounce of strength I have. I don't. Instead, I stand up and say nothing. I try to hide the hurt his words inflict, but I can't. My face falls. My body droops. I stalk off to his bedroom at the back of the cabin.

"What's the matter, baby girl? Can't handle the truth?" Nico calls after me.

I can hear the humor in his voice, and that's what cuts me the deepest. The scars from the pieces I managed to stitch back together are torn open once more. My heart lays at my feet. Each beat seems to get slower and slower until it finally stops.

I rummage through my clothing, still in my bag, until I find the warmest clothing I can find. Maybe if I put leggings on underneath my jeans, I'll stay warmer longer as I'm trekking through the snow. Nico said he was a couple of miles or something out of town. Maybe if I can make it to the town, I'll be able to find someplace to stay and ride out the rest of the storm. Then, I can call Christian to come get me. He was smart and flew into Denver two days ago. I wish I'd been able to book a flight sooner. I was honestly lucky I got the one I did. Who knew it would get canceled?

I let out a breath as I take the clothes out of the bag. I plan to leave the clothes I was wearing yesterday here because they're still in the dryer. I just want to leave. It was foolish of me to think for a moment there was any chance of reconciliation between us. I'd rather live with the knowledge of knowing he was the one that got away over trying to work it out with someone who hates me as much as he does.

I glance out the window. The snow is coming down heavier than it was last night. That sucks a lot for me, but hopefully if I follow the main roads, I'll get there.

I take Nico's sweatshirt off and put a bra on. I can already feel the biting air. The fireplace is wonderful, but it doesn't heat the entire cabin. I do my best to block the cold air from my mind. I start to think of warm beaches and sand. Anything to keep the precious body heat I have.

I'm reaching for a long-sleeve under shirt and my sweater just as the door starts to open. Like it's on a swivel, my head snaps to the door. My eyes land on Nico's dark gaze. He leans against the doorframe and crosses his arms over his unfairly broad chest.

"What are you doing?" His eyes drop from mine and land on the bag on the bed I haven't zipped up.

My gaze, though, is completely frozen on him. My mouth goes dry, and I stop mid-motion. No words formulate. I feel like I just got caught by my dad trying to sneak out of the house. I'd expect my heart to be racing right now.

Only this time, it doesn't. It feels nothing. Maybe his words earlier really did kill me this time...

Chapter 5

❄ Nico ❄

For several moments, I stand in the doorway watching Noelle. She looks like a deer in the headlights. Like she was just caught doing something wrong. Her expression is a mix between bewildered and pissed.

My breath catches. She's still the most beautiful woman I've ever seen. She's standing in her pajama bottoms and a red bra that I know she bought for my eyes only. I was there when she tried it on. She was as red as the bra with embarrassment at the fact that her ample breasts spilled out of it.

It took a store associate to explain to her that it was supposed to be like that. It's meant to push her tits up and give her a sexy amount of cleavage. The support is the perfect amount, and what she considers spilling out is really just the bra making her more sexy than she's used to.

I narrow my eyes for two reasons. The first is because I want to know why the fuck she packed that bra, and why she's wearing it right now. The second is because I'm pissed she even still has it. It was supposed to be just for the two of us. She only ever wore it when she wanted to sexily seduce me. The very thought she's wearing it for any other reason infuriates me.

"Of all the bras you own, Noelle, why that one?" I pinch the bridge of my nose and close my eyes, breaking the spell between us. I can hear her clothes rustling as she changes.

"I can wear what I want. You're not going to have to worry anyway."

I bark out a bitter laugh as I open my eyes again. Unfortunately for me, she's got her sweater on. My dick is as unhappy about that as I am. "Where do you think you're going? Out there?" I gesture towards the window. "You'll drown in the snow. It's almost up to my windows. Which, just so you know, are four feet above the ground. And let's not talk about the fact that you'll fucking freeze to death and won't be found until the snow melts."

She shrugs. "Then, I guess that's my problem." She starts shoving the clothes she removed from her body into the bag. She zips it.

My jaw ticks. I don't take well to my words being thrown back at me. She knows that. "You're not leaving, Noelle."

She turns her own furious glare on me. Her gray eyes are as stormy as it is outside. "You can't keep me here. I can do whatever I want. You lost the privilege of having anything to do with me when you accused me of cheating on you."

I scoff. "Kind of hard to accuse you of anything when I saw it with my own eyes! It's not an accusation at that point. It's a fucking fact!"

She picks up her bag and slings it over her shoulder. Her face is red with anger. Her eyes look like they could pierce the strongest armor. "I never cheated!" she screams at me. "Just because I'm twelve years younger than you doesn't mean I don't have morals and can't control my impulses! Which I never had for your brother or anyone else!"

She storms towards me and forces her small body past me. The only reason she succeeds is because I'm taken aback by not only her outburst, but her blatant as fuck denial. I follow her as she stomps towards the front door. She's quick for someone as tiny as she is, but I catch up to her before she gets too far.

I grab her arm and spin her around before dropping my hand from it like she just scalded me. I can feel my own fury building. "How the fuck can you deny any of this? I saw it! I saw you sitting on that bed wrapped in a towel with Christian's head between your legs!"

"I never cheated!" she screams. "I hurt my ankle getting out of the shower! I slipped! I practically knocked myself unconscious! Did you know he took me to the hospital after that? No! Because you were too busy being an asshole to us! You were too high on your horse and too fucked up to even talk to us! No matter how many times we tried! You completely destroyed us, Nico!"

"The fuck I did! You hurt your ankle my ass! It didn't look like he was looking at your fucking ankle!"

Tears pool in her eyes, but I'm not sure if they're from the fact that my words finally cut through her and she knows she can't deny facts, or if it's because she's furious I'm not falling for any of the bullshit.

She doesn't say a word. She drops her bag and reaches into the back pocket of her jeans. She unlocks her phone and thrusts it into my chest with a force that might hurt anyone else.

"Fuck you, Nico. You can keep the phone. If I'm gonna die out there, I may as well do it right. A stupid woman rushes out into the storm of the century without a phone to call for help." She laughs wryly and emotionlessly. "I can see the headlines now."

I take the phone with no intention of actually looking at it. She's not leaving the house. She won't need the damn phone anyway, but as I'm about to throw it against the wall, something catches my eye. I pause as she picks up her bag and continues to the door. I look at the image she pulled up of someone's foot. Hers. I'd know it anywhere. I don't even have to see my name tattooed above it on the lower part of her leg.

It's obvious she sprained it. So obvious. It's bruised to hell and swollen to the size of a damn baseball. "Come on, Noelle. How the fuck do I know this wasn't last month?"

"You know, I knew you'd ask that. It's the stubborn cop in you. So go ahead. Scroll up. Look at the details. It shows you when the image was taken. And after that, swipe left. You'll see several more images. One of them is when I was in the hospital."

"Again -"

She cuts me off like I hadn't even tried to say a word. "If you look closely on the one with the silly selfie with me and Christian, you'll see the computer in the background. It shows the date right on there."

"Noelle -"

Again, she rolls right over me like I hadn't attempted to speak. She continues to put her boots on, not looking at me at all. "Oh. And before you say anything about how happy we both look together, keep in mind that I'd just lost you, I had a concussion, it wasn't just a sprain, it was broken, and I'd fractured my wrist during the fall. I was anything but happy. You'll see that if you look closely enough. I appreciate your brother, though. He really tried to help me through all of that."

I do what she says and scroll through, but only out of purely morbid curiosity. As she said, the images are all date stamped with the very day I walked away. The emergency room images are the same. One of the images, I can see her wristband. It has the date and time she checked in. The image of her with my brother, though, is the one that breaks my heart. While they both are trying to act silly, I can see just how upset and hurt they are. Their eyes look dead.

Kind of like how Noelle's look right now.

I'm starting to panic.

Fuck...

What did I do?

Fuck... Fuck! Fuck!

I need to fix this.

I'll talk to Christian later. Right now, I need to make this right with Noelle.

My girl.

I take a deep breath to stop the rising dread. "Noelle, stop." I drop her phone on the couch and walk towards her.

She shakes her head and holds up a hand. "Don't. Don't do this. I'm barely holding on, Nico. I've been clinging to a thread for a long time. It's frayed and about ready to break. I can't fight with you anymore. Every time I look at you, I feel like I might actually die from the hurt." She swallows a sob and closes her eyes, but doesn't drop her hand.

I reach out slowly and take it. It's trembling; all of her is. I did this. I broke us both because I walked in on something I couldn't process. I didn't listen when our friends tried to talk to me. I didn't listen to my parents. More importantly, I didn't listen to Christian and Noelle. I didn't listen to reason. I believed I knew what I saw and didn't give a shit about what either of them were telling me. I thought it was just two people trying get out of fucking up after being caught redhanded in said fuck up.

I should've listened.

I pull her closer, keeping her hand in mine, and cup her cheek with the other. "Noelle, I'm so sorry, baby girl."

She shakes her head, the tears finally spilling as she pulls her hand free. She takes several steps back. "You don't get to call me that anymore! And you don't get to apologize after this long and expect everything will be fine!" She grabs her coat and starts putting it on.

My chest actually fucking tightens at the very thought of her walking away from me. What's more, though, is the panic I feel at her being out in the storm. I can't handle the idea of anything happening to her. I thought it was because I'm just that kind of person, and it might have something to do with it, but it has a lot more to do with the fact that I care about her. No matter what I tell myself, I've never stopped loving her.

I can't.

She's the other part of my soul. The piece I never knew was missing until she was gone. The anger and hurt filled the void for a little while, but the second I heard her sweet, soft, and very hesitant voice behind me in the airport, that was it. I felt the black void more prevalently than I've ever felt anything in my life. I took her up on her offer to drive out here and share the car she rented not because I had no other choice. It was because I didn't want another one. I wanted to spend time with her again. My heart needed it.

Trust that fucker to know exactly what I need when my mind is being a stubborn fucking dickhead.

I take a deep breath as she slings her bag over her shoulder again and turns for the door. She yanks it open, but I slam it shut again. "Noelle. No. I'm not letting you go out there in this. I'm fucking not letting you go, period."

She turns towards me. Mistake number one on her part. I cage her against the door and lock it as my gaze meets her piercing stare. Mistake number two for her. She's fucking sexy when she's pissed, and since I woke up with her in my arms, I haven't been able to get my cock, or the rest of me, to behave.

"You can't keep me here against my will. It's called kidnapping."

"Wrong. It's called saving your fucking life. If you go out there, you will freeze. You won't make it to town. The snow is too deep. You come across a drift, it will be taller than you. I'm certain they pulled the plows, but in the rare case some asshole is out there driving in this shit, and you, by some rare miracle manage to make it to the Interstate, you will be hit. You *will not* be seen in time for someone to stop. And that's only if the plows haven't been pulled. Judging from how much snow has fallen, though? They have. Realistically, you're not making it ten feet out that door."

She pushes as hard as she can against me, but this time, I don't budge. And that is her final mistake. Three strikes. I'm done fucking around. I grab both of her wrists and use my body to pin her against the door. I lean down and kiss her with a level of passion I've been holding back since the day I walked away.

The second my lips meet hers, I'm a goner. I make a solemn vow to fix everything I fucked up because I can't live my life without her.

As I swipe my tongue over hers after forcing my way into her sexy mouth, she watches me with wide eyes. I know one thing. If she's done with me for good, I won't survive it.

Chapter 6

❄ Noelle ❄

The first thing I feel when Nico starts kissing me like I'm his air and he'll die without me, is a sense of calm wash over me. Like it's all going to be okay again. Like everything I've ever wanted to happen is happening. Our reunion. Us getting back together. All of the love I once had for him that has never died. It's only multiplied exponentially until the weight of it nearly crushes me.

The second thing I feel is the overwhelming anger I've had for him for a long time. The sense of betrayal I've felt at the very idea he could possibly think I'd ever do something to hurt him. The pain that he bestowed single-handedly on my heart the very moment he showed he didn't trust me.

While I want to throw my arms around him and kiss him just as deeply and passionately as he is me, the simmering anger wins out. I pull away quickly with narrowed eyes. My hand moves on its own and connects with his face. Hard.

His face snaps to the side. It's like he moves in slow motion as he turns back to me. At first, his eyes register shock before fury. The low growl that comes from the pit of his stomach sounds demonic. While I should be terrified, I'm not. I'd be lying if I said I'm not slightly turned on.

"I'll let that slide because I deserve it," he says low and dangerously. "Do it again, though, I'm taking you over my knee."

My eyes widen, and my pussy clenches. Just the memory of being over his knee and the deliciousness that came from it has my panties melting off my body. My mouth both waters and becomes as dry as the Sahara Desert. He's the only one who can quench my thirst. He's always been my lifeblood. Being in such close proximity for the past twenty-four hours has brought everything within me to the surface.

I don't know how long we stand in our little faceoff, but it's me who finally can't take anymore. I don't remember dropping my bag, but I'm grateful I did. I launch myself at him. I throw my arms around his shoulders and spin us both so he's the one against the door. Even standing on the tips of my toes, though, I can't reach his lips. I need them. I need him. I've missed his taste, his touch, all of him. I've missed him.

Nico's eyes seemingly ignite in fiery passion seconds before his lips meet mine. He grips my butt as he kisses me until I see stars while he's lifting me. I wrap my legs around his waist. He spins us until it's me against the door once more.

"You're wearing way too much," he growls as he nips my lower lip and grinds into my center.

"Oh God, Nico." I push against his hard length as his lips crash to mine once more.

He reaches behind him and grabs my foot. He unties the lace with one hand and tugs off my boot. I gasp into his mouth as he tosses it back on the floor next to his own. He does the same with the other one, keeping me pinned between him and the door while he ravishes my mouth.

"You're not going out in this, Noelle. I'm not letting you." He doesn't give me the option to answer him before his tongue is wrestling with mine once more. It's a battle he knows he'll win. I'll submit to him every single day for the rest of our lives.

I moan in answer to him and press even closer to him, but it's still not enough. Trusting him to not drop me, I let go of his shoulders and unzip my coat. I wiggle my way out of it, being sure not to break our kiss. A kiss I've dreamt about countless times. It's haunted me, but at the same time, it's kept me going.

I toss my coat onto the bench next to me where I was sitting to put my boots on. I wrap my arms back around him and grind myself against his growing cock. I need him inside me more than I need to breathe.

Nico has always been good about reading me. He knows my every need and desire even before I do. So, I'm not at all surprised when I find myself floating through the air while his lips mold themselves to mine. Nico lets down, but I'm ready to let go. I don't know how I stop myself from sliding down his body.

Nico pulls away slowly. We both are slightly out of breath, but there's no way either of us are finished with each other. He lets me go, and I whimper at the loss of his touch, but it's short lived. Nico strips his shirt off and sits down on the couch. He tosses the shirt over the arm of the couch at the same time he's grabbing me. I can't help but notice his gaze hasn't left mine until this very moment. The moment they start to roam up my body.

"Fuck, sweet girl." He settles me in front of him between his legs. "We need to get these clothes off."

I bite the inside of my cheek to keep from giggling. "But it's so cold outside."

His grin is wicked and full of promise. "I'll keep you warm."

Seconds later, Nico has my jeans and leggings pulled down and tugged off. He tosses them onto the arm of the couch with his shirt. My panties follow, and I can't stop the giggle from bubbling out of my mouth. It quickly turns to a gasp, though, when he flicks the button on his jeans and his cock springs free. I don't have any time to admire him, though. He grips my hips and has me straddling him faster than I can show his dick any appreciation.

"Too many clothes still," I whisper. The tip of his dick is nudging my pussy, waiting to be granted entrance.

"Agreed." He pulls my sweater off. The long sleeve shirt I had under it is gone next. I figure he'll leave the bra on, he loves it, but he removes that next. "Much better."

I moan the second his mouth latches onto one of my nipples. His tongue flicks back and forth as he sucks. My fingers tangle in his short hair. I tug just a little. His large hands move to my bottom, and he guides me down on top of him. He slides into my pussy, but it's not an easy feat. I'm small and very tight. His dick is thick and somewhere between eight and nine inches. My pussy clamps around him. He'll have no choice but to work his way into me.

"Nico...," I whisper. I wrap my arms around his shoulders as tightly as my pussy is squeezing his length as he thrusts gently. I spread my legs as wide as I can make them. The wetter I get, the deeper he slides, inch by glorious inch, until he's buried balls deep inside me.

"Fuck, you feel better than I remember. How is that possible, beautiful girl?" He buries his face in my neck.

I love when he calls me that. He's the only one who's ever called me that. He's the only one I'd ever let call me it. I've never been one for sweet pet names, but when they fall from his lips, it's like honey that I'm on my knees waiting to lap up.

I don't even need to tell him that I'm ready for him to move. Nico just knows. He begins thrusting slow and deliberately. We both hold onto each other like we need each other to stay afloat in rough seas. We breathe against each other's necks like it's the scent from one another's skin that keeps us alive. Each and every thrust he gives me seemingly heals another crack; another hole.

As he puts each piece of me back in place and repairs my soul, the thrusts get faster, deeper, and harder. The little bit of control I have is snapped in two. I hold onto him like he's my lifeline as I ride him for all I'm worth.

There's no talking. Only the sounds of him slamming into my pussy again and again. Our moans turn into growls of pleasure. Our lips meet each other's over and over, exploding into an inferno of passion and devotion. Our lovemaking is as intense as it used be, but it's so much more this time. This time, we're both pouring all of our souls and feelings into it. Everything we've locked up for so long.

I meet him thrust for thrust as I rock back and forth over his dick and slam down on him. My pussy pulses around him and clenches tighter and tighter, making him moan. His thumb touches my clit, making me jerk into him. With the perfect amount of pressure, he rubs. I buck into him wildly.

"Nico!" His name is the first word either of us has spoken since he dropped me onto his dick. "Ahhh!" I scream. My thighs tremble, followed closely by my entire body.

"Fuck, Noelle. Oh fuck, baby. Be my good girl and come for me." His voice is deep and dominant against my neck.

I throw my head back and slam down on him hard, burying him as deeply as I can. "Nico! Oh God, yes! Yes! Nico!"

"Noelle!" Nico bellows.

I feel a river of come start flowing from his cock into me. Our hips jerk against each other as I experience an Earth shattering orgasm more intense than any I've ever felt before. It's like the black hole in the universe exploded and sucked us both into it, swallowing us whole. Only the colors are brilliant, and it's not as scary as scientists believe. It's beautiful.

I don't know when he pulled out or how he got us to the floor in front of the fireplace. I couldn't explain when he started the fire that's currently burning and keeping us both as warm as we were when I was bouncing on him. All I know is wrapped in his arms with the blanket wrapped around us is all I've ever wanted. I could die happy right now and feel like my life is complete.

Nico is the greatest present of all time.

Chapter 7

❄ *Nico* ❄

The next morning, after spending most of the night making the sweetest love to the woman who's always owned my heart and soul, I grunt and grumble as I drag a tree into the house as quietly as possible. The storm isn't slowing down. I spent a lot of time shoveling a path from the house to this tree. Luckily, it came down sometime last night, so I didn't need to cut it down. I dragged it to the garage to trim it.

I pause for a moment thinking I hear Noelle moving. After a few moments of silence, I continue tugging the tree inside. Thankfully, the garage is attached to the house, so once I got the tree in the garage, I was safe from the elements howling outside.

It seems like hours pass, but I finally have the tree up. I wouldn't bother with this, but I want to make this Christmas special for Noelle. She loves Christmas. She loves everything about it, but mostly, the time she gets to spend with people she cares about.

The thing is, she doesn't have family. Her parents passed away just after we started dating. After a lot of investigation, given they were only in their fifties, it was discovered that natural causes was the cause of death. She has no siblings or any other family that she knows about.

That didn't stop her from going all out for Christmas. The first one was a little bit hard on her, but she spent it with me and my family as well as a couple of my friends. She was happy with that during the duration of our relationship. I heard that the last couple of years, she spent Christmas alone. I spent it with my family, but still made it clear I didn't want to speak to Christian. He respected my wishes. The holidays were a little awkward, but we made it work.

At least I had them. Noelle had no one, and that was no one's fault but my own. I destroyed her, and then kept breaking her again and again with every single holiday she used to spend with me and my family. I went about my life. Noelle's was at a standstill. She volunteered to work just so she didn't have to be alone.

Not anymore.

From here on out, Noelle is never going to be alone again. I have a lot of time to make up for, but I'm willing to put in the work. She's worth it. She's worth everything and so much more. I'm going to prove it to her.

Once I get the tree set up, I go back to the garage for Christmas decorations. It may seem odd that I have any, I don't live here year round, but the last time I was here, the General Store was having a massive blowout sale. On a whim, I bought a lot of Christmas stuff. As soon as I got it back here, I sat asking myself why the hell I bought any of it. I played it off as I was just being nice to my friend and supporting his business.

I know now that it was fate leading me. No one really understands how fate works, but sometimes, she takes hold of a hand and leads. We have no choice but to follow, and that's just what I did. Now, I understand why I bought all of this stuff. It was to prepare for this moment.

Once I have everything in, I put my coat away. I strip my wet clothing and put it in the washer. I start it and walk naked to my bathroom.

I peek into the bedroom and see Noelle still sound asleep. It's barely ten in the morning. I don't blame her for being out like a light. We were catching up on all of our lost time until almost five in the morning. The only reason I was up doing anything is because I couldn't fall asleep. I was thinking of all the ways I could make it all up to her and show her just how sorry I am. This was the number one way I could think of.

I quickly finish my shower and dry off. I wrap a towel around my waist and stride to my bedroom. My breath catches when I see Noelle putting her silky hair in a messy bun on top of her head.

"Goddamn, you're beautiful."

She lets out a quiet squeak as she turns to me. She clutches the blanket wrapped around her to her chest. "Nico, you scared me."

"Sorry, baby. That wasn't my intent." I give her a sexy grin and wink that has her giggling.

The sound goes straight to my dick. I ignore it and stride to my dresser. As much as I want to bury myself inside her again, I know she needs a break. Before she finally passed out from exhaustion, she whispered that her pussy bone hurt. I couldn't help but chuckle because of how cute she said it, but I know from experience that she's going to be walking on the slower and more careful side today.

"It's too cold for wearing such thin pajamas." She visibly shivers.

I glance at her. She's not wearing anything right now but my comforter, but I understand what she means. Her pajamas are a thin tank top with fleece bottoms. She expected to be in a warm hotel room where she can adjust the heat. I slide on a pair of gray sweatpants and remove the towel. She licks her lips and drops her eyes very obviously to my dick as I grab a sweatshirt.

I laugh. "I'd show you what you do to me, but I know you're hurting."

She blushes. "More just irritated than anything else, but you're right. I'm not sure I can take more right now." She looks down.

I grab her a pair of my sweats and a sweatshirt and walk to her. I sit down on the bed next to her and set them in her lap. "Put these on. Come out to the living room. I have a surprise for you." I kiss her softly as I get up, then kiss her forehead before I grab a sweatshirt and leave her to get dressed.

Not that I want to. I'd love to watch her. But I have one more thing to do before she gets out here. I hurry to the living room and put a couple of logs on the fire so she's warm when she comes out. I then rush to the kitchen when I hear the bathroom door close. I grab some bacon out of the fridge, grateful once more for the amazing community we're in. After I start cooking it, I take out ingredients for waffles. I wasn't sure how long I'd be here, but there's enough food for at least three weeks.

"Thank God for that," I say to myself. I smile when I hear her come out of the bathroom just as I start mixing the batter.

"Mmm... I smell bacon."

I glance over my shoulder with a grin. Her nose is adorably sniffing the air. "Mmhmm." I turn and pour batter into the heated waffle maker.

This was a tradition I started with her the first Christmas we were together. She loves bacon with waffles. If she could, she'd eat it for every meal every day, but it became one of our Christmas traditions. Every Christmas Eve, I'd make it for her. And after I left, it was something I never gave up.

When I put it on my grocery list, I didn't think anything of it. Now, I feel like it was another fate thing. This entire thing was all something that was meant to happen. Maybe it wasn't our time then. I don't know. All I know is I'm never letting her go again. She's my forever.

I smile down at her when she appears at my side. She sniffles as her eyes meet mine. "You remembered."

My grin widens, and I lean down to give her a sweet kiss. "Confession time. I never stopped doing this on Christmas Eve. I couldn't let it go."

"Me either," she whispers. "I thought about you all of the time. I missed you every day. But it was always worse around the holidays. Even though I chose to work and actually had a good time being around so many people, I still missed you like crazy. Last year, we ended up calling the police for something. I stayed in the background, but I was wishing so hard that it was you who showed up." She looks down and shakes her head. "That was so stupid of me."

"No, sweet girl. It wasn't stupid of you." I pull the waffle out of the maker and add more batter before turning and wrapping my arms around her.

I kiss the top of her head and feel her melt into me when her arms slip around my waist. With one hand, I flip the bacon, but I keep her close, swaying gently with her. She needs the comfort, and I just need her.

"I'm so scared I'm going to wake up. Like I'm just having a dream, and I'm going to wake up in my car buried in snow and you not being there."

"First of all, I wouldn't have left you, Noelle. I don't care if you were my mortal enemy. I never would've left you there. Second, this isn't a dream. I know because I've pinched myself several times and have the marks to prove it."

She giggles, and it's such a sweet sound. Seconds later, after she begins to pull away, she gasps. "Nico, no! You got a tree? How did you get a tree?" She squeals and runs towards it.

I laugh as I start plating things. "It came down last night. Luckily, the wind was blowing the opposite way of the power lines and the house. It was a pretty small tree, too. I think it's only around seven feet."

"It's perfect. And it smells amazing!"

I grin and turn with the plates. I bring them to the living room and set them on the table before going back to get some orange juice. Just as I'm opening the fridge, the inevitable happens. The power goes out.

"Fuck," I mumble.

"Oh no…"

I turn when I hear the fear in Noelle's voice. She's looking at me like she might cry. I smile reassuringly. "Don't worry, baby. We're all stocked up with gas for the generator. We'll be just fine."

She visibly relaxes. "You have a generator?"

I nod. "Most everyone out here does. It was the first thing I was told to invest in when I bought this place. Glad I did. It's come in handy a few times. Come grab the drinks. I'll get the generator going. I thought we could eat breakfast and then tackle decorating the tree."

Her smile is so wide. So pretty. Brighter and more beautiful than any Christmas lights in existence. "You have decorations?"

I nod. "I don't know why I bought them, but I'm going with Santa. He must have had a hand in making my wish come true."

She giggles as I wink and hurries to the fridge while I make my way to the garage. I can't help but smile at my analogy. Maybe fate has nothing to do with this.

Maybe it was Santa setting this all up all along.

Whatever it was, I know that it led me back to the other half of me. My home.

The End

About Melony Ann

Melony Ann began writing short stories and poetry as a child. She continued honing her craft over the years until she took the plunge and began publishing her work, despite having severe anxiety.

Melony writes contemporary romance stories that are full of suspense and a lot of steam.

When she isn't writing, she is loving her family and working to make her life something she deserves.

Melony believes that if her writing can inspire just one person, then all of her hard work is worth it.

Her hope is that her writing allows each and every one of her readers to escape for a little while. To dive into a different world one book at a time.

Books By Melony Ann

Available Now

The Beautiful Dream Series
Loving You
My Love, My Heart
Softening Lyric
Undercover Temptations
Captain Charming
Breaking Boundaries
Crashing Into You
Tactical Inferno
Ravishing Our Queen
Cherished By The Texan
Unveiling Our Passions

The Crane Family Series
The Reluctant Mafia King
Sweet Lies
Billion Dollar Love Story
Be Mine
Protecting Her
Dangerously Forbidden Love
His Heart
Love In The Dark

The Deimos Trilogy
Connor's Legacy
Aryan's Alpha
Kade's Redemption

The Forbidden Temptation Series
The Detective's Forbidden Temptation
The Running Back's Forbidden Temptation

Social Media Links

Follow me on:

Facebook
/jason.mel.authors

Instagram
@melonyannauthor

Tik Tok
@authorsjasonmel

Website
www.melonyannauthor.com

Nikki A Lamers

Romance
Author

Sinfully Sweet & Spicy
www.NikkiALamersauthor.com

Happy Reading!

25 Men Of Christmas
An Unforgettable December

by Nikki A. Lamers

Blurb

Dean always goes after what he wants, but when he steps in to help his best friend, modeling for a December countdown to Christmas calendar, a photo shoot for a good cause, he runs into Leah - his best friend's little sister. Despite being warned to stay away from her, Dean finds himself uncharacteristically flustered and distracted by the firecracker that is Leah.

Leah has worked hard for her position in her company and is determined to make her mark with the Christmas fundraiser, but with Dean's presence stirring up her long-held feelings for her secret crush, she's finding it harder and harder to stay focused.

Will Dean be able to resist the temptation of Leah or will he give her a real chance? Or is he just the player everyone assumes? Will Leah be able to stay clear of distractions and prove what she's capable of? Will she finally get the chance she's always craved with Dean this Christmas?

In Nikki A Lamers' 25 Men of Christmas, An Unforgettable December, find out what happens when the known player and his best friend's sister come together in this contemporary romance novella. Join Dean and Leah as they fight for a chance at love that might be more than either of them bargained for.

Chapter 1

❄ Dean ❄

"Need some oil?"

I glance at the guy out of the corner of my eye, making sure he's talking to me before shaking my head. "No thanks."

"You'll look better on camera," he adds, quirking his eyebrow.

"Don't need it." I run my hand through my inky black hair. For the fifteenth time, I wonder how I ended up getting manipulated into being here. Every guy around the room is dressed, or half-dressed in some Christmas theme.

There's a Jack Frost across the room, elves at various levels of fucked-up, someone I assume is Scrooge, and a guy painted green. The Grinch is great, but seriously? And I'm wearing red Santa pants with black suspenders and boots, my chest bare.

He shakes his head and shrugs. "Suit yourself."

My phone vibrates in my pocket and I pull it out, one of my best friends lighting up the screen; the guy responsible for me being here. Swiping, I answer, accusing, "How the fuck could you do this to me, Joe?"

His laugh echoes through the line. "Who was I supposed to send? Christian? While Bree is home with the baby? She would kill me."

"What about you?"

"My sister is on the crew! No way in hell I'm getting half naked in front of her, no matter how good the cause."

"Isn't she only a year younger than you?"

"Yeah, she's twenty-six. So what. That has nothing to do with it. She's still my little sister."

"I'm sure there was someone else you could've asked."

"Sure, but you owe me and it's easy for you to take off work."

I groan in frustration. "Yeah, yeah."

I owe him a lot – him and Christian. They're always there, no matter how much I fuck up. They've been my best friends since our freshman year of college. They've seen me at my best, and my worst. Christian is now married with a kid, and Joe just started dating someone new, so they haven't been around much, but I know they would be if I needed them. Just like I'll still do anything for both of them. That won't ever change. It's why I'm here.

"How's it going anyway?"

"It's like being in the locker room at the North Pole." I'm unsure how else to describe it.

He laughs. "Have fun but be good – it really is for a good cause."

"What is that again?"

"You each represent a different cause throughout the month of December as a countdown to Christmas. The program goes all year and there has already been tons of marketing done for the fundraisers, but this is a last-minute add-on they'll share at the fundraiser event they want you at on Thursday night."

"Next Thursday? That's fast."

"It is, but this is specifically for another push. They're working with non-profits for the homeless, terminally ill, a separate one for sick kids, food for the hungry, gifts for the holidays for kids and families, clothes, school, and office supplies for those in need, military families, families suffering from domestic abuse and a few others."

How can I back out on something like that? No way! I heave a sigh. "Fine. I'll deal!"

"Stay away from her, Dean. She's been warned about you for years, so she wouldn't touch you with a ten-foot pole."

"Why does everybody think I'm such a player?"

He ignores my question believing the answer is obvious. "You know I appreciate you. Thanks for doing this, Dean." I grunt in acknowledgment. "I gotta' go. We'll catch up later."

"Sure, asshole." I disconnect the call and slide my phone back in my pocket.

In the next instant, a hand slips into my pocket and pulls out my phone. I spin around in protest. "Hey!" A petite blonde with her hair pulled back in a French braid drops my phone into a black and red bag and slings it over her shoulder as she puts her hand up halting my movements. "That's my phone."

"No phones allowed on set."

I smirk. "On set?"

She rolls her gray eyes. Taking a step back she slowly assesses me from head to toe. Pulling a bottle out of her bag, she squeezes something into her hand and mumbles under her breath, "You need oil."

Gesturing behind me, I begin, "I already told…" I gasp as her hands connect with my chest and start rubbing, sending a shock right through me. Clearing my throat, I attempt to do what I do best. "If you wanted to touch, all you had to do is ask."

Her eyes dance as she glances up at me from underneath her long eyelashes, a splash of freckles over the bridge of her nose bouncing as she laughs. "Nice try, Santa."

I flash her an innocent smile as she steps back with a shake of her head. "This isn't me trying, beautiful." The guy behind me laughs, but I ignore him, my eyes fastened to her.

She hands me the bottle. "You can finish yourself or ask one of the guys for help."

"Wait, what?"

"Make sure you get your back." She smirks. "You'll get your phone back after you're done."

My eyes remain glued to her perfect ass as she impossibly disappears in a room full of men. Damn!

Sighing heavily, I glance down at the bottle in my hand. Is she kidding? My eyes shift to my half-oiled chest. Apparently not. She didn't even flinch. Relenting, I do what I'm told, rubbing oil on my arms, and grabbing a towel to wipe my hands.

"Dean Chambers."

Guess I'm doing this.

Chapter 2

❄ Leah ❄

"Today went fantastic," Scarlett proclaims, pushing her long, wavy, red hair over her shoulder. "It's almost worth missing out on Black Friday shopping."

I huff a laugh setting down a box of Christmas decorations on top of another box before sitting on the opposite end of our oversized tan couch that barely fits in our living room. "You think that because you got to do makeup for a lot of guys."

She grins. "Not just guys, hot men! I think my favorite were the ones who needed oil rubbed all over their muscles."

My face heats instantly, my fingers trembling at the reminder. Dean fucking Chambers. He hasn't changed a bit. Remembering his abs, I admit that's not exactly true. What the hell was my brother thinking sending him? I get it. It's probably not his first modeling job with that lean, firm body, strong jaw, eyes making me melt without even trying and a killer smile, but he's trouble.

"Oh, what are you blushing for, girl? Did I miss something?"

Of course, Scarlett notices. She hasn't only been my best friend since middle school, we've been roommates for over eight years. Every breakup, success and failure, we've endured together. No one knows me better. I heave a sigh. "Well, you know when Davis backed out at the last minute because he heard I went on a date with Beau?"

"I still can't believe that jealous idiot."

"Whatever." I roll my eyes. "Anyway, I called my brother and he asked one of his friends to help."

"Oh, was that the guy I saw you rubbing down?"

"I was not rubbing him down."

She bursts out laughing. "He's hot!"

"Yeah, but he knows it. Besides, he's a player."

"Joe told you that?" She arches her eyebrows in challenge.

"Yeah, but it's not like he's making it up. He lived with the guy all through college and a couple years after."

"He can't be all bad. This event you're doing is for a good cause, or technically a lot of good causes."

"It's my job!"

"A job that you fought for and a Christmas fundraiser you pushed for, planned everything and have been working your ass off to boost donations. A lot of people will benefit because of you."

"No, it's because of everyone who's been working hard to get it done in time for Christmas and the people willing to donate their time and money for the causes. I'm just doing something I believe in. Besides, I want to do a good job to prove my worth. I've been there over three years, but this is the first big project they've given me. I'm so nervous about everything falling into place. I need it to go well."

Biting my lower lip, I run my teeth over it in thought. She's right, but Joe calling in a favor doesn't scream good guy. Then again, If it wasn't for Davis quitting on me at the last second, I wouldn't have been so screwed.

I didn't have any time to find another December 5th and I haven't seen many men around here who fit what we need. The printer already says we're way behind. At least printing is the final thing on the list besides last-minute details. I'm not about to let this fall apart now. I've worked too hard.

"It will go well and you're young. You need to take a break so you don't burn out before you turn thirty."

"So, I have time." I shrug and she narrows her eyes at me. My lips twitch in amusement knowing she's about to react. "Well, I'm only twenty-six. Taking a break can be my New Year's resolution."

She plants her hands on her hips, narrowing her eyes. "What am I going to do with you," she mutters, shaking her head. "Maybe we should invite some of the guys over to help us decorate for Christmas. We are busy and it would be fun," she suggests making me laugh. "But it's Friday, Leah. You can't do anything for the next couple days. Forget decorating, we're going out for a drink." She jumps up, tugging on my arm.

"Hey!" I argue, knowing it's pointless.

"Quit whining. You need it! And you owe me."

"Fine!" I relent, letting her drag me towards the door. "At least let me put on some shoes."

"Whatever," she huffs in mock annoyance.

I tug on my black city boots sitting by our front door and glance in the mirror, dusting my nose with powder, and applying mascara and lipstick as she waits, watching. "Where are we going, anyway?" I slip my ID, debit card, and phone in my back pocket.

She loops her arm through mine as we walk out the door. "Not far. We need to be able to walk home together later."

"That's not an answer." She laughs. "Scar!"

"A few of the guys were talking about going out to the restaurant that turns into a dance club at night."

"The guys? Like from the shoot today?" My eyebrows hit my hairline.

"Of course."

"I'm not dressed to go out for something like that."

Sighing, she halts her footsteps, staring at me. "Yeah, you are. You look hot in those jeans."

"But I'm wearing a button down. I look like I'm ready to go to work."

"Unbutton it and show off your lacy black cami underneath."

"It's almost winter in Maine!"

"Almost is nothing like the real thing and you know it will get hot inside. Roll up your sleeves, tie the bottom in a knot and take it off when you're hot. You need this or I might strangle you before Thursday."

"Gee, thanks," I grumble, deadpan. With an exaggerated sigh, I fix my shirt so I look more like I'm ready to go out, even with my hair pulled back. "I know I've been stressing, but can you blame me? It's not just that

I want to prove myself. So many people are depending on these funds. I don't want to disappoint anyone."

"You won't. It will go amazing knowing you, but not if you don't destress."

"You're probably right."

She grins, picking up her pace. "You know I am."

Chapter 3

❆ Leah ❆

It's not long before we enter the already crowded bar. License plates from all over the world plaster the left wall, interspersed with Christmas decorations, likely wherever they fit. I'm curious if they used to be on cars, or if they had them made.

To the right is a long oak bar adorned with garland wrapped with red lights, the same decorations framing the back of the bar with an eighteen-inch porcelain tree centered among the liquor bottles. A large wreath with colored lights hangs in the back of the club, the tables removed to make up a dance floor. It's small but it works.

Scarlett weaves us expertly through the sea of bodies towards the bar, ordering two lemon vodka and sodas. "Here," she offers moments later.

"Thanks."

"Cheers!" She grins holding up her glass and we both take a drink.

"Hey, it's makeup girl and Wonder Girl!" a deep voice proclaims as he throws his arms over both our shoulders, almost making me spill my drink. "Oops, sorry." He gives me an apologetic smile.

"Wonder Girl?" I arch my eyebrow at the familiar guy with brown hair and eyes. He shrugs giving me a look I'm sure he's used to get what he wants. "David, right?"

"She remembers me!" He grins, his arm dropping from Scarlett.

"Well, we did see you a couple hours ago." She smirks.

"Glad you guys made it. Can I buy you both a drink?" We laugh, holding up our drinks and toast one another again. "Next round."

Scarlett leans in by my ear. "Try to relax."

"I'm here, aren't I?"

She laughs, looking around. "Oh, Ben is here. I'm going to go say hi. You're good here?" she asks and spins on her heel without giving me a chance to respond. Glancing back at me, she winks.

I flip her off and take a sip of my drink, already starting to warm up from all the body heat in here. I look up at David his arm still draped over my shoulders. "So, have you done a lot of modeling?"

His eyes light up as he begins to ramble. "Not a lot, but I've done a few jobs. You may have seen me in the ads for the department store? They wanted me…"

The cacophony of voices and music filling the small space drown out his voice. I take the time to look around searching for other familiar faces. Scar's right, it's hot in here. I slide out from underneath his arm and slip out of my shirt, tying it around my waist as he turns to the bar and orders another drink.

I spot some of the other models and crew from today and some of the younger staff from my company, Charming Affiliate Marketing. Thankfully, the senior staff doesn't appear to be here, so I'm comfortable enjoying the night. The room definitely has more women than men. I'm surprised by how dressed up everyone is too, hinting someone shared there would be models here tonight.

My gaze lands on a woman a couple feet from me with long, dark hair wearing a short, tight, black dress with spaghetti straps and two-inch platforms. Why would you wear that to go out to a random bar in Maine this time of year? Maybe she heard the model rumor.

She pushes into the guy standing in front of her and presses her lips to his. The guy's hands reach around her, one tangling into her hair and the other cupping her ass, pulling her into him while she pushes closer, not caring her dress has nowhere to go. My eyes widen as they start making out, not giving a damn who's surrounding them. His lips move to the crook of her neck a flop of black hair falling over his face making me gasp.

Is it him? No way. "Dean fucking Chambers," I mutter under my breath. I should've known.

Ripping his lips away from her skin, his steel blue eyes crash into mine with a spark of surprise. I gasp, realizing I said that much louder than I thought. Damn. A lump forms in my throat and my stomach twists. I hate that just a look from him has my body reacting, especially when he just had his tongue down another woman's throat. Apparently, I have no shame.

"Wonder Girl." He grins pulling away from the woman, as she glares at both of us.

My heart begins to thrash against my ribcage, my eyes glued to his. This man. Shit, I'm in trouble.

Chapter 4

❄ Dean ❄

The moment my name leaves her lips, I know it's her before I look. "Wonder Girl." I grin as I mumble the name I've been hearing out of the guys mouths all damn day wondering how she'll react. She pinches her full lips, attempting to hide behind her drink as she takes a sip. She's heard the name, but she doesn't appear to know why.

She looks hot as fuck in a lacy black tank, accenting her ivory skin. I take a step closer to her as the woman who threw herself at me latches onto my arm, trying to claim me, but that shit doesn't work with me. "Dean," she whines, "I thought we were busy."

"Nah, I'm good. I'm talking to Wonder Girl." She huffs as I disentangle my arm without looking in her direction.

She steps into my space again and Wonder Girl rolls her eyes dramatically. "Are you really that desperate?"

I huff a laugh before I can stop myself. The woman glares at her. "How dare you! Who the hell do you think you are?"

"There's plenty of other models here. Is he really worth getting hit over?" She challenges, ignoring her question. I'm not sure if I should be pissed at the insult or turned on.

"Screw you both," the woman mutters as she spins on her heel and stalks away.

I laugh and step closer again. She smirks as she takes a step back looking up at me from underneath her long eyelashes, her eyes swirling with blue and gray. "Thanks for the save."

"Didn't look like you really wanted it."

"Like you said, she's obviously here to hook up..."

"With a model," she interrupts.

"You know that's not my actual job, right?" I quirk a brow, for some reason needing her to know I'm more than my face. "I'm just here helping out a friend."

"And taking advantage of the benefits."

"Hey, is it my fault women throw themselves at me?" She may be right, but the words coming out of her mouth feel like a punch to the gut.

Let alone, I let the woman kiss me hoping to get this firecracker out of my damn head.

She gives me a look and opens her mouth, probably to call me on my shit, when David steps up to her and drops his arm around her shoulders, making me stiffen. He's one of the assholes who made that fucking bet. She glances up at him, her body not folding into his like I've seen other women do all night. Thank fuck. He lightly swirls a drink hanging it over her shoulder. "I got you another drink, Wonder Girl."

"Thanks." She glances at her still half-full glass and downs it. My jaw drops as she sets the empty glass on the bar and changes the subject as she takes the drink from him. "And why does everyone keep calling me that?"

"We saw how hard you were working," David claims, telling her a partial truth.

"Well, thanks," she murmurs, accepting his response as she takes another drink.

I clear my throat, refusing to walk away while this douchebag is anywhere near her. "It's nice to see you taking a break."

"You sound like my roommate."

"Your roommate?" I arch my eyebrow in question.

"Yeah, I need to go find her. I'll see you guys later!" She dips out from under David's arm and I breathe a sigh of relief. My gaze drops to her ass and back up as she waves over her shoulder.

Moments later, she hip checks a petite redhead and her arms go up in the air as they dance. I'm not able to take my eyes off her. I could watch her move all night. My dick jumps in anticipation, but I ignore it, knowing I should keep it professional. David groans beside me reminding me he still has his eyes on her along with other assholes in this room. For some stupid reason it pisses me off.

"Maybe she's not as much of an ice queen as we thought," David comments.

I narrow my eyes on him. "She just has fucking standards."

He laughs. "Or maybe she's a bitch and needed some loosening up."

"What the fuck?!" I shove him in the shoulder and he stumbles back, wide-eyed.

"Dude?!" he grunts, holding his hands up in surrender. "Don't be such an asshole."

"Treat her with some fucking respect!"

He smirks; the look making my stomach roil. "I'll happily fucking worship her."

Without thought I grab him by the shirt and shove him up against the bar, glaring at him. "What the fuck did you just say?"

The bartender yells, "Hey, assholes!" Instantly, he's behind David. "Settle the fuck down or get the hell out!"

My eyes narrow on David, his hands up as if he's innocent and his lips twitching in amusement. He's trying to piss me off. "Watch yourself," I warn before I release him with a shove and step back, stalking towards the dance floor to find her.

Chapter 5

❄ Leah ❄

Making my way through the crowd, I find Scarlett talking to her cousin, Ben. I hip check Scar and grin up at him. "Hi Ben. You're here."

"Hey, Leah! Good to see you." He leans down, giving me a hug.

"Of course, he is, I wasn't lying about that. His boyfriend is one of the models."

"Really? Who's your boyfriend?"

"Jacob." He grins.

"He's so nice and hot too."

"Yes, he is."

"Why did you leave David? He looked like he wanted to eat you for dinner." Scarlett wiggles her eyebrows.

I scrunch my nose up in disgust. "Exactly. He was giving me creep vibes and he's too into himself."

"That sucks." Scar frowns. A new song comes on and she jumps. "Oh, I love this song! Let's dance!"

I nod and finish my drink setting it down on a table behind them, the alcohol suddenly hitting me hard. I guess it has been a long time since I've let loose. My hips begin to sway and I raise my arms in the air, closing my eyes as I get lost in the music.

A firm hand falls to my hip and a warm front presses against my back, moving with me. I try to pull away, but I feel sluggish, so I lean my head back and look up, finding another face or two that I recognize as one of the guys I worked with today, but I can't remember his name.

"You can really move," he tells me.

"Thanks," I mumble my throat suddenly dry. The room starts to spin, so I stop.

"Are you okay?" Scarlett steps in front of me, but I can't focus on her moving form.

"Um, yeah." I gulp and tap the hand gripping my hip hard, desperate to escape and breathe. "I think I just need water. I'm going to the bathroom."

"Okay, I'll come with you."

"No, I'm okay, I'll be right back." I look towards the back corner, keeping my focus on my destination, rushing towards the bathroom.

As I push through the door, the room spins and I stumble to the sink. I plant my hands on each side of the porcelain, taking a couple deep breaths, trying to calm my stomach and stop the dizzy spell. Desperate for a reprieve, I splash my face with cool water.

The door swings open, someone walking in. I lift my head, glancing in the mirror and gasp, David catching my gaze in the reflection. "You're in the wrong bathroom," I mutter, my words slurring.

"No, I'm looking for you. I heard you might need help."

I shake my head, my movements wobbly. "No."

"Are you okay, Wonder Girl?" His voice sounds anything but sincere. "You don't look so good." He steps towards me and I try to step away, but I fall back against the wall of the bathroom stall. "Just relax. Let me help you feel good," he urges, planting his hands on the wall, next to my head, closing me in.

He runs his finger under the strap of my cami, making me feel naked. "No, no, no," I stammer as a prayer.

The door hits the wall with a bang, but my limbs are either too weak or too slow to react. "Get the fuck away from her!" Dean's voice echoes against the walls.

"I heard her calling for help," David claims, stepping away.

"Dean." I gasp for breath, relief consuming me.

"Asshole," Dean grunts as everything goes peacefully black.

Chapter 6

❄ Dean ❄

Grateful the police are gone and I got my statement over with, I slide down the wall next to my bed, sitting on the floor with my knees propped. My hand runs down my face to the back of my neck, rubbing it as I stretch, trying to release the tension.

I haven't slept on the floor like this since college, but there was no way in hell I was leaving her side. She looks so beautiful, peaceful, as I watch her chest rising and falling methodically in sleep. My old black Imagine Dragons concert t-shirt looks sexy as hell on her, along with knowing she's wearing a pair of my boxer shorts underneath the dark gray sheets covering her legs.

She begins to stir. I shove myself off the floor and lean against the wall as her eyes flutter open. She groans and wipes her eyes, looking around the room. "How are you feeling?" I ask gently.

Her head snaps to me and she winces from the movement before her eyes go wide. "Dean?"

I pinch my lips tightly together and give her a stiff nod. Does she not remember? Shit. "There's some water and aspirin on the nightstand if you need it," I offer, attempting to give her time to process.

She reaches over, downing the aspirin and the entire glass of water. "Why does my mouth feel like I ate sand? And why am I here? What happened?"

Heaving a sigh, I drop down onto the edge of my bed, looking at her anxiously. This is not something I want to tell her. I was hoping she would remember. She looks back at me, her blue-gray eyes lighter, more vulnerable, hitting me hard as they begin to narrow. "You don't remember anything?"

She shakes her head pulling her knees up to her chest, the sheet going with her like a shield. "Not really, we didn't...um..."

"No!" I insist with a hard shake of my head. I don't want her to think the worst of me.

Her eyes suddenly widen in fear and she gasps, pulling the sheet even tighter around herself. "David...he...he..." she stammers, not able to get the words out.

"He didn't do anything. Well, that's not exactly true, but he didn't touch you. I got there before anything happened."

Tears spill down her cheeks and she looks away, staring out the window. "I'm so fucking stupid!"

I inch closer, not wanting to startle her. "No, you're not. It's not your fault."

"I took a drink from him. Just because I was working with that asshole for a day doesn't mean I know anything about him. I know better than to take a drink from anyone. How could I be so stupid?"

"Stop!" I'm desperate to help her feel better. "You were surrounded by people you knew. Why wouldn't you trust that you were safe?"

Her narrowed gaze swings back to me. "There's two rules I've been taught to always follow to protect myself when going out. Don't go anywhere alone and don't ever take a drink from anyone you don't know really fucking well. Apparently I broke both those rules."

I reach up and wipe the tears from her cheeks, no longer able to hold back. "It's not your fault he's an asshole."

"What happened to him?"

"I don't exactly know. I wanted you out of there and the police don't tell you anything."

"The police?"

"Yeah, they were here early this morning to take my statement. I didn't tell them you were sleeping in the next room; I didn't want to wake you. But he won't come near you again."

"How do you know?"

"I hit him and left him with the bouncer, telling them he put something in your drink."

Her eyes widen and she reaches for my hand, tingles shooting straight up my arm as she runs her fingers over my cracked and bruised knuckles.

"Thank you," she murmurs without meeting my gaze.

"You don't have to thank me."

"Why am I here, Dean? Why didn't you just bring me home?"

"I was going to bring you home, but you passed out in the Uber before you could tell me where you live. I guess your roommate figured you'd tell me. No way I was taking you back in there to ask."

She looks up, into my eyes. My chest tightens at the range of emotions passing through her teary gaze, fear, gratitude, relief, and heat. "Thank you."

Not able to stop myself, I reach up and cradle her face in my hands, wiping her tears with my thumbs. "I'm just glad I was there."

A soft whimper escapes her lips before she presses them to mine taking me by surprise. I don't waste a second, kissing her back. My lips move in a slow rhythm over her soft full ones. She moans, the sound sending heat throughout my body, my dick jumping in excitement.

My tongue juts out, wanting a taste but she pulls back, denying me. "I'm sorry, I shouldn't have done that."

I quirk a brow, hoping she doesn't regret our sweet kiss that felt anything but.

"After last night, my mouth just tastes gross."

Relief floods me. "There's an extra toothbrush under the bathroom sink if you want."

"Thanks." She scoots to the edge of the bed before looking back at me, her cheeks flushed. "Um, my clothes?"

I give her an apologetic smile. "You threw up on your jeans and tank, so I tossed them in the wash. You still have your bra and panties on, but I thought you'd appreciate something to wear."

Her face turns brighter with each word I utter. "Um, thanks?" She squeaks as more of a question, making me chuckle.

"Don't worry, I didn't look more than I had to. Not that I didn't want to." I don't want her to think I'm not interested.

She clears her throat, changing the subject. "So, Scarlett knows I left with you?"

"Your roommate?" She nods. "Yeah, she knows. Although, you might want to call or text to let her know you're okay."

"She knows I'm safe with you."

My eyebrows draw down in confusion. "Why would she know that?"

Her puzzlement matches mine. "Because you're Dean. I'm sure Joe asked you to watch out for me." Her gaze drops to the floor as my heart plummets.

"Joe?" I ask as reality slams into me. "You're little."

"What?"

"I used to call you *little* Leah."

She grimaces. "He's barely a year older than me. I've just always been small."

"Fuck," I mumble under my breath. "I knew you were working there, but I didn't expect you to be all grown up."

"Wait. You didn't know I was Joe's sister?"

"It's been a long time since I've seen you." I know it's a weak excuse. I'm such a fucking idiot. I said I would watch out for her, but I didn't realize she looked like this.

She huffs and pushes off the bed, stalking into the bathroom without another word. "Fuck." I run my hand through my hair in frustration. "I'm sorry, Leah!" Without a response, I sigh heavily, trudging towards the kitchen to make us breakfast and get some much-needed coffee.

Little all grown up is hot as sin. I'm fucked.

Chapter 7

❄ Leah ❄

My reflection glares back at me as I untangle my hair from yesterday's braid. I look like I got run over by Santa's sleigh taken over by rogue elves who then jumped out and danced to Jingle Bell Rock on my head. It's the same way I feel. I'm pissed at myself for being so stupid. Never again.

But Dean... I sigh, not knowing if I'm irate or relieved. He wasn't watching out for me because I'm Joe's little sister, but because he wanted to. I always knew he was a good guy, but he's also a player. Charm comes so naturally to him. It felt like he was interested in me. That's what he does though, right?

Then again, maybe he wouldn't have kissed me back if he knew who I was. Maybe it's good he didn't know because that kiss... I couldn't stop myself with the way he was looking at me and what he did for me. But what now?

Sighing, I shove away my question. I'm thankful for him, no matter who he is to my brother.

I walk out of the bathroom, finding his bedroom empty. Grabbing my phone, I see a few missed calls and texts. Ignoring the others, I open one from my roommate.

Scar: Are you okay? I'm worried!
Leah: I'm okay. Just woke up. Dean didn't have our address.

Scar: The police want to talk to you right away to take a statement.

I grimace, setting my phone down as the smell of bacon hits my nose. "Mm," I murmur, following the scent to the open living space, a combined, living, dining, and kitchen, the white granite countertop separating the kitchen from the rest. "Smells good." I drop onto a stool, leaning on the counter. "Is anything for me?"

He chuckles, the deep sound making my stomach flip. "I made you breakfast. Scrambled eggs, bacon, and toast. Is that okay?"

"That's sweet. Thank you!"

"No problem. I'm sure you need it," he mumbles, keeping his back to me.

I can't argue with that. I spin on my stool taking in the large Christmas tree sitting in front of a picture window, the branches bare of decorations or lights. "You have a Christmas tree."

"Of course, don't you?"

"Not yet. Thanksgiving was just two days ago. I've been busy. When did you have time?"

He plates the food, setting one in front of me and another next to it. "I got it on Thanksgiving."

"What was open?"

He sits down next to me. "This is Maine, Christmas trees are everywhere." I arch my eyebrows and he laughs. "My parents have a ton of trees. I cut it down on their property."

"Now that makes sense." I nod, realizing I don't know much about Dean besides what Joe has told me over the years. Most of Joe's stories constitute drinking, parties, women, bad decisions, or a combination.

Then again, last time I saw him was probably their college graduation. He obviously didn't remember me. Maybe he's changed. The woman from last night flashes through my mind making me grimace. Maybe not...

"You don't like my cooking?"

I blush and shake my head as I finish chewing. "No, that's not it. I was just thinking about something."

"Something?"

"My brother."

196

"I can see how Joe could put that look on your face." He smirks, making me blush a deeper shade of red. "Or are you thinking about how he told you to stay away from me, warned you about me, told you I'm a player and then you woke up in my bed?"

"What?" I gasp, wide-eyed.

He waves his hand like it's no big deal. "It's fine. Your brother has seen me at my best and my worst. But why don't you come to your own conclusions about me?"

"It's not like that."

He puts his fork down, his plate empty and focuses his full attention on me. "You sure about that?"

"When you mentioned your parents' property, I was thinking how I never knew that about you."

"So, you don't think I'm an asshole or a player?"

"No," I retort, my nose wrinkling without my consent. He chuckles. "You're obviously a good guy."

He winces. Standing, he grabs his plate, moving towards the sink. "A good guy but a player."

"You did have your tongue down some random's throat when I saw you."

He barks out another laugh and turns, facing me. "So, since I'm such a good guy, why don't you spend the day with me?"

"You don't want my company. I have a terrible hangover."

His shoulders slump. "I'm sorry that happened to you."

"I'm okay thanks to you. I just want to put it behind me. I will never be that stupid again."

"Are you going to the station to give your statement?"

"I guess I have to," I concede, my chest suddenly tight. "My roommate said they were at my place this morning."

He strides toward me, putting his arm around me, and rubs soothing circles on my back. "Yeah. I can take you."

"That's okay. Scarlett will go with me."

He nods, pursing his lips. "Well, junk food and movies are a great cure for a hangover if you want to hang out later."

"Do you want to?"

"I'm asking, Leah."

I lick my lips. "I don't know..."

"Give me a chance to show you I'm not who you think and at the same time, I can help you forget about last night."

My heart squeezes. I don't know if this is a good idea, but when I look into his eyes, I can't say no. "Okay."

"Yes?"

"Yeah, I'll text you when I get home. Now, can I have my clothes?"

He laughs and kisses me on the top of the head, eliciting a gasp from my lips as tingles shoot from my head to my toes. "Sure, but you look good in my shirt," he calls over his shoulder. My entire body heats as he leaves to fetch my clothes. I watch, holding my breath until he disappears.

Damn, that man...

Chapter 8

❄ Dean ❄

My hand remains poised above the door, ready to knock, but questioning everything about being here. This is Leah. She's not a woman I can fool around with, but me being here, doesn't mean anything will happen. I need to make sure she's okay. I huff a laugh.

Who the hell do I think I'm kidding? Yeah, I want to check on her, but I want something to happen. I can't fuck this up. Joe is too important to me. Maybe I should get to know her more to see if there could be something…it's been a long time for me.

The front door swings open. Leah's red-headed roommate stands in front of me, grinning like a Christmas elf. "Are you going to stand there raising your hand all night or are you coming inside?"

A laugh escapes as I give her a crooked smile, attempting to act like she didn't catch me fighting with myself at their front door. "Hi, is Leah here?"

She nods, calling over her shoulder, "Leah, Saint Nick is here!"

Does she have a date tonight? "I'm Dean."

She giggles and waves me off as she steps back. "I know who you are."

Leah stumbles into the room in light blue flannel pants with Santa hats on them and a white tank with three red buttons between her breasts, drawing my attention. She gasps, her gaze meeting mine. "Oh, hi."

My smile falters. She doesn't seem very happy to see me, but at least she doesn't have a date if she's in pajamas...or maybe she does. "Hey, I thought we had plans for a Christmas movie night, but I didn't hear from you..."

"I'm so sorry. I was exhausted after..." she pauses shaking her head.

"Well, if you're okay, I'm going to meet my brother and sisters for a drink." Scarlett stops and stares at Leah, waiting.

"I'm fine, Scar."

"In that case, don't wait up!" We remain silent as her roommate exits.

"I'm not good company tonight."

"I thought that was why we were going to watch Christmas movies."

She arches her eyebrows, her doubt obvious. "You, Dean Chambers, want to stay in on a Saturday night and watch movies with Joe's little sister?"

I flinch, quickly trying to hide it. "I want to stay in with you and do whatever the fuck you want as long as it will make you happy and help you forget about assholes and police stations."

She sighs, giving me a fake smile. "You don't have to do this."

"You're right, I don't." I step towards her until I'm in her space, looking into her eyes. This isn't about anyone but you.

Her breathing picks up its pace, becoming ragged before she suddenly clears her throat and takes a step back. "Okay, do you want something to eat or drink?"

I grin, holding up the bag in my hand. "I brought ingredients for Christmas corn."

Her eyes sparkle and she dives for the bag. "No way! That's my favorite!"

I laugh. "I know. Your brother used to ask me to make extra for him so he could give it to you for Christmas."

Her mouth drops open. "He told me he made it himself." I shrug and she rolls her eyes.

"It's not hard. You just mix fresh popcorn with red and green chocolate candies. Then, drizzle it with melted white chocolate and either the red and green sugar or sprinkles while the chocolate is warm."

She reaches for my hand and tugs, shooting sparks up my arm as she drags me towards the kitchen. "Well, let's go already!"

Dropping my hand, she pulls out a large bowl as I dump the contents of my bag on the counter. "So..."

She crosses her arms protectively over her chest. "Go ahead, get it over with and then we don't talk about it again. Agreed?"

"Yeah. How are you?"

Releasing a heavy sigh, she claims, "I'm fine. I'm tired, and I've had a hangover all day, but I'm fine. The police station sucked. They don't think they have enough to press charges since I didn't go to the hospital and have a blood test to confirm what was in my system and there was no real proof that he put anything in my drink. I'm pretty sure the asshole got off with a warning."

"What?" My blood instantly boils as I drop the candy into the bowl, staring at her, mouth agape.

"Stand down, Saint Nick. I'm fine thanks to you." She shakes her head, turning her back to me. "I'm done talking about it."

I sigh, running my hand through my hair. She'll be pissed at me if I bring it up again and that's the last thing I want. I should've hit him harder. "So, what's with this Saint Nick shit?" I ask, attempting to appease her, but I'm not forgetting what that asshole did even for a moment.

She giggles. "One, you in your *25 Men of Christmas* outfit and two, you coming to my rescue."

The corners of my lips twitch up in amusement. I lean back against the counter, my finger tapping on my bottom lip as I rake my eyes up and down her body. "Well, I could always put on the outfit for you and do things to your body to show you I deserve that name."

Her face heats and her breathing quickens, giving me the desired effect. "Dean," her voice catches. With a shake of her head, she clears her throat and picks up the popcorn mixture, striding towards the living room. "You're definitely no saint."

I chuckle, following. "You got that right."

She sets the bowl on the coffee table and swipes the remote, flopping onto the couch. I sit next to her, draping my arm across the back of the couch and setting the bowl in my lap as she flips through a few movies. "What about Elf?"

"Sure." Laughter will do her good.

A smile tugs at her lips as she relaxes, leaning towards me and the popcorn mix, popping some in her mouth. "Mm," she moans. I lick my lips, my mouth watering as her tongue juts out. "This is so much better than I remember."

My dick twitches and I clench my jaw. This will be harder than I thought. I fist a handful of popcorn and stuff it in my mouth, suddenly in desperate need of a distraction.

Chapter 9

❄ Leah ❄

Sunlight peeks through my closed lids making me groan in protest. Did I forget to close my blinds? I'm hot as hell and reach up to wipe the drool from my mouth when my pillow moves. My eyes flash open, Dean's dark scruff inches from my face, his sweet musky scent filling my nostrils. I'm afraid to breathe, realizing I'm draped over his chest. I must've shifted when I fell asleep. What do I do?

He moans, his hand sliding to my ass. Reflexively, I arch into him, his morning wood pushing into my stomach, eliciting a gasp from my lips. "Leah?" Dean rumbles.

In a sudden panic, I push up and jump off the couch, my knee colliding with Dean. "Fuck!" He grunts, his knees pulling up as he covers himself, rolling onto the floor in pain.

"Oh, my God! I'm so sorry!" I can't believe I did that! His face turns so red, it's nearly purple before lightening, while I incessantly apologize. When his breathing appears back to normal and he no longer looks like an exploding tomato, I approach tentatively. "I'm so sorry. Are you okay?"

"I'll let you know if I'm able to have kids one day." I wince. "It's a joke, Leah, I'll live."

"I'm sorry."

He exhales harshly and sits up, leaning against the couch. "Did I try to feel you up in my sleep or something?" he asks giving me his sexy crooked smile.

I laugh. "No, I just woke up. I guess you startled me."

He huffs a humorless laugh. "I'll have to remember not to scare the shit out of you if I want to protect my balls."

My face heats and I look away. "I'm sorry I fell asleep on you."

"I'm not. I'm just sorry with how you woke me up."

Damn this man. "So, what are you doing today?" I ask, hoping the teasing stops.

"Spending the day with you."

My eyes fly back to his. "What?"

"I thought we were spending some time together and you were giving me a chance to show you who I really am?"

"Yeah, but I have a lot of work to do for the event Thursday."

"Okay, you work, while I go home and shower. I'll pick you up later for pizza and a Christmas tree."

"You don't have to."

"I know." He stands, stepping towards me. "I want to."

My heart skips a beat and I relent. "Okay."

He grins making my stomach twist. I bite my lower lip, holding back my groan. He wraps his arms around me, pulling me close. Smiling, I hug him back and melt into his chest as if the spot were mine. He kisses the top of my head and steps back. "I'm leaving before you change your mind. I'll text you when I'm on my way."

I wave as he walks out the door. My entire body sags as I exhale, collapsing onto the couch behind me. "What am I doing?"

"Morning!" Scarlett announces making me squeal in surprise. "Sorry, didn't mean to scare you. I wasn't sure if that sexy man was still here with all the noise you two were making this morning. I didn't want to walk in on anything."

Groaning, I trudge towards the kitchen needing coffee. "It's okay. Apparently I'm on edge this morning."

"Where's Dean?"

"He just left."

"You two seemed cozy when I walked in last night?"

"What am I doing Scar? I can't go there with him."

"Yes, you can!"

"But Joe…"

"Your brother doesn't own him and he's obviously into you."

"But he's a player. I know I've gone out with a few different guys lately, but I like being in a relationship. Sex is a big deal. I can't pretend it's not."

"I'm pretty sure with him, everything would be a big deal." She wiggles her eyebrows making me laugh. "And have you seen those hands? Can you imagine what he can do with them? And his tongue…"

"Stop!" I toss the kitchen towel at her and grab a full mug of coffee from under the Keurig.

She laughs. "It will be worth it."

"Well, he's picking me up later for pizza and a Christmas tree."

She quirks her brow. "Christmas tree?" I nod, my lips twitching. "You need to stop thinking so much. Have fun! You trust him. What could possibly go wrong?"

"Famous last words…"

Chapter 10

❄ Leah ❄

Dean pulls through a tall, wrought-iron gate, down a narrow drive into the woods. "I never took you for a serial killer," I mumble under my breath.

He bursts out laughing, the sound shooting tingles throughout my body. I glance at him out of the corner of my eye, his crooked smile remaining as he stares at the road ahead. "I did bring my ax." He gestures towards the back of his truck.

I glare at him, his responding chuckle making me impossibly hotter. Damn him. "Where are we?"

"My place."

"You live in the woods?"

"This is my parents' property. They have over three-hundred acres here. I have a house on the back of the property, far enough away from the main house."

"I didn't imagine you living at home." He clenches his jaw, making my stomach churn. "Not judging. Just surprised."

He relaxes slightly. "Well, it's not like they're ever here."

"Why? It's so beautiful!"

He shrugs. "Yeah, it is. This is only a small piece of it. I always said one day I'd build my own house, but it's just me. My parents have another place in Colorado, New York, California, and England, but this is where I want to be."

"I had no idea."

"Most people don't unless I grew up with them or they know my parents. Joe and Christian know, but I don't like to talk about it."

"Can I ask why?"

He parks the car in front of a small cedar house and twists his body to look at me. "For starters, my parents are assholes."

"I'm sorry."

He waves me off, like it's no big deal. "Don't be."

I bite my bottom lip, attempting to hold back my reaction. "Your other reasons?"

"What?"

"You said for starters, meaning that's not the only reason."

"I did." He sighs. "The simplest explanation is people change when there's money involved. I've learned who my real friends are over the years."

"I'm sorry," I murmur, my heart breaking for him.

"Stop apologizing. It's a good thing. Anyway, let me set the pizza inside and we'll go get you a Christmas tree."

"Aren't we eating first?"

"Not if we don't want to be chopping down trees in the dark."

"True."

Taking my time, I climb out, waiting for him. He returns, pulling an ax out of the back of his truck. A mischievous glint shines in his eyes as he stares at me, his voice monotone. "Let's go."

I giggle, stepping beside him. "Don't you want a coat?"

His crooked smile slips out. "Nah, I have plenty to keep me warm."

Surprising me, he reaches down, grabbing my hand, entwining our fingers together. My heart pounds erratically and I attempt to focus on the trees while I get my heartbeat under control. "So, where are the best trees under eight feet?"

"This way," he directs with a gentle tug.

Strolling hand in hand down the dirt path, covered in fallen leaves, the scent of pine thick in the air, I smile to myself, the moment surreal. I've had a crush on this man for a long time, but I've also repeatedly been warned. He's been so caring, protective, perfect…maybe the warnings are unjust.

His phone rings, breaking the silence. Dropping my hand, he pulls it out glancing at the screen before quickly slipping it back in his pocket, the message unanswered. Unfortunately, he wasn't fast enough. "Who's Lace?"

If I weren't staring at him, I might not notice his flinch, but I do. "No one important."

Maybe the warnings are spot on. "What about this one?" I point to a tree, about a foot taller than Dean.

"You sure?"

I nod and he steps up to the tree I've claimed as mine, for no other reason than it's decent and my head tells me not to believe in happily ever after.

What am I doing, especially after that phone call? Does he want to be here with me?

My muscles tense as I watch him take out his frustrations in a few swings, the tree falling, landing with an echoing thump. Grabbing the tree in one hand, the ax in the other, he turns towards his house with me trailing behind.

The silence is no longer peaceful between us. I quicken my pace just to keep up and I hate it.

Chapter 11

❆ Dean ❆

The moment the text from Lace, a late-night hookup, came through, the air shifted. Leah looked physically pained and quickly tried to hide it. She's too damn good for me. I wasn't kidding when I said Lace was no one important. She uses me for my body. I've learned sex is something I can control and that works for me.

We walk into my place, the living, dining, and kitchen area in an L-shape with the couch and recliner in front of the TV to my right, a table behind it to my left, with the kitchen back on the left. I make my way into the kitchen, turning on the oven and sliding the pizza in to warm it up before daring a glance at Leah. She tugs her white coat in as if she's cold, protecting herself from me.

Heaving a sigh, I step closer, planting my hands on the counter as I watch her looking around my place. "I should take you home." The words are out before I think it through.

"What? You want me to go?"

The look on her face makes me wince and I shake my head. "No, but you don't look like you want to be here anymore."

"I'm sorry."

"Stop, there's nothing to apologize for."

She offers me a sad smile, squeezing my heart. "Why me?" My eyes widen in shock. "I mean, you could have anyone you want and with me, things could get sticky. So why me? Is it because of what happened the other night?"

I scoff, my disbelief apparent. "I think the better question would be why I should stay away from you. You're way too good for me, Lee."

"That's not true." She rolls her eyes dramatically, reminding me of when I first met her. I was at her house and she walked through the door, looking young, but fierce. She still has the same fire in her eyes. I never want to be the one to take that away from her; it's one of the things that makes her so special. "And Lee?" she quirks a brow.

I shrug. "A different nickname for the sexy grownup Leah." I tuck a loose blonde lock of hair behind her ear, stepping into her space. She looks up at me with wide eyes, her breathing picking up its pace and her eyes deepening, making my body stand up and take notice. "You're beautiful, smart, and determined. You work your ass off to get what you want; you would never expect someone to just hand it to you. You make me laugh without even trying and your heart is pure gold."

"Dean," she whispers my name, the sound hitting like an electric shock.

My body moves without thinking. Cradling her face in my hands, I lower my mouth to hers. Moving my lips slow and fluid, I relish the warmth, the sweet taste, the spark as she kisses me back, moaning softly into my mouth. Her tongue juts out, licking my lips and I'm done for.

I pull back barely breathing. "You're too good for me, but damn I want you," I growl over her lips, holding her heated gaze. Without delay, I mold my mouth to hers, my tongue slipping inside, finding hers in an eager dance. With our teeth clashing, tongues licking, and mouths sucking, I pull her to me, lifting her up, and setting her on the counter for better access. I step between her legs and she tugs frantically at my hair, her tongue matching mine, tasting like mint and vanilla; spicy and sweet like her.

The oven beeps, piercing our bubble. Startled, I break our kiss, breathing heavy. I stare at her, her chest rapidly rising and falling, her cheeks flushed, and her hair no longer perfect.

When did she get so fucking gorgeous?

I step over her discarded coat and pull the pizza out of the oven. Why is her coat on the floor and when did she take it off? Or was that me? I run my hand through my hair, exhaling harshly. I need to slow the fuck down.

"Hungry?"

Chapter 12

❄ Leah ❄

What the hell just happened? And can we do that again? I've never been kissed like that, with so much passion, desperation. His kiss breathed life into me and I don't want to live without it after diving into the waters.

Does he kiss all women like that? Women like Lace?

"What's wrong?" Dean asks, his eyebrows drawn down in concern. I remain silent, looking at him with confusion. "Your face is scrunched up like you're upset."

Lace. I nod and lie through my teeth, "No, I was just thinking about something for the event."

"Need help with anything?"

I laugh, my body relaxing as we sit at the counter, eating pizza and talking about work. It feels normal. Exactly what I need. "Yeah, there's still a ton to do. I just hope it goes smoothly. Working with twenty-five different organizations is a lot. We have one person from our company overseeing two or three each and I'm coordinating the kickoff event, along with the *25 Men of Christmas* calendar we're giving out Thursday. You'll also be able to buy a digital copy, but it will only be available for the month of December."

"What did you do with the last six days of December?"

"The earlier promo shots we did, plus some group shots filled in the last few days perfectly."

"I can't believe you're getting it done so fast."

"It took a lot of persistence and begging."

"Well, I'm impressed. I've been working for my family business for a long time and it takes weeks for me to get any quality printing done."

Pursing my lips, I stare at him in thought. "What is it you do exactly? Joe never told me what your family business is."

He grins. "One of the reasons I know I can trust him."

I startle, taken aback. "Because he didn't tell his sister what you do?"

He chuckles softly and shrugs. "Yeah." I narrow my eyes, but he only laughs harder. "I told you before, people are assholes when money is involved. My family owns a lot of land and they've invested in different businesses over the years. One of them is private jets."

"Jets?"

His stare grows more intense as he elaborates. "That's what I do. I use my business degree to run Chambers Luxury Fleet. It's a private jet sales and rental company."

"Hm," I mumble, more curious than anything. "Can you fly them?"

"I have my pilot's license."

"Wow." He continues watching me closely, like I'm under a microscope, but I'm not sure why. "Do you like what you do?"

He leans back, licking his lips and drawing my attention. My gaze snaps back to his eyes as he clears his throat. "Yeah, I do. I like the freedom it gives me. I enjoy flying and traveling. And I think I'm damn good at the business side of things. We work with mostly corporate or rich assholes; sometimes both." He smirks. "But I handle it and do it well."

"I'm not surprised." His features soften. "But didn't you go to University of Southern Maine?"

He huffs a laugh. "You know I did."

"Why?" He quirks a brow. "It's a great school, I'm just surprised you didn't end up somewhere more...elite."

"It's not me. I wanted to be somewhere I could blend in, somewhere people didn't know me, or who my family was, and like you said, it's a great school. It also gave me a chance to enjoy college without the pressure of my family name."

"Well, from the stories I've heard, you took full advantage of that."

He flinches, quickly hiding it. "Yeah."

"No one ever knew?"

"People found out, but I could usually tell by the way they treated me. I got sick of being used in one way or another. Joe and Christian were the only two that never asked for anything from me except my friendship. We always have each other's backs. I will never do anything to put that in jeopardy."

His words are a slap to the face. It's not like I would ever tell my brother we kissed, but I guess we can never be anything more and I'm already too deep. I've had this stupid crush on him for years. It's time to change the subject.

"That explains why you helped me out at the last minute."

"I'm happy to play Santa to help you with anything you desire." A crooked grin covers his face making my heart skip a beat and my skin heat. Attempting to ignore him, I take a bite of my pizza, but this sexy man and his playful innuendos are not easy to overlook.

What am I going to do?

Chapter 13

❄ *Dean* ❄

"Ding!"

The elevator doors slide open but I hesitate, wondering if I should be here. Leah might not appreciate me just showing up, but I get the feeling, she'll work right through lunch to make sure everything is perfect and she needs to eat. For some reason, I need to be the one to take care of her.

Someone bumps into me as they step past me, jolting me out of my thoughts. "Sorry," the guy mumbles. "Hey, you're one of our models, aren't you?"

I lift my head, glancing at a tall, thin guy with brown hair and eyes. "I guess I am."

He laughs. "Not your normal thing? So, what are you in for today?"

"Just checking in with a *friend*." I grimace, the word feeling wrong on my tongue.

"Need help, finding your *friend*? They won't let you by the front desk without an appointment."

A heavy sigh escapes my lips, his words making me second-guess myself again. But I'm here. I don't hesitate. "Leah Abrams."

He grins, nodding his head. "Leah," he murmurs, dragging out her name, succeeding in pissing me off. I bite my tongue, waiting for the doors to open. "Follow me."

He shows me to a large conference room. Leah stands at the front, intently studying pictures spread out in front of her and some jackass looming behind her. "Leah, you have a *friend* here to see you," the guy announces, further irritating me.

She lifts her head, straightening. Her gaze crashes with mine, a smile immediately tugging at her lips. "Dean, what are you doing here?"

I approach, feigning my usual confidence. "Hey, I thought you might be hungry and with the event Thursday night, I was fairly confident you would skip lunch if I didn't force it on you."

She laughs, the sound going straight through me. "You're right." She steps away from the tables and towards me, forcing the dickhead to move back. "Thank you." She smiles up at me, the look making my dick jump.

I clear my throat. "So, are you going to eat, or do I need to force-feed you?"

"Well, your timing is perfect. I can take a few minutes with you." She grins, turning back towards the dickhead. "You can take lunch and we'll finish up this afternoon."

"See you in a bit," he calls, her focus already on me and I fucking love it.

She looks gorgeous in black pants, a matching blazer, and a red silk tank underneath, with her hair pulled up into a messy bun, a pen sticking through it. I point to it, arching my eyebrows in question.

A blush covers her cheeks as she grabs the pen and tugs, her hair spilling over her shoulders. "I just needed my hair out of the way. We were looking through pictures we want included with the decorations and my hair kept falling in my face. It's easier, and..." She shakes her head, her nerves going along with it. "What's for lunch?"

The combination of her nerves and her confidence is like my favorite candy on Christmas morning, making me want to do something stupid like lay her out on the conference table and claim her as mine. Shoving the thought away, I focus on lunch. "I wasn't sure what you would want, but I got a chicken salad sandwich with cranberries and a turkey club with cranberry dressing."

"What if I don't like cranberry?"

"It's Christmas-y. You don't have a choice."

She laughs. "Well, it's a good thing I love it, then."

"Yeah, it's a good thing your brother is my best friend."

She gives me a look and giggles, stepping past me. "Come on, we can sit down here."

She reaches for the chicken salad and I hand her a water, sitting down next to her. "I hope it's okay I just showed up."

"It's sweet. Thank you."

I nod. "When do you actually start decorating for Thursday?"

"Luckily, we get in to start setting up Wednesday morning. There's no way we would get it done in one day."

"Are we still decorating your tree tonight?"

She groans. "If I ever get out of here. I keep telling myself, a few more days and then someone else takes over."

"You need to make it to Thursday night. Let me help you."

"You've already done so much."

"Not enough if you're still stressed," I claim, my hand falling to her knee, tingles shooting up my arm. She turns to me, her blue-gray eyes darkening like the sea, pulling me in. I lean towards her, caressing her cheek and pressing my lips to hers. Her hand falls to my arm as she kisses me back.

"Would you look at that..." his deep voice grumbles as he steps into the room. Leah pulls back and jumps up, as the world crashes around us. I move with her, her body trembling. "All I had to do is pretend to be a hero and it would be Merry Fucking Christmas to me."

I lunge, but her arms wrap around my waist, urging me to stop. "Don't," she pleads so quietly I almost don't hear.

"What the fuck are you doing here?" I challenge, stepping in front of Leah, attempting to block her from view. He has no right to ever look at her again.

"I was invited. I have an event to attend on Thursday and I have a meeting with my new contact."

Leah gasps, pressing further into my back. "You're not going to the event," I command like I have every right.

He laughs. "But I did nothing wrong in the eyes of the law. You, on the other hand..."

Before I have a chance to realize what's happening, Leah is in front of me, stalking towards him. "You stay the hell away from him and me or I will make your life a living hell," she threatens with conviction making me cower.

"Damn, I bet you're a firecracker in bed."

Unexpectedly, she lunges for him with a growl. My hand wraps around her waist, lifting until her feet leave the floor. "Let me go."

"I think he's the one who needs to go," I argue, my blood boiling.

He laughs, waving as he walks out the door, Leah collapsing into the chair.

Fuck!

Chapter 14

❄ Leah ❄

Why would they let him come into the office? After what happened, I don't understand. My boss's words echo in my head. "He's gone. This time he won't be back."

I groan, running my hands through my hair. I hate that he's in the calendar, but there's not enough time to replace him. Thankfully he's banned from the event and office."

A knock at the door startles me out of my thoughts. "Coming!"

I yank it open, my heart skipping a beat at the sight of Dean standing in my doorway with a lopsided grin. "What are you doing here?"

"Are you at least a little happy to see me? I brought hot chocolate." He waves two cups in front of me.

"Of course, come in." He steps past me, handing me a cup. I close the door and take a sip, moaning in appreciation, "Mm."

"You're trying to kill me?"

My eyes fly open, spotting the heat in his eyes. I grin. "For the record, I would've let you in without the hot chocolate, but this gives you bonus points."

"I'll take it." We make our way to the couch and sit down, the boxes of decorations still unopened in front of the tree. "Is your roommate home?"

"No, she's out with friends."

He nods, his voice soft, asking, "You okay?"

I meet his gaze and sigh. "Yeah. I think I'm more mad than anything with how it was handled."

"I agree with that." His jaw clenches and he gives a slight shake of his head. "So, I have the rest of the week off, and thought I could help you with the event."

"What? Do you ever work?"

He chuckles, shrugging his shoulders. "Of course, but I am my own boss and you are my priority."

"Dean, I can protect myself."

"I know. You've proven that, but I won't get anything done after today. This is for me."

I scoff, knowing that's only half the truth, but I don't care. "Fine, but I have to clear it with my boss."

He winces. "I already did. I introduced myself and asked if I could help."

"Introduced yourself?" I know his statement means more than he's claiming.

Shifting uncomfortably, he runs his hand through his hair. "Yeah, my name and company."

My heart sinks, knowing he gave up his anonymity for me. "I'm sorry."

"Don't," he warns, his jaw clenching as he stares at me, pleading. I snap my mouth shut. My stomach twists, gulping down the sudden lump in my throat as realization slams into me. He really cares about me, but what does that mean for him?

I nod, my gaze veering towards the tree. "Well, you brought the hot chocolate. How about we turn on some Christmas music and you can help me decorate my tree?"

He grins, the tension easing out of him. "I like that plan."

I flip on the satellite holiday radio station and connect it to my speaker, a new version of *All I Want for Christmas* blasting throughout the room. Dean wiggles his eyebrows playfully, making me laugh as we open the boxes, finding the ornaments. "Are these all yours?"

"Mostly. Scarlett has a few, but she has all her decorations in the box against the wall."

I pull out a reindeer ornament, and he grabs a Santa, bringing it close to his face. "See the resemblance?"

Another giggle escapes and his mouth drops open, feigning offense. I only laugh harder and he's soon joining in. "I like playful Dean."

He steps closer, reaching over me to hang Santa on the other side of the tree. As he brings his hand back, his fingers graze the side of my face. "I like laughing Leah." Did he just say he likes me? My heart races, but he steps back without leaning in, smiling at me.

Trying to shake it off, I grab a roller skate, reminding me of a Christmas when I was small. "One Christmas, I begged for roller skates. I asked Santa for ones with pom-poms and told my parents my life would be over if I didn't get them." He laughs. "I know, but I could be dramatic when I wanted. Anyway, I got the roller skates. I was so excited, I had to try them right away, but since it was freezing outside my parents told me I had to wait. So, I got creative." I shrug. "How could they honestly expect me to wait to use the present I'd been begging for?"

He laughs again, the sound giving me goosebumps. "So, I snuck down into the basement and tried them on, trying to skate around on the cement, but we didn't have the space for it."

"Oh, no."

I nod. "Yeah. I lost my balance, my arms flailing like a windmill and fell hard, breaking my arm and slicing my elbow open. I was afraid I'd get into trouble, so I hid down there crying until Joe found me and convinced me to come upstairs by telling me he ate all the candy from my stocking."

Dean's head falls back, laughing. "Joe?"

"I know, right?" I grin. "Anyway, it worked. While I was looking in my stocking, my dad found me covered in blood like something out of a horror movie and brought me to the hospital. I never wanted to roller skate again.

"The next Christmas, Joe got me this telling me it's the only skate I should ever have. Of course, after that I had to prove him wrong and saved up my money to buy a new pair of skates since my old ones were too small. Then, I finally learned how to skate.

"That's one of my favorite Christmas memories; obviously not getting hurt, but realizing how strong I am."

"Determination is beautiful on you, Leah."

My stomach flips. "Thank you. I always find a way to stand up and push forward. I won't let anyone or anything keep me down."

He moves towards me, the intensity shining in his eyes overwhelming. "Damn," he mumbles, running his hands over my hair, grasping my neck, and tipping my head back. He skims his thumb over my lower lip. My breath catches as he tips his head down, kissing me soft and slow, as if he has all the time in the world igniting me from the inside-out. I moan, pushing up on my tiptoes, attempting to get closer, but he pulls back. Dizzy from his kiss, I drop back on my heels, slightly stunned.

That kiss felt nothing like the player I've been warned about.

Chapter 15

❄ Dean ❄

The next day, I stayed at the office with Leah as she worked into the night. There was no way in hell I was going to leave her side. I would find every excuse I could to help. She'll be fine. Her strength is attractive as fuck, but I needed to see this through for my own sanity.

Hopefully she won't kill me for what I did with her *25 Men of Christmas* calendar. Sometimes it's good to be known; this was one of those times.

Working alongside some of her staff, we unload the decorations followed by a truck of calendars, placing them on a table at the front of the event venue.

"December 5th, you're looking fine!" Scarlett smirks.

I shake my head in amusement. "Gee, thanks."

She continues flipping through the calendar and suddenly gasps. Her gaze wavers between me and the calendar. "You did this, didn't you?"

"Yup," I murmur, popping the p.

"Did she see this yet?"

"Nope."

"Damn…" She spins on her heel and yells across the room. "Hey, Leah, your calendars are here. You should see these."

She stops what she's doing and rushes over. "Are they okay? Please tell me they're okay."

Scarlett holds her hand up. "Whoa. Nothing to worry about."

Leah picks up the calendar, pausing a little longer on December 5th, causing my lips to curve up. I can't help it. She continues skimming through, until she reaches December 21st and screams, the calendar flying out of her hands onto the ground. "What is that?"

"That," Scarlett points to the discarded calendar, "is Saint Nick making sure the devil didn't end up in your calendar."

She turns to me with wide, teary eyes, my heart clenching. "Dean?"

I blush, nodding, not sure if she's happy, pissed or a little of both. In the next instant she crashes into me, squeezing me tight. My arms fall to her back as my cheek rests on top of her head, my pent-up breath leaving me.

"Thank you," she rasps, her breath catching.

"Anything for you," I whisper, unsure if she hears me.

She pushes back, stepping out of my embrace and wiping a tear from her eye. "But did it have to be my brother?"

My head falls back as I burst out laughing. There's my girl. The simple thought causes my heart to thunder in my chest as my laughter slows, reality slamming into me. I'm falling for Leah. Clearing my throat, I clarify, "So you're not pissed I messed with your calendar?"

She grins. "Nah, just that it's my brother." She scrunches her nose up. "But how in the world did you get Joe to agree?"

I smirk. "I have my ways."

She shakes her head, giggling, the light sound going right through me. "In other words, I don't want to know." I shrug, unapologetic. I would do it again in a heartbeat to protect her. "Why don't you come help me with the auction room?"

"Lead the way."

We cover the tables, alternating red and green tablecloths before spreading out the various auction items. She gasps. "You donated a private jet?"

I chuckle. "Not exactly. I donated a private jet for a one-week getaway in California wine country. I couldn't exactly donate one without the other."

Her smile lights up the room. "Thank you!"

I nod, not wanting the praise. She reads me right, changing the subject. "So, we talked about one of my favorite Christmas memories the other day, but you never told me yours."

"You're right." I continue working, not wanting to meet her gaze as I confess. "Honestly, my favorite memory is watching you, Joe, and the rest of your family the year Joe brought me for Christmas Eve. It was our sophomore year of college. Christian was home with Bree and his family. Joe knew my parents were gone." I smile at the memory. "I've never had a Christmas like that, where it's really about family. Your house had the kind of love and laughter that I barely caught glimpses of growing up."

Leah's hand falls to my arm, her voice soft, squeezing my heart. "Dean?"

I shake my head and force a smile. "It's okay, I can't complain. I haven't had a bad life at all. They just didn't believe much in holidays."

"That sucks."

I laugh. "Yeah, it does, but I turned out fine."

"Well..." she murmurs, dragging out the word.

I reach for her and she giggles as I squeeze her side.

She settles as my arms inch around her, like that's exactly where she's meant to be, the feeling foreign. "Dean?"

"Hmm?"

"What about this Christmas? Do you have plans?"

"Right now, I'm focused on you." My lips find hers, my hands weaving into her hair. Slipping my tongue out, she meets me in the middle, giving me a sweet taste before she falls back on her heels, breathless.

She licks her lips, her gaze hungry. "Come home with me tonight."

Groaning, my dick stands at attention, ready to follow. But it's Leah!

I can't dive in before knowing I'm really what she wants. "Fuck, I want to, Leah. But I need you to be sure. Joe is my best friend. I can't fuck that up. I can't do that to him. And I sure as hell can't do that to you."

Her face falls, looking rejected. "Okay."

"Leah." I palm her face in my hand, needing her to look at me. "I want you."

"I know."

"What about this… Take the day to think about what you want. You're busy. We have the event tomorrow and after this is over, if you still want this, I plan on keeping you in bed."

She looks up at me, thoughtful. "I can do that, but I'm not about to change my mind."

A salacious grin tugs at my lips, "I sure as fuck hope that's true."

She pushes up on her tiptoes, giving me another chaste kiss and walks away, my dick throwing insults my way.

Chapter 16

❄ Leah ❄

I'm so nervous, but not for tonight's event. At this point, I've done all I can. I'm sure there will be a few last-minute fires anyone can handle, but I expect it to go well. It's Dean that's making my stomach go haywire.

I can't stop running my fingers over the red silky fabric of my A-line dress. Spaghetti straps trail to a V-neck accented with a fitted, lace, floral overlay, while the bottom fans out just enough so I'm able to move around freely. I've opted for a two-inch heel, wanting to be closer to Dean's lips. Hopefully they won't be my downfall.

Ugh, I sound ridiculous, even in my own head. I've crushed on him for so long, and now that he wants me, how do I jump in and protect my heart? Doesn't he get it? But there's no way I'm changing my mind. It's Dean.

I wonder what Joe would say if he found out. My stomach drops, but I shake the thought away.

Scarlett walks into the bathroom, her eyes meeting mine in the mirror. "Everything looks fantastic! You did such a great job."

I grin, spinning around. "Thank you. You look gorgeous, Scar."

She curtsies in her shimmering dark green mermaid dress, her red locks hanging loose around her shoulders. "Thanks. So do you. Dean will have a coronary when he sees you."

My cheeks heat. "Are the models done with the prep?"

She smirks. "Is Dean done? Yes, but not everyone is yet. I'm sure they'll be ready when the doors open."

I nod, breathing deep and exhaling slowly. "Then, a little more lipstick and let's go." She laughs and we both reapply before slipping out the door, my eyes bypassing the white lights, Christmas trees, wreaths, garland, and the rest of the Christmas decorations, drifting towards the National Safe Haven Alliance, where I know Dean will be standing in support. He's wearing a classic black tuxedo with a red vest and bow tie taking my breath away.

"Is there anything he doesn't look good in?" Scarlett asks.

"No," I answer honestly. My stomach twists as he turns, meeting my gaze, his eyes blazing from across the room. "I should go say hi before he gets busy."

"You do that." She giggles, walking in the other direction.

My heart thrashes against my ribcage as I approach, Dean's eyes never leaving mine, holding me captive. "Wow," he mutters under his breath. "Leah, you're absolutely breathtaking."

My skin heats as I smile adoringly up at him. "Thank you. You look pretty good yourself."

"Thanks." He grins, leaning down, placing a kiss on the corner of my lips. Goosebumps instantly erupt across my skin. "This looks incredible, Lee. You've done a really good thing."

"Thank you. I just want it to go well."

"It will."

Joe steps up between us with a wide grin. "Leah, this is, wow."

I turn to my brother, smiling. "Thanks for coming."

He smirks, gesturing to Dean. "This guy twisted my arm. I couldn't say no."

"Well, thank you both. I should go check on everyone else." They wave as I walk away, ready for the night to be over before it even begins.

Soon the night is in full swing, the rooms packed with supporters of the various organizations and the local media. The *25 Men of Christmas* calendars, alongside the men themselves, are the night's biggest success. I should be happy, but my gaze keeps drifting to Dean, finding him taking pictures with women and sometimes men hanging off him, laughing, talking, and having a good time. I shouldn't be surprised. He's gorgeous, and he's doing exactly what's been asked of him. Unfortunately, the jealous pull I have in my gut doesn't give a damn and wants to claim him in front of everyone.

I attempt to push the thought away when a memory of Joe warning me flashes in my mind. *Dean always could talk a woman into doing almost anything he wanted.* My stomach churns, but I remind myself, I'm the one who started this. If anyone is trying to do the convincing, it's me.

I know what I want.

Sighing, I push my doubts away and make my way around the room, posing with each organization and model, documenting the event. As I move to step away from Joe, he wraps me in a hug, whispering in my ear, "I'm proud to be your brother."

"I love you." I'm too choked up to say more before I make my escape.

By the time I circle back to Dean, the night is almost over. He gives me a crooked smile making my heart pound, his arm falling around me as we pose for another picture. "You're a busy woman tonight, everyone wants a piece of you."

"I was just thinking the same about you."

He waves away my comment. Taking a deep breath, I catch his gaze, making sure he knows my intentions. "I haven't changed my mind. I know what I want." His eyes flash as he stares down at me.

His Adam's apple bounces as he gives me a firm nod. "I have no doubt in my mind about what and who I want. Tell me when you can go. I'm not leaving without you."

My stomach tightens. The end of the night drags, the seconds ticking by.

Chapter 17

❄ Dean ❄

My hands press against Leah's doorframe vibrating with need, waiting for her to unlock it. "Is your roommate home?"

"I think so…"

The key clicks and we push inside. Spinning her around, I pick her up as I kick the door closed behind me. "Wrap your legs around me." She does as I say, tossing her coat on the floor as she kisses and licks a path down my neck, searing my skin.

"First door on the left."

I shove inside her room, turning her around, pinning her against her door, devouring her mouth. My tongue slips inside, tasting, licking, exploring, desperate. Pushing her dress up, I press my body to hers, groaning as my cock rubs against her heat, feeling like I could burst before we begin.

Her head falls back against the door as my hands begin to roam, my body holding her in place, not bothering to remove her sexy as sin dress. My hands skim over her breasts, her belly, her ass, not sure what to explore first.

"Dean," she whimpers, my name a frantic plea as she tugs my hair. The sound goes straight to my balls.

"Fuck, Lee, I need you."

"Please. I can't wait anymore." She shoves my tux jacket off my shoulders and I pause, grabbing a condom from the inside pocket before I shake it to the floor. She slides her hand down and rubs me through my pants, making me groan. "Please."

Reaching down, I slide her panties to the side, finding her soaked. "Fuck, yes." I drop my pants and boxers, rolling on the condom, still holding her in place. With a quick yank on the sides of her panties, they fall to the floor. I line up, looking into her eyes for consent.

She arches towards me, pressing her lips to mine, giving me what I need. I plunge inside, not able to take it slow, not yet. A guttural groan leaves our lips. Grasping her knees, I push them towards her chest and thrust, determined to make her feel as good as she's making me. My balls slap against her heat as my dick dives deep inside her, my vision starting to blur.

"Dean," she screams, tugging my hair, my shirt, anything she can grab. I move faster, harder, deeper, eager to see her come undone in my arms.

My balls start to tingle, letting me know I'm close. "Lee, I can't...hold...on...please." White flashes, body burning, and my balls explode. My movements become erratic as her insides squeeze my cock. We groan, pushing, thrusting, desperate, until she collapses against me, both of us panting for breath.

Holy fuck that was hot.

I take a minute to get my bearings before I release her knees. Kissing her softly, I let her slide down my body, her dress falling into place. She looks up at me, slightly timid, making my lips twitch. Leaning down, I weave my fingers into her hair, kissing her deeper, trying to let her know I'm not going anywhere. "You okay?"

She nods awkwardly, making me chuckle. "Yeah, just, wow..."

A cocky grin lights up my face as I kick off my shoes and step out of my pants. I remove the condom, tossing it in the garbage by her desk. "We need to get you out of that dress."

"But we just..."

I nod, not able to wipe the smile off my face. "Yeah, but now I need to take my time and cherish every bit of you I didn't get the chance to explore."

She whimpers, the sound vibrating through me. "Okay."

My fingers caress her shoulders, between her breasts, her skin velvety soft. "I didn't even see you yet. There's so much to do."

"Dean," she moans. She turns around, moving her hair to the side.

I reach up, unzipping her dress. Tracing up her spine, I slip her straps off her shoulders, letting it pool around her feet, her heels her only accessory. When she doesn't move, my arm wraps around her waist and I pick her up, tossing her lightly onto her bed. She giggles and rolls over, looking up at me.

Stopping, I take in her beauty, her blonde hair splayed above her head like a halo. Her flawless ivory skin, full breasts, taut pink nipples, curve of her waist and a thin strip leading to her sweet pussy makes my heart stop and brings my dick back to life. "You're so beautiful."

She blushes that shade of red I love so much. "What about you? I think you need to take off all your clothes."

I glance down, my shirt, vest, and tie still in place, two buttons ripped off making me chuckle. With her eyes on me, I peel them off, crawling over her as if she's my prey. She reaches up, tugging me to her lips, her tongue slipping inside. Moaning I pull back, leaning on my left arm and kissing my way to her breast, while my other hand skates across her skin. My tongue sticks out, swirling around her nipple and sucking it into my mouth, my hand, rolling and pinching her other one, craving her soft sounds as she arches into me. Releasing, I switch sides, giving each the same treatment.

I move down her body, my fingers finding her wet folds. Groaning, I slip inside, her answering moan making me harder. My mouth finds her clit, as I add a finger, curling them inside. My tongue juts out, licking, savoring her sweet taste.

"Dean!"

Circling her clit with my tongue, I move in slow, deliberate strokes, relishing every sound, every taste, every reaction. She bucks underneath me. I lay my palm on her stomach, pinning her to the mattress as I work her body. She screams, just before her insides squeeze my fingers and her juices explode on my tongue, continuing my assault until her body gives in, melting into the mattress.

She laughs. "What are you doing to me?"

My lips tug upwards. "What we both want."

Reaching for me, her hand slides up and down my shaft. "How are you hard again?"

"You." She starts to slide down my body, but I stop her with a shake of my head. "One more orgasm from you with me inside you."

She jumps out of bed, reaching into my tuxedo pocket, and finding five more condoms. Arching her eyebrows, she questions, "Confident?"

"Hopeful." I shrug, nonapologetic.

She comes back with one, tearing it open, and rolling it on before straddling me and easing herself onto my cock. My body heats as I watch her move. Taking control, I flip her over, pressing my lips to hers. Our tongues fight for dominance as we move in a slow, sensual rhythm. My hands drift to her breasts, rolling her nipples between my fingers, increasing our pace. As my balls tighten, my hand slides lower, circling her clit.

Breaking our kiss, I plead, "I need you to cum."

Our breathing becomes rapid, matching our thrusts, the sound of skin slapping against skin echoing in the room. "Dean." Her body convulses around mine, squeezing me, milking me urging my body into bliss.

My vision blurs, my body goes taut, burning like a raging inferno as I fall over the edge once again. I pump into her a few more times, breathing heavily, and collapse next to her.

I catch my breath, disposing of the condom and rush back to Leah, pulling her into my arms. My lips brush the top of her head, whispering, "I didn't know it could be like this." She doesn't respond, but I don't care.

We have all the time in the world.

Chapter 18

❄ Leah ❄

My eyes flutter open, my body wrapped around Dean causing a smile to tug at my lips.

"Good morning, Lee," his deep voice rumbles as he runs his hands through my hair.

"Morning." I lift my head, looking up at him.

He pulls me close, pressing his lips to mine, soft and slow as he cradles my face in his hands. "Mm," I moan, my body burning instantly.

"Ready for another round?" He flips me over, his lips falling to my neck, my back arching, curving into him as he wakes me up in every way.

A knock at the door, causes a soft growl of protest to escape his lips.

Another knock, a little bit louder interrupts his movements, my brother's voice silencing further protests. "Leah, are you home? I need to talk to you about Christmas and you're not answering your phone."

My eyes widen in panic. Joe can't see Dean here. "Just a minute!" I yell as I scramble out of bed and throw on my clothes. I glance at Dean, staring at me, unmoving. "What are you doing? You have to get out of bed. You have to hide."

"What?"

"You need to hide. Joe can't see you here."

His mouth falls open, like he's about to argue, but he does as I request, making his way into the bathroom. "I'm too old for this shit," he grumbles under his breath, making me wince.

"I'm sorry," I whisper, as the door closes softly behind him.

Sighing, I rush towards the front door and yank it open, my brother leaning against the doorframe. "Took you long enough," he grumbles pushing off and stepping inside.

"Sorry, I was up late with the event and it's been a long couple months. I needed the sleep."

"I'm sure you did. It looked like everything went great. The place was packed. Did you get a good read on the impact?"

I smile. "It went really well. All the organizations are thrilled with the results so far. There's still more time."

"That's great, Leah. I'm proud of you."

My brother wraps his arms around me, giving me a hug, making me smile. "Thanks, Joe."

He releases me, taking a step back. "By the way, how did it work out with Dean?"

"He was fantastic! Thank you so much for sending him." I rave.

"You two seemed pretty cozy before the doors opened." Joe's eyes narrow.

"Yeah, I've just gotten to know him better since I've been working with him." My heart races and I begin rambling, trying to wipe that look off my brother's face. "But, you know Dean, he relished every moment with so many women and even a few men drooling over him all night. I'm sure he's happy with all the phone numbers he got from doing it."

He laughs humorlessly, his hand running along his jaw. "Sure…"

My stomach churns, my entire body on edge as he assesses me. "I'm sorry to kick you out, but I have to get ready to go meet Scarlett. We're going Christmas shopping. She stopped at her parents, but I don't want her waiting too long."

"Okay, I just need to talk to you about Christmas."

"I've just been busy, but with the event over, my big part is done and it's someone else's responsibility now. I promise, I'll respond and we'll figure out Christmas later, but I have to go."

"Okay, okay, I can take a hint. I'll catch up with you later. Great job, Leah."

"Thanks," I mumble, walking him towards the door, anxious to get him out of here. "Bye, Joe." He waves as I close the door behind him.

Heaving a sigh, I make my way back to my room and find Dean by my bed pulling his shirt on. "Where are you going?"

He stops and looks at me with complete disappointment and betrayal, causing my heart to drop into my stomach like lead. "You're just like everyone else. Once a player, always a player, right? I'm the guy you want to brag to your friends that you fucked but you're too embarrassed to tell your family about."

"It's not like that!"

"It's not? Were you planning on telling Joe?" I don't answer and he huffs a humorless laugh. "Joe's one of my best friends. You think I would fuck around with you and risk losing a guy I consider a brother? You were never just another girl, but the feeling is obviously not mutual. I can't believe you of all people used me like everyone else. Fuck this!"

He steps around me, leaving me standing with my mouth open and tears streaming down my face. My door slams shut, the vibration shaking me, as my entire body is consumed with guilt.

What did I do? I sink to the floor regretting everything in the last five minutes.

Chapter 19

❊ Dean ❊

I stalk through my front door, my body tired from cleaning up around the property, but still vibrating with anger and betrayal, unable to rest. After taking a quick shower, I throw on jeans and a long-sleeved t-shirt. I need to find something else to do to get Leah out of my damn mind.

Grabbing my phone, I text Joe and Christian a message I'm sure they won't ignore. Confessing anything to Joe is stupid, but I do it anyway.

Dean: I'm fucked. I fell for someone and she screwed me over. Join me for a drink at Benny's?

Ten minutes later I walk into the dimly lit bar, already flooded with twenty-somethings. I push my way to the front, ordering a double shot of whiskey and whatever's on tap. I down the shot followed by the beer, immediately ordering myself another round. Grabbing the second shot, I tip my head back and swallow before he hands me the beer.

I slide my card across the bar. "Start a tab?"

He nods, taking my card.

Just as I turn, a petite blonde steps in my path, fluttering her eyelashes. "Excuse me," I growl, stepping past her as if she's the blonde who scorned me.

I spot a booth in the back and make my way towards it as another woman calls my name. "Dean!" Not even bothering to turn my head, I lift my hand and flip her off.

"Shit man, you're in fine form tonight," Joe mutters stepping beside me.

I slide into the booth, laughing manically and take another gulp of my beer. Joe slides in across from me holding his own. How'd he already grab a beer?

"I was on the other side of the bar when you walked in. By the time I reached you, you downed a couple tall shots, a beer and pissed off two women. What the fuck is going on?"

"That's what I'd like to know," Christian mumbles sliding in next to Joe.

"I get it, Christian."

"Get what?"

"I finally get why you were so fucked up when you lost Bree."

Christian runs his hand over his face and shakes his head. "Okay, but this shit didn't help and I became an asshole, someone who didn't deserve Bree."

"Who cares since she was just using me, right? Who the fuck knows why, but she's like everyone else. I thought her of all people would be different," I spit my words with venom.

"Why? Who is she?" Joe probes.

I shake my head. "Doesn't matter. I'm not good enough to share with anyone she cares about. Sleeping with a model apparently gives you bragging rights."

"This girl slept with you because of the modeling thing I conned you into doing?"

Christian chuckles. "I heard about that. If she's that shallow, she's not worth it."

I slam my fist down on the table, making both of them jump. "She is worth it!" I mumble under my breath, "I thought she was."

The two of them look at each other before focusing on me. "Look," Joe starts, "maybe you read her wrong."

I clench my fist, wanting to take a swing at my best friend. Christian raises his hand, attempting to calm me down. "Maybe whatever happened was a misunderstanding. If I know anything from experience, it's things aren't always what they seem. If you've really fallen for this woman, fight for her. Don't follow my example. Believe me, it will get you nowhere."

"Really?" I challenge, my disbelief apparent. After all, he's married to the love of his life. I down my beer and stand. "I'm getting another beer. Want anything?"

"No thanks," they reply.

I stalk towards the bar, finding an open spot, focused on getting so drunk, I forget. "Double shot of whiskey and another beer."

A woman presses into my right side. "Want to buy me a drink?"

"Fuck no." Her friend behind her laughs, but I ignore her.

While waiting, I catch sight of her walking in and freeze, her eyes widening the moment she spots me. The bartender slides the beer and shot across the bar. "Can I have another one of these?" I hold up the shot. He pours, sliding it over. Grabbing it, I offer it to the woman who laughed when I shot her friend down.

She shrugs, taking it from me.

We toast, downing the shot. Feeling Leah's eyes burning into the side of my head, my fingers twitch, wanting to hurt her like she did me. Stepping forward, I press my lips to the woman in front of me, taking her by surprise, but she kisses me back. I tear my lips away from hers, grabbing my beer. "Thanks."

When I'm almost back to the table, I stumble over my feet at the sight of Leah and Scarlett. "Shit." Grabbing a chair, I sit down at the end of the table. "Well, isn't this a *nice* surprise."

Joe gives me a look of warning, but fuck that. "Um, maybe we should go. We're supposed to meet up with Scar's friends anyway."

"They can wait." Scarlett waves her hand dismissively, a mischievous sparkle in her eye. "Where's the girl you were just making out with?"

"Which one?" My words hit their mark, Leah not able to hide her flinch. But it leaves me feeling empty. I glance at Christian and Joe; Christian narrowing his eyes on me, seeing too much, and Joe watching his sister.

With a heavy sigh, I run my hand through my hair. "You're right, Christian. I fucking hate it, but you're right." I shake my head and down my beer. "I gotta' go."

Christian stands. "I'll drive you."

I walk out, not bothering to say goodbye.

Chapter 20

❄ Leah ❄

Scar glances at me with a sympathetic smile. "I'm getting a drink. Want anything?" I'm too choked up to respond. "I'll surprise you."

The moment she walks away, I turn to Joe with tears cascading down my cheeks. "Leah, what's wrong?" He slips into my side of the booth, wrapping me in his arms. "Who do I have to kill?"

I shake my head. "No. This is my fault. All my fault."

"What?"

"I fucked up, Joe. I really fucked up and I don't know how to fix it."

"Talk to me. Tell me what's wrong."

I gulp down my nerves. "Just promise you'll listen before you say anything."

"You know I can't do that, but I promise I'll listen to everything you have to say. Please talk to me."

I nod, wiping my tears away. "Okay... I've had a crush on Dean since the first time you brought him home."

His eyebrows hit his hairline. "I'll kill him."

"No!" I shake my head. "He didn't do anything wrong."

"If he hit on you, he sure as hell did!"

"It was me, just listen!"

"Ugh! Fine!"

"He told me about his family, and how people always use him for his looks or his money, except you and Christian. I was so stupid!"

"Explain, Leah!"

"When you sent Dean to the photo shoot, that night a bunch of us went out. Dean saved me from that asshole you replaced."

"What?" Joe's eyes widen and I quickly shake my head, pushing past it.

"Nothing happened, but that's probably because of Dean."

"Fuck, Leah!"

"Anyway, he watched me close after that and we hung out a lot. I really got to know him. At first he said he couldn't go there because you're like a brother to him, but…I think he really had feelings for me, Joe, and I pretended like he was nothing." I wince, remembering my earlier words. "He got mad and left. He looked at me like I killed his puppy, but I just didn't want to get hurt. I was protecting myself and now he hates me."

"You and Dean?" he asks, his face pale.

"Yes, but…no, I don't think he'll forgive me."

Joe sighs heavily, running his hand through his hair. "When did this happen?"

"Yesterday morning."

He exhales harshly, muttering under his breath. "That explains why he's so fucked up. I've never seen him like this." He groans, dropping his fist on the table. "Fuck my life. You're right about one thing. I think he did have feelings for you."

His words only make me cry harder. "Did?"

"Does…"

"What am I going to do?"

"First, breathe. After you calm down, you can fix this, but really? Dean?" I glare at him, wiping my stream of tears away. He puts his hands up in surrender. "Okay, Okay. We'll figure it out."

Scarlett returns, holding out a credit card. "I closed the tab for your table on Dean's card."

My eyes widen. Scarlett just gave me a reason to show up at his door.

Chapter 21

❄ Dean ❄

My head feels like I lost a boxing match, and my mouth tastes like I ate cotton balls doused in kerosene. I need to get up to grab aspirin and hydrate. Groaning, I roll over, realizing too late I passed out on the couch and collide with the floor.

"Fuck!"

Peeling my eyes open, I push myself up, and stumble into the kitchen, straight for the painkillers. A knock at the door gives me pause and I brace myself against the counter, choking down the aspirin.

Another knock. "I'm fucking coming!"

I yank open the door finding a wide-eyed Leah looking gorgeous in black leggings, boots and an oversized white sweater underneath her unzipped winter coat. "What the fuck are you doing here?"

She startles, but clenches her jaw, determined. "Can I come in?"

Without a word, I shove off the door frame, stalking towards the kitchen. Grabbing a bottle of water, I return to the couch. I chug the contents, tossing it on the table before I lay down, closing my eyes. The soft click of the door closing and tapping of her approaching footsteps, echoes like thunder in an impending storm.

"Can you please put a shirt on?"

I look down, realizing I'm in nothing but boxers and smirk. "No."

"You left…"

"Can you talk a little quieter?"

"You left your credit card with the bartender."

Prying my eyes open, I glance at her out of the corner of my eye, my card in her hand. "Thanks, you can leave it on the table."

She huffs. "You're not going to make this easy, are you?"

"What?"

"Dean…"

"You used me. What the hell am I supposed to do with that?"

"I'm sorry."

I nod, her words hitting me hard. "Great."

"No, I'm really sorry. I didn't mean what I said to Joe. I was just trying to protect myself after all the stories I've heard…"

I wince. "Yeah, stay away from the player."

"I don't think that of you."

"You sure?" I sit up, wincing at the movement. Staring at her, I clench my jaw. "That's exactly who I used to be."

"But not anymore."

I don't respond, I don't have to.

"Please." Her voice catches, squeezing my heart. "I know I said some stupid things, but I didn't mean them. Please let me make it up to you."

I heave a sigh, running my hand through my hair. "Fuck, please, don't cry, Leah. I can't handle seeing you cry."

"Please forgive me."

The sincerity in her eyes appears genuine. I can't say no. "Why don't I get dressed and we'll order some food and talk."

Her body sags in relief, making my chest tight. "Thanks."

"We need to figure out how we can…be *friends*." The word feels like poison on my tongue.

Chapter 22

❄ Leah ❄

He trudges towards his room, his words echoing in my head and squeezing my heart. He wants to be friends?

Jumping up, I follow him. "No!"

He pulls a t-shirt out of his dresser and pulls it over his head. "What?" he asks sounding exhausted.

"I don't want to be friends."

His jaw ticks. "What do you want?"

"I want you to come to my parents' on Christmas Eve."

He shakes his head. "Tell Joe I'm good."

"It's not him asking, it's me."

He blanches. "No, thanks."

"Dean, I want you to come as my boyfriend."

He freezes, staring at me. "What did you say?"

I gulp down the lump in my throat. "I want you to come to my parents' on Christmas Eve as my boyfriend."

In an instant, he closes the distance between us, grasping my arms and staring into my eyes, begging for clarity. "Leah?"

"Dean, I've had a crush on you since the day I met you. I'm sorry for what I said. I was afraid. I know it's no excuse, but I swear I didn't mean it. I'm crazy about you. I just want a chance."

He presses his lips to mine, my entire body sagging with relief as I melt into him, returning his kiss. He pulls back, a cocky smirk on his face. "You've had a crush on me since we met?" My cheeks heat, but I nod, letting him relish the moment. "You're going to have to tell your brother."

"He, um, already knows."

"What?"

"After you left my place, I was upset. Joe told me he was going to meet you. I was coming to apologize, but I saw you kissing someone else." My stomach roils at the memory.

He winces. "Fuck, I'm sorry. I only did that to piss you off."

"It's my fault."

"No, I'll take credit for my stupid decisions. I'm sorry."

The candor in his eyes tightens my chest. Clearing my throat, I continue, "Anyway, when you left. I couldn't stop crying. I told Joe everything."

"Everything?"

My body heats. "Not everything. But I told him I really like you and I'm the one who messed up. He said he thought you had real feelings for me. Is it true?"

He steps towards me and cradles my face in his hands. My heart beats rapidly, blood rushing in my ears. I focus on the sound of his voice. "Fuck yes."

I giggle, relief consuming me. "Good."

"Leah, you make me feel alive. You're gorgeous, smart, driven." He brushes his lips over mine, giving me goosebumps. "Your strength and courage are sexy as hell." His lips press against mine. "I've never met anyone like you." He kisses me hard, making me whimper. "But most of all, you make me feel like I'm home."

A soft sob escapes my lips as I crash into his mouth, attempting to push my tongue inside. He pulls back, stopping me. "You don't want to do that. I might still be a little drunk. I need to eat, drink some water, and brush my teeth."

Laughing, I give him a chaste kiss. "Okay, I'll order us some food, while you brush your teeth."

"Deal."

Chapter 23

❄ Leah ❄

Mindlessly, I draw patterns on Dean's chest, a little in awe I'm here. I press my lips to his side, a deep rumble coming from his chest. "Leah."

Lifting my head, I smile as his fingers run through my hair. "I like being able to kiss you anytime I want."

He grins. "You can do more than that."

"Oh?" My hand slides down to his thick cock as my lips trail down his body.

He moans, "That's not what I meant. You don't have to do that."

"I know." With wide eyes, I watch goosebumps erupt over his skin, loving that I'm the one getting this reaction. I tug his boxers down, his dick springing free, already hard.

"Lee," he groans as I lick from base to tip. My tongue circles the end before sucking him into my mouth, hitting the back of my throat. "Fuck…" His hand tangles into my hair. I release him slowly, sucking him in again and again, relishing his look as he starts to lose control.

Suddenly, he pops out of my mouth and I'm on my back. His lips press to mine, his tongue delving inside. I moan, my entire body tingling with anticipation… with need. He pulls back, yanking my shirt off in one swift movement. His lips fall back to my neck as he unclips my bra, tossing it on the floor.

"I wasn't done."

"Later."

"Dean," I moan, my body curving into every touch, lick, kiss. His hands roam my body, setting me on fire, my core burning for him.

His hand skims over my breasts, down my belly and into my pants, his fingers rubbing my clit and sinking deep into my pussy as I pant for breath.

"You're fucking soaked."

I don't respond, I can't. My leggings and underwear quickly disappear.

He reaches over and I soon hear the crinkle of the wrapper as he rips open the condom, rolling it on. He hovers over me, kissing my lips, my jaw, my neck and back again. "Please, look at me."

I open my eyes, holding his gaze, feeling him at my entrance. "Please."

Granting my wish, he pushes slowly inside, my eyes rolling back in my head. My vision clears and I meet his stare. His expressive blue eyes reveal so much causing my heart to beat faster as he thrusts inside. My body arches, moving in sync with his, like we were born to be together.

My body and heart vibrate like never before, reacting to him, claiming him as he claims me. Our breathing escalates as he attempts to maintain the torturously slow pace.

I can't take anymore.

I wrap my leg around his back, urging him on, moaning as he fills me up. Holding me close, he kisses me, quickening our pace. With our bodies slick with sweat, he slides so deep, triggering something deep inside me. My insides tingle, burning, the feeling intensifying in my core, before I'm exploding, convulsing, and squeezing him, tipping him over the edge along with me.

"Leah," he grunts, his movements erratic. My insides milk him as we both ride out our high.

My body liquifies into the mattress, my limbs useless as he collapses by my side. He stands, tossing the condom and returning to me with a sweet kiss. "Damn, woman," he murmurs, pulling me into his warm embrace.

Sated and breathless, I giggle, wondering how we got so lucky, grateful he's mine.

I glance at Dean, knowing I'm falling in love with him. But I can't tell him…yet. I don't think he's ready to hear it. I've always known if I ever had this chance with him, he would be the one man I would never be able to let go.

Chapter 24

❄ Dean ❄

My heart thrashes against my ribcage. Why the fuck am I nervous? This is Joe's house. Leah's. I've been here so many times, although, neither of them actually live here…

The door swings open and I smile. Leah stands in the doorway, beautiful in a red, scoop-neck dress, trimmed with black velvet, hugging her curves. "You look gorgeous."

"Thank you, so do you." She pushes her blonde hair behind her ear and smiles. "I saw you through the window."

I shrug, grinning. "I like the cold."

"Apparently." She laughs, holding out her hand. I take it, instantly calm as she tugs me inside. "Merry Christmas." Pushing up on her tiptoes, she presses her lips to mine.

"Merry Christmas."

"I just can't get used to this," Joe grumbles as he walks into the foyer.

Chuckling, I kiss her again before looking at my best friend. "Figure it out. I'm not going anywhere."

He nods. "Good." I step back from Leah and we give each other a hug with a hard pat on the back. "Don't fuck this up."

"I won't."

"Merry Christmas, brother."

Brother. The single word slams into me like a freight train. If Leah and I marry one day, Joe would really be my family. I gulp down the lump in my throat. "Merry Christmas. Is there somewhere I can put these?" I hold up a bag filled with Christmas presents.

"Let's put them under the tree in the family room," Leah suggests, leading the way. We step into the room filled with their family; their mom, dad, aunts, uncles, cousins, and grandparents.

A chorus of, "Merry Christmas," sounds from around the room, overwhelming me yet again.

I smile, each of them greeting me with a hug, while Leah places the presents under the tree.

"It's December 5th!" Leah's grandmother cheers making me blush uncharacteristically. Joe groans.

"We're delighted you're here. You're good for our girl. She's so happy," her mom gushes.

I glance at Leah, enjoying her blush. "Mom..." she warns, entwining my fingers with hers.

Chatter, banter, laughter, and love remain prominent as the night continues filling my heart.

Because of Leah, the missing pieces of my life are falling into place. The way she embraces my heart like a treasure; like I'm worth it is everything. I look down at her, my chest tight.

She meets my gaze. "Dean?"

"I love you, Leah." Her eyes widen, a soft gasp escaping her lips as I pull her into my arms. "I don't expect you to say it back, but I need you to know I'm in love with you. You have given me the world by just being you and I will work my ass off to be the Saint Nick you deserve."

She laughs and I silence her with a sweet kiss.

"I love you, too, Dean."

My eyes widen, her words better than any Christmas present. This is a first for me. I'm never letting the feeling go.

"And don't you know by now? You've already given me everything, Saint Nick."

The End

About Nikki A. Lamers

Award Winning Author, Nikki A Lamers grew up in Wisconsin and lived in Florida for a few years before ending up on Long Island in New York where she now lives with her husband and their two teenagers. She has always loved to write and curl up with a good book. Since meeting her husband, they enjoy spending time in Maine every year and exploring different places.

The Unforgettable Summer won the Imadjinn Book Award for Best Romance and the Firebird Award in four categories including Best New Adult Fiction, Series, second for Summer/Beach Read and third in Contemporary Fiction Novel. Unforgettable Nights also won the Firebird book Award in three categories including, Best New Adult Fiction, Best Contemporary Novel and second for Series. Now with six books in the Unforgettable Series, you have the chance to fall in love with the characters just like her!

Breaking Cycles is a spin-off from The Unforgettable Series and changes location to the Carolinas. The first book in Mending Shattered Hearts series is again a stand-alone novel. Each book will have different main characters, so follow along or find your favorites and dive right in.

Dreams Lost and Found and Finding Home are part of a duet that hits close to home for the author. The main character Samantha was adopted as an infant, just like Nikki. Although Samantha's story is not her own, she enjoyed writing every word. Now, Nikki is having fun working on her next book, in the Mending Shattered Hearts Series with Declan's story, as well as a new series she will be sharing soon.

Books By Nikki A. Lamers

Available Now

The Home Duet
Dreams Lost and Found
Finding Home

Mending Shattered Hearts Series
Breaking Cycles

The Unforgettable Series
The Unforgettable Summer
Unforgettable Nights
Unforgettable Dreams
Unforgettable Memories
The Unforgettable One
Unforgettable Mistakes

Social Media Links

Follow me on:

Instagram
@nikkialamersauthor

Tik Tok
@nikkialamersauthor

Website
www.nikkialamersauthor.com

And subscribe to her newsletter for the latest updates:
https://www.nikkialamersauthor.com/contact

The Perfect Package

by Samantha Michaels

Blurb

One phone call changed my entire life…

When I landed my dream job with the Philadelphia Flyers, my life honestly felt perfect. Even though the man I thought was my future was no longer at my side.

That was a long time ago, though. I haven't seen Nick in a long time. I worked my way into a job I love. I have my own place in the city, and I still live close enough to my dad to see him whenever I want.

So, when I get a call that my dad is in the hospital, I rush to his side. I have little information about what happened. When I walk in and see Nick standing in the room, I go through a multitude of emotions in the span of seconds.

He was my first love. My one true love. I've never forgotten him. Neither has my heart. With the holidays fast approaching, it's like no time was lost between us.

We both quickly realize that we've never stopped loving each other. The sparks between us ignite once more, but with life changing so much around us, I fear I'll be spending another Christmas without him.

Prologue

❄ Holly ❄

(Thirty Years Ago)

"He asked me! He asked me! He asked me!" I shout as I come flying into the house after school.

"Honestly, Holly. You scared me half to death," my mom, Alice, says from the kitchen. At five-foot-eight, I tower over my mom. I had this crazy growth spurt in my last year of elementary school, thus ending my chance of ever being accepted, or even having a single friend. That is until the new kid showed up in our first year of middle school.

Like me, he looked older than his thirteen years. He was already six-foot-tall. His long, sandy brown hair hung past his shoulders, making him look just like those musicians I love so much. It took me about five seconds to get lost in his crystal blue eyes. There was just *something* about this boy.

"Sorry, Mom."

"Now, what were you shouting about?"

"Nick asked me to be his prom date!" I bounce up and down.

Mom hugs me and says, "Oh, honey, that's wonderful. How about we go dress shopping on Saturday?"

"Okay." I furrow my brows in concern when I see my mom stumble a little. "Why don't you rest? I can take over making dinner."

"I'm fine, sweetie. Why don't you run along and get your homework done?"

I look at her for a moment, still concerned. "Well, yell if you need me," I say quietly. She nods and gets back to cooking.

Grabbing my backpack, I head into my room and sit at my desk. I know my mom's sick. I've overheard her telling my dad more than once. But for some reason, she tries to hide it from me. I grab my calculus book and knock that homework out first. I'm just finishing when I hear my dad's car pull into the driveway, so I head out to the kitchen.

After setting the table, I help my mom put dinner into serving dishes. Even though it's just the three of us, she insists on everything being fancy. I carry everything over to the table so she can sit down and rest for a moment.

"There's my two favorite girls," my dad says. With a broad smile, he hands my mom a bouquet of mixed flowers.

"Holly has some news," my mom says, smiling weakly.

"Oh yeah?" my dad asks. He puts on a brave face for her. So do I.

"I'm going to the prom. With Nick." The smile that spreads across my face is genuine. I do all I can not to squeal.

Dad gives me a hug. "That's wonderful. He's a nice boy."

After dinner, I take our dog for a walk around the neighborhood. Mom seems to be getting weaker. It was all I could really think of during dinner. I heard her tell my dad the tumor isn't getting smaller, and that scares the hell out of me.

When I get back, Mom's asleep on the couch and Dad's reading the paper. I wave so I don't wake her and go to my room. I'm sitting on my beanbag chair reading the latest book in the *Sweet Valley High* series when I hear a knock.

"Come in."

My dad opens the door. His mouth is tight as he sits down on my bed. "I don't need to tell you Mom's sick, do I?"

I put my book down and look at him. "No, Dad. I've heard you two talking." My stomach is in knots.

"I may need your help caring for her. Can I count on you?" I see tears forming in his eyes, and my heart shatters.

"Absolutely." I hesitate for a moment. "Can I ask you a question?"

"Anything."

"What exactly's wrong?"

My dad lowers his head. "It's breast cancer. And it's inoperable."

My chest tightens. "Daddy, is mom gonna die?" I nearly whisper. Getting the words out is hard.

"Oh honey." A tear slides down his cheek.

I fold my hands in my lap. "Please. Tell me." I choke back the lump in my throat.

"There's a very real possibility. We just don't know."

I hear my mom coughing. Dad races out to check on her after patting my leg.

Things go downhill fast.

❄ ❄ ❄

I try to skip the prom, but Mom insists that I go. She wants to see me and Nick dressed up. Somehow, she hangs on long enough to see her only child graduate at the top of her high school class. During my valedictorian speech at graduation, I focus my speech on my mom and her strength. There isn't a dry eye in the house. A week later, she's gone.

I spend my summer helping my dad around the house while he is at work. The hardware store is more popular than ever. Our small town is like one big family and they are all there for my dad as he navigates life without his partner. The day he drives me to Penn State's main campus is tough for us both.

"I'm so proud of you," he says as we are bringing the last load of my stuff to my dorm room.

"Are you sure this is okay? I can come home and go to school locally."

Dad shakes his head. "No way. This is your dream, and I won't let you give that up. I'll be fine."

❄ ❄ ❄

Four years later, I walk across the stage after earning a bachelor's degree in marketing. The look on my dad's face brings me to tears. The radiant smile was in direct contrast to the sadness in eyes. My mom was, and still is, the love of his life. Dating someone else wasn't, and still isn't, an option. We both wish she could have seen me graduate college.

After graduation, I land my dream job, marketing and public relations for the Flyers, Philadelphia's National Hockey League team. But, the job requires a lot of time and travel, leaving me little time to help my dad. I spend the off-season with him, helping around the house so he could keep running the store. But doing everything alone is taking a toll on him. I can see it clearly.

After I started the job with the Flyers, Nick and I split. He was never much for academics, doing just enough to graduate. Where he did excel was in the trades. He loved everything about trucks and large construction equipment, both operating and repairing them. He ended up getting a job with our local township, and he loved it. I think about him often. But life goes on.

Chapter 1

❄ Holly ❄

(Present Day)

It's the Friday before Thanksgiving, and I'm sitting in my office at the Flyers arena finishing up a few things before I head back to my old stomping grounds for the holidays. No matter how old I get, my dad insists on me coming home for the season. And while I'll never admit it, I get excited when it's time. From the time I was a little girl, we would decorate the tree together on Christmas Eve, and we still do.

And without fail, I come out every year to way too many gifts under the tree. Growing up, so many of my friends had to deal with divorce, step-parents and step-siblings. I was one of the lucky ones. My parents were truly soulmates, and I always hoped I'd find what they had. But this job just doesn't allow for a relationship. So, here I am. At least I have my dad.

I'm just finishing up the last promotional piece on my list when my assistant, Dave, pokes his head in.

"Phone call. They said it was urgent," Dave says.

"Thanks. Put it through."

I hear the phone buzz and pick up the receiver. "Holly Anderson."

"Ms. Anderson, my name is Josie, and I'm a nurse at Abington Hospital. Is Mark Anderson your father?"

I squeeze my eyes shut. I can't handle... I take a deep breath, refusing to allow my mind to go there. "Yes. Is everything okay?"

"Your father's in the ER. He slipped off of a stepladder and injured his hip."

My heart skips a beat and spikes at the same time. "Oh no. I'm leaving now and should be there in about an hour."

"Very well. Park at the ER, and when you come in, they'll bring you back."

"Okay," I say, far calmer than I feel, and disconnect. I've told my father countless times to stop climbing ladders, but that stubborn man won't listen!

I stop by Dave's desk as I hurry out and fill him in. "I may need to take some time off to care for my dad. I'll let you know as soon as I can."

"Call me if you need anything," Dave says, giving my hand a reassuring squeeze.

I force a smile as I head toward the elevator bank.

I race to the hospital and park at the ER. After I give my keys to the valet attendant, I sprint inside.

"May I help you, ma'am?" I glance at the receptionist's name tag.

"Good evening, Rose. My name's Holly Anderson. My father, Mark Anderson, was brought in after a fall."

"Right this way." She buzzes a door open for me, and I see someone walking towards the doors from a nurse's station.

Josie, the nurse who called me, walks me to the stall where my father was taken. I hurry into his room, and my jaw drops when I see who's standing there.

"What are you doing here?" I ask. I stare at him wide eyed, my heart beating rapidly. My stomach does a couple of somersaults as I do my best statue impression. "Where's my father?"

"They just took him for x-rays," he says, his voice deep and raspy. I nod as I listen to a voice from my past.

My high school boyfriend.

Nick Daniels.

"H-how did you know he was here?"

"I work for him now."

I raise my eyebrows. *When did that happen?* Instead I say, "Oh." I shake my head. *Oh, that's all I can manage to say. What an idiot.*

I'm about to ask Nick something else when I see an orderly wheeling my father back to the stall. The words die on my tongue, but I'm still hyper aware of Nick still near me.

"Talk about a sight for sore eyes," Daddy says when he's back in the stall. "Thanks for coming, sweetheart. Now, where's my hug?"

I purse my lips. "First, tell me where you were injured. I don't wanna hurt you."

"Just my hip." My dad shakes his head from side to side.

"Your father's a lucky man," the orderly tells me after he gets my father settled in the bed. "Mr. Anderson, can I bring you anything?"

My father flashes his million-dollar smile and says, "No, thank you." The orderly nods and heads out of the stall.

I turn toward my father. I narrow my eyes and plant my hands on hips. "Now, mister, didn't I tell you no stepladder?" I scold.

My dad rolls his eyes at me.

"What did I tell you about rolling your eyes?" I tease.

Daddy looks at Nick and says, "I'm in trouble now."

I turn toward Nick. "And you! You need to keep a better eye on him."

Nick looks at his feet.

"Sweetie, it was an accident. It wasn't anyone's fault."

I fold my arms across my chest. I'm about to respond when a doctor walks in. "Mr. Anderson, I'm Dr. Davis. I have the results of your x-ray." He nods at Nick and me before he continues. "Do I have your permission to speak in front of your guests?"

"Yes," My dad says.

"Your x-ray shows a fracture in your hip. You were fortunate it's not a full break, but you will need to take it easy. I'll also want you to schedule some physical therapy. The details will be in your discharge papers."

My dad's eyebrows shoot up as he shakes his head. "I can't do that. I run a hardware store, my only source of income."

"Well, I'm afraid you don't have a choice. You need to give your hip time to heal," Dr. Davis says, his voice stern.

"I can run the store," Nick says.

"I know you can, but I can't ask you to do that alone," my dad says.

I dart my eyes between my dad and Nick. I know what I need to do. There's no question. "I'll help."

"Honey, you already have a job," Daddy says.

I flash him a stern look. "I'll take a leave of absence. We have a family care program for just such a situation."

I watch as my dad turns his palms up and juts his hands out in front of his chest. A long, low sigh escapes his lips. "I surrender."

Dr. Davis nods. "Very well. I'll have Josie prepare your discharge papers, then we'll get you out of here."

"Thank you, doctor," my father says, holding out his hand. I smile. My dad, always the gentleman. And definitely my hero. "Honey, can you drop me at the hardware store when we're done here?" my dad asks.

Is he kidding? I'm convinced there's no more stubborn man on this entire planet than my father. "Absolutely not. You need to rest, young man," I tease, a smile playing at my lips.

"But my car."

"After we get you settled, I'll drive Holly to the store to get your car," Nick says. He locks eyes with me and smiles.

My insides turn to goo. "Thanks."

After signing the discharge papers, Nick pushes my father's wheelchair out to the parking area. He waits with us until the valet brings my car.

After helping me get my father loaded, Nick says, "I'll meet you at the house." He gives my shoulder a squeeze, setting my skin on fire. Nick's face floats through my head the entire ride back to my dad's house.

A few minutes after I pull into the driveway, a pickup truck pulls in behind me. I'm strangely excited that Nick's still a truck guy. I always felt like a queen sitting in his truck when we were dating. Strange, I guess, but something about being up higher than a car just felt regal back then.

Or maybe it's because I lost my virginity on an old mattress in his truck bed! My face heats up as I remember that amazing night. I hear my father clear his throat, and I scold myself for having those thoughts with him in the car.

Nick helps me get my dad settled in his bed, then drives me down to the hardware store so I can grab dad's car. We head inside for a minute so I can get his car keys.

"So, when did you start working here?" I'm grateful he does, especially with my dad getting older.

"About a year ago." Nick sits down for a moment. I join him.

"I thought you loved the township."

Nick sighs loudly. "I did, but about a year ago, they hired a new supervisor."

I nod. I've read countless articles about management being the number one reason people leave a job. "Not so great, huh?"

Nick laughs. "Now there's the understatement of the century."

I lean toward him and whisper, "Well, I for one am grateful you were here with my dad tonight."

"Anything for you." His eyes widen. "I mean for him!" he quickly corrects.

I smile as he stares at his feet. I can't help but think, and hope, he was right the first time. "Well, I hope my dad's been a better boss for you then."

He nods, still looking down. "Oh yeah. He's great. I'm sure your staff feels the same about you."

"Guess you'll find out, huh?" I wink at him.

"Yes, boss," he responds, a smirk on his face.

I let out a sigh. "Well, I guess I better get back to my dad in case he needs anything." Plus, I need to get away from Nick. I'm not sure if it's nostalgia or something else, but my mind is a mess right now. I need to turn my focus to my dad.

Nick gives my hand a squeeze. "In all seriousness, you need any help with him, call me. He has my number."

I nod, grab my father's keys, and get up. We walk out of the office together. I watch as Nick sets the store alarm then locks the door when we get outside. Nick walks me to the back parking lot.

"I'll take care of opening in the morning so you can take care of your dad."

I nod feeling a little pressure release from my chest. "Thank you so much. For everything."

"My pleasure." Nick smiles at me again, and my panties melt. Talk about fine wine! He waves as I get in Dad's car and head home.

Chapter 2

❄ Nick ❄

I get home and plop myself down on the couch. My dog, a goofy black lab named Pepper, jumps up next to me and lies her head in my lap. I smile as I pet her head.

"Today was a crazy day, Pepper." She looks up at me. "I sure didn't expect to have to take Mr. Anderson to the hospital." I sigh, and Pepper gives me lick on my hand. "But even more, I didn't expect to see her. Holly. The one and only love of my life. How the hell am I gonna work with her day in and day out?"

Pepper looks up at me again, and I smile. I'm so glad I have her to talk to, but I really miss having a woman in my arms. Specifically, one particular woman. It took every ounce of strength not to wrap my arms around Holly tonight.

I turn the TV on and flip through the channels. Nothing catches my eye, so I shut it back off. I yawn, the events of today catching up to me. After I take Pepper out to go potty, I head off to bed.

❄ ❄ ❄

The next morning, I grab a shower. Of course, all I can think about is Holly, forcing me to take things into my own hand. Literally. After my release, I clean up and head to my bedroom to get dressed. One thing I love about the hardware store is being able to wear jeans. I grab one of the company polo shirts out of my closet, then throw on my socks and sneakers. I top my look off with a splash of *The One* by Dolce & Gabbana.

Grateful that I'm able to bring Pepper to work, I pack up a bag for her and head out to my truck. Pepper jumps into the backseat, and I start driving. When I get there, I set Pepper up in the back office, then get the store ready for customers. I straighten up the display that got knocked over during Mr. Anderson's fall.

About an hour after we open, I hear someone coming in the store. My heart skips a beat. Holly's a vision in her tight indigo jeans and waist-length, black, wool coat. She sheds the coat, and holy hell. Her black, long-sleeved v-neck tee shows off her best assets. My mouth waters, aching to taste her, but I push that aside. At least for now.

"So, what were you doing at the township when you left?"

"I had moved up to the top step," I say, grateful for the distraction. Though, her voice is just as sexy as the rest of her.

She flashes me a smile that makes my heart skip a beat. "Wow, that's great. What exactly did you do?"

"I ran the leaf site."

"Oh, so you were in charge of the place that made high school smell awful for four years." She laughs.

I grin. "Hey, we weren't as bad as the sewer plant."

"True." She pinches her nose.

I see a small smile appear on her face, and wow, still just as beautiful. I remember the first time I saw that smile. My family had just moved here the summer before middle school. The teacher sat me right in front of her in homeroom. When I walked into the classroom, she had her head buried in a book looking so damn cute in her jeans and Whitesnake tee.

Lunchtime rolled around, and when I tried to sit at what I soon found out was one of the cool kids tables, I was banished to where the 'weirdos' sat. I walked over, and the only person sitting there was Holly. Her gorgeous, chestnut brown hair, full pouty lips, and a rack that would make Dolly Parton jealous greeted me. Her nose was buried in a book.

"Hi. I'm Nick."

"Holly." She didn't even look up.

"David Coverdale has one of the best voices." At that, she lifted her head and looked at me.

"You're into rock?"

"What else is there? So, what's a pretty girl like you doin' at this table?"

She looked down at her chest and kept her gaze there. "The things you can't stop staring at. I've had them since fifth grade. Let's just say, the other girls want nothing to do with me."

"Well, their loss."

She looked up and smiled at me, and I fell. Hard. I'll never forget the first school dance. I somehow found the courage to ask her to dance. We lasted for one song before we snuck off to make out. She was the first girl I ever kissed, and I don't think I'll ever forget those soft lips.

Her voice snaps me out of my reverie. "Earth to Nick. Come in, Nick."

I shake my head. "Sorry. Need more coffee."

"Ha, I get that." She points to the counter. "And that's why you're lucky to have me."

I look over and see two extra-large Dunkin' coffee cups, and a box of Munchkins. "Cream and sugar?" Let's see if she remembers.

"Of course. I know how you like it." A wicked smile forms on her face, and my dick stirs. "Now, time for you to teach me the ropes."

How the hell am I gonna get through today working side by side with the object of my desire? "How about for today, you shadow me? Then after closing, we can go over stuff in detail."

"That works. I'll pay you overtime."

"No need. I'm happy to help out your father." My heart skips a beat when I see her kind smile.

"Well, then, please come have dinner with dad and me tonight." My stomach growls at the memory of her cooking.

"I'd love to."

She claps her hands in front of her sexy chest. "Great! You can keep Dad company while I get everything ready."

Holly walks into the office, and Pepper pops her head up. I watch Holly jump. Shit, I forgot to tell her.

"And who's this cutie?" Holly bends down and rubs Pepper's head.

I chuckle. "You just made a friend for life. This is Pepper. I rescued her from our local SPCA. I'm sorry. I forgot to tell you she was here. Your dad didn't want me leaving her home alone every day."

"I agree. Especially if she was hurt or abandoned by other people." That's my Holly, still the sweetest woman I've ever known.

"She was. I volunteer at the shelter, and the minute Pepper was brought in, I knew she'd be coming home with me."

Holly strokes my arm, and holy shit, her soft hand feels just as amazing as I remember. "My favorite kinda man."

I can't think of a single thing to say that isn't dirty, so I flash her a smile and head out front.

We have a steady stream of customers throughout the day. I'm relieved. It keeps my focus away from the beautiful woman who followed me around all day.

Most of her day was spent fielding questions about her father. After the last few customers pay for their orders, I lock the door and turn the open sign to closed.

I turn when I hear a loud sigh. "I hope word spreads about my dad's condition so I don't have another day of fielding questions."

I lay a hand on her shoulder. "I could tell it was getting to you. People love your dad."

She nods her head up and down. "I know, and trust me, I'm grateful." She lets out a loud yawn as she stretches her arms straight out to each side. "I didn't get much sleep last night."

"Your dad's gonna be fine." I squeeze her shoulder before dropping my hand.

"After all these years, you're still good at that."

That's what happens when you're soulmates. I've always known exactly what she's feeling, and she's always known the same for me.

"Just because we've been apart physically doesn't mean we haven't still been connected."

She crosses her arms on the counter in front of her and lowers her head. "I'm so tired."

I cover her hand with mine. "How about we save the lesson for tomorrow? I'll meet you at your dad's house and help you with dinner."

She barely raises her head and gives me a tired smile. There goes my heart again. "Thank you."

We walk back to the office. Pepper completely ignores me and runs right up to Holly. "Well, I guess the ladies are gangin' up on me."

Holly laughs, making Pepper howl. Holly looks at her and howls back. After a five-minute duet, Holly's doubled over, tears streaming down her face, and I'm grinning from ear to ear at the adorable interaction.

"You have no idea how much I needed that."

"I get it more than you know."

Her face gets serious. "I'm sorry. I can't imagine how you handled losing your parents. I'm a wreck, and all my dad did was fall."

I walk over to Holly and give her a hug. "You survived losing your mom. We're stronger than we realize."

"Yeah." She doesn't say anything else. Instead, she pulls away slowly and puts her coat on. Then, she fastens Pepper's leash.

I shut the lights off and set the alarm. We walk outside, and I lock the door behind us. Holly gets Pepper into my truck and shuts the door.

"I'll see you in a few. I just need to drop Pepper at home."

Holly shakes her head. "No, please bring her. I'm sure my dad would love to have her there."

I can't help but smile once more. "Cool, thanks. I just need to stop at home and grab her dinner."

"Okay. See you soon!"

Chapter 3

❄ Holly ❄

"Hey Dad," I yell as I walk in the front door.

"I'm bored." Annoyance fills his words.

I roll my eyes. This man does not know how to sit still. "I know, and I understand, but you need to rest."

"What if I go to the store and just sit?"

I put my hands on my hips and narrow my eyes at him. "Honestly! What am I gonna do with you? You have to rest. End of story."

Dad attempts to pout but ends up laughing. "Fine!"

"That's better. I'm gonna get dinner ready. Nick and Pepper will be joining us."

My dad wiggles his eyebrows. "Oh, is that so?"

I shake my head. "Stop. We're just friends."

"For now."

Oh great. Now he's trying to play matchmaker. But, there are worse things than being with Nick. I shake my head and growl inwardly at myself. *Stop it. You have other things to focus on.*

I turn my attention to mixing and forming the meatloaf and getting it in the oven. I start peeling potatoes just when I hear the doorbell.

"It's Nick," I hear from the other side of the door.

Butterflies start flitting around in my stomach. "It's open!" I call out.

Nick comes in, and I notice he changed his shirt. The loose, black button-down shirt looks amazing on him, and I feel my mouth start to water. After convincing myself it's actually dinner causing that, I get back to the potatoes.

Nick lets Pepper off her leash, and she goes right to the chair where Dad's sitting. Nick goes in and shakes his hand before returning to the kitchen.

"Put me to work, boss," he says with a wink.

I stick my tongue out at him, and I hear Dad laugh. He better behave tonight! "You wanna cut the potatoes as I peel them?"

"You got it."

"Thanks."

We get the rest of the meal prepared while the meatloaf finishes. Nick sets up TV tables while I put three plates together. After dinner, I clean up while Nick keeps Dad company.

He yawns when I return to the living room. "Think I'm gonna turn in early tonight."

"I'll get him," Nick says. "You rest."

"It'll be easier if we both do it," I say.

"Ah, togetherness," Dad says. I shoot him a look.

After I help Nick get my dad into the bedroom, I get the boot.

"I don't want my daughter helping me undress," Dad says.

My eyebrows shoot up. "But, Dad, Nick shouldn't have to do it," I say.

"It's no problem," Nick says. He's so sweet, and my wall crumbles a bit. After I leave the room, Nick shuts the door behind me.

I walk down the hall and stand in the doorway of my childhood bedroom gazing at the bright orange walls. Posters of my favorite musicians and Flyers players still adorned the walls. I think back to the whole room painting adventure. Dad let me pick the color, and he shouldn't have been surprised when I chose the same orange the Flyers have as part of their uniform. Dad affectionately referred to my room as The Carrot.

I head back downstairs and wait for Nick. I turn on the TV and as I'm flipping channels, I find *Beavis and Butt-head Do America*. It just doesn't matter how old I get. These two jokers still crack me up. I'm so busy laughing, I don't notice Nick come downstairs until I hear my name. I nearly jump off the couch, and Nick laughs at me.

I fold my arms across my chest. "Shut it!"

Nick sits down next to me, and by the time the closing credits are rolling, my stomach and my face hurt from laughing.

"That's exactly what I needed," I say, barely able to catch my breath.

"Do you remember how many nights we spent up in my bedroom watching this?"

"I remember more nights where we weren't watching."

"Holly!" Nick's mouth hangs open.

"Hey, you never complained." I smirk.

"I'd have been a fool if I did. I'm glad you were my first." He puts a hand on my shoulder.

"Me too." Holy shit. My stomach suddenly fills with butterflies just as it had the first time we went out. It's almost like being in this house has transported me back in time. Back when our biggest worry was which band tee to wear.

I try to suppress a yawn, but my exhaustion overpowers me. I can barely keep my eyes open.

"Sounds like you need some sleep."

"Really, Captain Obvious?" I stick my tongue out, and he laughs.

"Need me to get you ready for bed, too?"

My brain has a different answer than my mouth. "Uh, I think I can handle that all by myself."

He looks me up and down. "I bet you can." My jaw drops but no words come out. Nick laughs. "Get some sleep, doll. I'll see you Monday morning."

"No, I'll be in tomorrow."

"Don't remember that your dad stopped opening on Sunday, huh?"

I pause, suddenly remembering. "I guess not. I may still go in and just get familiar with stuff then."

"I'll meet you there. Then we can do some work with no customers there."

"I can't ask you to give up your Sunday."

"You didn't. Besides, I can think of worse things than spending some time with you."

My insides heat up. "Well, thank you. Just make sure you bring Pepper." I smile when Pepper's ear perks up at the sound of her name.

Nick puts his coat on while I put Pepper's leash on. Nick has her bag and a bag of leftovers, so I walk Pepper out to his truck. Once they're in his truck and backing out of the driveway, I head to bed.

Of course, sleep eludes me. All I can think about is Nick. I would give anything to have him lying in bed next to me. I sit up with a start. Holy shit, I'm still in love with him. All these damn years, and he's still the one. Now, I just need to figure out how to hide it.

❄ ❄ ❄

I'm awakened the next morning by the sexy sound of my favorite singer's voice, Dean Davidson. I get in the shower and get dressed. Of course, by the time I'm ready, the stubborn one managed to get himself downstairs.

"Why didn't you let me help you?" I scold.

"I can take care of myself, young lady."

I sigh exasperatedly. "You better not injure yourself worse. And don't think I'm budging on letting you come to the store."

Dad pouts.

"Keep it up and your face will freeze like that," I tease.

He laughs and takes a seat in his favorite recliner.

"What do you want for breakfast?"

"Would you mind cooking me an omelet?" Dad asks, his hands folded in front of him.

"Of course not. What do you want in it?"

"Ham and cheese, please."

"Coming right up." I pour Dad a cup of coffee and hand it to him then return to the kitchen and get his omelet ready. "Any toast?"

"One piece of wheat, sweetie."

When his breakfast is ready, I take his plate to the living room. "Are you sure you'll be okay without me for a couple hours?"

"Yeah. A couple of my buddies are coming by in a little while, so I'll be fine."

"Okay, great. I'll be at the store if you need me. Nick's gonna show me some stuff while we don't have to worry about customers."

"Oh, honey, you shouldn't have made him come in on a Sunday."

"I didn't. I mentioned that I was gonna go in and get familiar with stuff. He offered."

He smiles softly. "He still loves you, you know."

I shake my head. "Dad, please."

Dad puts his hands up in front of his chest. "Okay, fine. I'll drop it for now."

"Good. Now, behave. I'll be back later."

"Yes, ma'am," he teases.

❄ ❄ ❄

I pull up in front of the hardware store and see Nick sitting in his truck. I get out of my car and knock on his window.

"How about we go visit our old stomping grounds for breakfast?" Nick asks.

"Daddy Pops?"

"Yep."

"Let's go!" I bounce up and down and clap my hands before jumping in the truck.

Nick pulls away from the store and heads toward the diner. "How's your dad this morning?"

"Stubborn as always. He got himself downstairs while I was in the shower." I shake my head.

"Not surprised at all."

"Hey, where's Pepper?"

"I wanted to treat you to breakfast, so I left her home."

I lower my eyes and pout. "Poor Pepper."

Nick laughs as he pulls up to the diner. After we're seated and decide what we want, he smiles at me. "So, how long do you think we'll be able to keep your dad away from the store?"

I throw my hands up. "I'm honestly surprised we've kept him away this long."

"Me too."

"You two ready to order?" We look over when our waitress, Flo, comes to take our order.

I order scrambled eggs and a side of scrapple, and Nick orders a hungry man special. We also both order coffee. We sit and sip our coffee while we wait for our food and make small talk.

A little while later, Flo brings our food, and my eyes nearly pop out of my head when she puts Nick's breakfast in front of him. Three eggs, two strips of bacon, two sausage patties, home fries, and three pancakes!

"Damn, hope you're hungry," I tease.

"Child's play."

I finish my breakfast and just sit gawking at Nick. He finishes every last bite.

"Well, color me impressed," I laugh.

A shit-eating grin spreads across Nick's face as he rubs his belly. I shiver wishing it was my hands touching him.

Nick pays the check when Flo drops it off, and we head out to his truck. After we pick up Pepper, we head back to the hardware store, so Nick can teach me the ropes.

Ooh, ropes. I push the thoughts away. *Stop it, dirty girl.* I bite my lip to keep from laughing. I really need to figure out how to get my thoughts under control.

Chapter 4

❄ Nick ❄

"The biggest change I need to go over with you is the computer system," I begin when we're settled in the hardware store.

She picks it up quickly, but I still make her show me how to complete a sale. A nod when she's done, and she jumps up and down clapping. And damn does she look cute. I love how excited she gets.

She throws her arms around me, and I pull her in tight. Oh, how I've missed the feeling of her soft body against mine. My desperate desire to kiss her overwhelms me, but just as I'm about to caress her lips with mine, she pulls away.

I fear I've crossed a line when she takes off from behind the counter. I see her look over her shoulder and stick her tongue out at me. What the hell?

I see her run by in the next aisle over. She stops and sticks her tongue out at me again. Oh, she wants to play, huh? I grin and run after her. I'm close to catching up when I hear a thud. I race around the corner, and she's on her perky butt surrounded by a bunch of Christmas-themed car air fresheners, laughing her head off.

"I kinda took out the display." Her eyes dart off to the side.

"Kinda? You annihilated it!" I laugh. I walk over and hold my hand out to help her up. Instead, she tugs, and next thing I know, I'm on the ground with her.

I join in her laughter as she scoops up a pile of the air fresheners and throws them up in the air.

"Guess I'm more like my dad than I even knew." She grins from ear to ear.

"No more visits to the ER." I give her a stern look, but that only makes her laugh louder.

"Then you'd have to take care of me, too."

My heart skips a beat. If only she knew I want to take care of her for the rest of our lives. "That wouldn't be the worst thing in the world."

She flashes the smile that's gotten me through my darkest days. A warmth spreads over me. I watch as she starts to clean up the mess. I get up and put the display back together. We sort out the air fresheners and put them back on the display.

"I don't know what came over me," she says.

"It was fun. But can I get serious for a sec?"

"Sure."

"I was afraid you pulled away because of me."

"Why would you think that?"

"Because of what almost happened."

"Oh, you mean this?" She throws her arms around my neck and lightly brushes my lips with hers. I grab the back of her head and pull her closer. I can't stop myself. I feel her open for me, and I slide my tongue into her pretty mouth. I feel her tongue dancing with mine as she moans.. I've wanted this, wanted her, for so fucking long.

Without warning, she breaks the kiss and pulls away. "I can't," she whispers.

I look at her confused. "Why not? I know you felt what I do."

"But the timing. I can't. Not right now. I'm sorry." She lowers her eyes and shakes her head.

I tell her I understand, but in all honesty, I don't. I know she's worried about her dad, but that doesn't mean her life has to stop. I don't wanna blow this, so I won't push her now.

"So, do you think there's anything we need to add or change here?" she asks, changing the subject. "You were here a lot more than me, so I trust your judgment."

"Honestly, I wouldn't change a thing. Your father has a loyal clientèle because of how this store is laid out and what he carries. Plus, and I think this is the biggest draw, it's a more personal touch. You have that same flair with people he does, so I know you're gonna be amazing."

"I wish I had the same confidence, but I promise, I'll get there."

"I'll be with you every step of the way helping. Is there anything you were thinking of changing?"

"Changing, no. But I was wondering if any thought had ever been given to adding a delivery service."

"I think that's worth discussing with your dad."

She nods. "That can be a down the road thing."

"Yeah. So, is there anything else you want to go over today?"

"Maybe just a quick walkthrough to check inventory. Not exactly exciting, but needed." Holly looks at me and giggles. "We could make it fun?"

I can't help the smirk and my dick stirring in my jeans. "Strip inventory?"

Holly rolls her eyes at me. "Is that all men think about?"

"Oh, like women don't." I smirk as I look her up and down.

Holly bats her eyelashes at me and puts her hands on her chest. "Not meee," she sing-songs.

"Sure. So, if not naked inventory, what were you thinking?"

She smiles and takes my hand. "Come on." She starts skipping down the aisle.

"I am not skipping."

"Why not?" She giggles as she keeps going.

I give in and skip next to her, also joining in her laughter. I love seeing her happy and carefree. She's been so stressed since her dad's accident. Not to mention the way her chest bounces as she skips. Hey, I'm a guy, give me a break!

"All the shelves look full to me," she says, still giggling.

"Um, that's not how it works." I shake my head at her. "We should be counting."

"Such a party-pooper," she says, a fake pout on her pretty lips. Lips that I ache to kiss again. "Seriously, though, do we have sheets, or how does Dad do it?"

"Everything's in the computer. Your dad would print the sheets when it was time to check things. But he only does full inventory quarterly. Just looking at the shelves is enough for today." I smile, waiting for the storm.

Sure enough, she puts her hands on her hips and narrows her eyes at me. "You are a turd!"

Mimicking her favorite gesture, I stick my tongue out at her then take off running. I don't hear her running after me, so I turn the corner and almost shit my shorts. She jumps out from the next aisle.

"You're in big trouble now," I tease.

"That's what you think."

I wag a finger at her. "Keep it up. I dare ya!"

"I'm not afraid of you. I'll just rig you up an outfit like they did for Mr. Hart in *9 to 5*."

"Oh yeah, I can see explaining that one to your dad." We both laugh.

I hear Holly's cell ring, and she races up front. I check a few more shelves. She joins me when she's done, her shoulders hunched forward. She frowns but doesn't say anything.

"What's wrong?" I put my hand on her arm and squeeze lightly.

"I'm banished."

I raise my eyebrows. "Banished?"

"From my dad's house. You know his friends that moved to Florida?"

Nick nods. "I remember how down he was when they left."

"Well, when they found out about his injury, they flew up to see him. He wants time to just hang with them." I shrug my shoulders. "Guess I'll just drive around."

"Don't be silly."

Holly crosses her arms across her chest. "What the hell do you mean? What else am I gonna do? I'm not drivin' all the way to Philly then turn around and come back."

"I just meant you're welcome to come to my house."

She lowers her arms and stares at her feet. "I'm sorry. That's kind of you to offer, but then I'm putting you out."

"Nonsense. I'd love the pleasure of your company." *And I know exactly how I'd love to pass the time.*

We look over when we hear Pepper bark.

"See? Pepper agrees," I tease, and Holly giggles. "I was planning on making fettuccine alfredo for dinner tonight. Sound good?"

She rubs her sexy tummy. Once again, my dick starts to harden. "Yum."

I put my arm out, and she links hers through mine. "Shall we head out?"

She looks at me and smiles sweetly. "We shall. Of course, I have nothing with me. Mind if I make a quick stop at Target and meet you at your house?"

I get Pepper leashed up while Holly turns all the lights off. After she locks up, we head to our vehicles, and she follows me home.

❄ ❄ ❄

I pull into my driveway, park, and after jumping out of the truck, I take Pepper inside. Holly pulls in about half an hour later.

I raise an eyebrow. The sigh tugs on my heartstrings. "All good?"

"Yeah. Can I tell you something horrible?" She flops down on my couch and stares at the floor.

I sit next to her and take her hand in mine. "Of course."

"I feel terrible thinking this, but I'm kinda relieved." She sighs again.

I nod, knowing where she's going with this. "He can be stubborn."

She raises her head and gives me a weak smile. "How do you always know?"

I give her a reassuring smile. "Nothing wrong with feelin' that way sometimes. Your dad needs the rest."

She lays her head on my shoulder, and I melt. "Thanks."

Her stomach growls, and I laugh. "Guess I need to get dinner started."

She joins in my laughter. "Can I help?"

"Of course. My pots are in that cabinet." I point at one of the lower cabinets as we both get up and head for the kitchen.

I grab the sauce and pasta while Holly gets a couple of pots out. And there goes my brain again picturing her as my wife as I've done countless times before. Making dinner together then heading off to bed for dessert. I really need to keep my dick at bay. But alas, he tends to have a mind of his own! And he misses his first love.

"Where were you just now?" Holly asks as she laughs. Damn I love that sound.

"Oh, uh, nowhere." I feel my cheeks heating up.

"You're a dude, so I'm guessing I know," she says with a wink. I chuckle because she really doesn't.

After we finish dinner and clean up, we head into the living room. I turn the TV on and put the Flyers game on. The next two and a half hours are filled with alternate universe Holly emerging. A steady stream of swear words and trash talk stream from her pretty lips.

"Some things never change," I tease.

She gives me the finger, and I drop my jaw. "Obscene finger gestures from such a pristine girl," I tease, quoting one of our favorite movies, *The Breakfast Club*.

She giggles. "I think we both know I couldn't be further from pristine."

"Mmm, I sure as hell do, beautiful."

She smiles at me as she stands. "I guess I'll go find a hotel now."

I wrinkle my brow. "A hotel?" I stand with her.

"Yeah, I told ya I was banished."

"Shit, I didn't realize you meant until tomorrow. Well, you're welcome to my guest room." *Or my bedroom preferably. There's nothing I need more than this woman in my arms.*

Holly hangs her head and whispers, "Thank you."

I put my hand under her chin and gently lift her head. As I gaze into her beautiful green eyes, I'm filled with an overpowering combination of love and lust. I let myself lose control, pulling her tight against me as I crush my lips to hers.

This time, though, she doesn't pull away. I feel her lips part, and I gently thrust my tongue into her mouth. Fuck, she tastes so good.

Just as I'm deepening the kiss, her cell rings, snapping us back to reality. She looks at the screen. She inhales and exhales loudly before she answers.

Chapter 5

❄ Holly ❄

"Dad, is everything okay?"

"Yeah, honey. Just need to talk to you about something."

"I can be home shortly." I jump at the chance to not take Nick up on the offer of his guest room. I know what will happen if I stay. Especially if he keeps looking at me like he is.

"Where are you?"

"Well, since you told me not to come home, Nick invited me for dinner."

"I'm sorry. I just needed some time to talk to the guys. You don't need to come home. Just need to talk."

There goes that idea. "It's okay, so what's going on? And are you sure you don't need me to come home?" I nearly plead.

"No, but could you put me on speaker? This really pertains to both of you."

I bite my lip at the serious tone. "Hang on." I put the phone on mute for a moment and look at Nick. "Dad wants to talk to both of us. Is that cool?" Nick tilts his head. "I'm as puzzled as you are. I'm putting the phone on speaker now." Nick and I sit back down on the couch, and I put the phone on speaker. "Okay, Dad, go ahead." I look over at Nick, and he shakes his head back and forth.

"My injury has given me some time to think about things." Nick grabs my hand and gives me a supportive squeeze. "I'm moving to Florida," Dad continues. My mouth drops open. Nick's does the same. We just sit and stare at each other. "Hello? Holly? Nick? You still there?"

I shake my head in shock. "Oh yeah, you just surprised us. What does that mean for the store?"

"I want you two to take over."

Nick sits up straight, and I raise my eyebrows. "Um, well," I begin.

"I obviously don't need an answer yet. I need to heal up a bit more before I go. But I think we all agree that it's time. I'm gonna let you go now and get back to my guests."

All I can manage to say as I slump is, "Okay."

"Night," Dad says and disconnects.

I drop my phone in my lap and just sit there staring at Nick. After what seems like an eternity, I finally recall how to speak. "What just happened?"

Nick shrugs. "Um, I have no idea."

We both laugh, still in disbelief at what we just heard. "Don't get me wrong, I'm grateful that Dad came to his senses, but I'm honestly shocked."

"Well, we definitely have some stuff to talk about. But, and I hope you feel the same, I need to sleep on this."

"Oh, I completely agree." My mind returns to what we were doing when my phone rang. I take a deep breath and exhale slowly. "Uh, I think we need to talk about somethin' else."

Nick gazes at me, but doesn't say anything for a few minutes. He finally sighs and says, "Yeah we do."

"I think I know where that was headed. And I need you to know, I wanted it. I still want it, but after that phone call, I don't think it's happening tonight."

"I want it, too. I want you so much. But I'm willing to wait."

I run my fingers down Nick's handsome face. "I do need to ask a favor, though."

He smiles at me. "Anything, sweets."

"I don't wanna sleep alone tonight."

Nick doesn't say a word. He gets up, scoops me up into his arms, and carries me to his bedroom.

"I could get used to that," I tease.

"Mmm, my pleasure." Nick gives me his panty-melting smile. And yep, that's exactly what mine do.

"I gotta go grab my bag from my car."

"Sit tight, I got it." I smile at the man who's always made my toes curl. When he comes back, I grab the tank top and shorts set I bought out of the bag.

"Need me to leave while you change?" Always the gentleman.

"Nah, you've seen me before." My cheeks redden. Did I really just say that without thinking? What the hell?

Nick sits on the bed and gazes at me as I lift my shirt off, and I hear a wolf whistle. I roll my shirt in a ball and hurl it at Nick's head.

"Hey!" He rubs the spot where the shirt hit him.

I roll my eyes at him. "Oh please, no way that hurt!"

"Maybe I'm just really tender." *Well, that is true. Not in the way he's saying, but in the absolute best way possible.*

I remove my socks, sneakers, and jeans, leaving me standing in just my bra and panties.

I smile when I see Nick's jaw drop. Then panic sets in, and I try to cover myself with my arms.

"No, baby, please don't cover up."

"But I saw your face." I lower my eyes to the floor.

"Trust me. That was a good jaw drop. You're still the most stunning woman I've ever laid eyes on."

Nick grabs his cell, and I hear one of my all-time favorite songs, *Is This Love?* by Whitesnake. He walks over to me.

"Dance with me, my angel." He wraps his arms around me and pulls me close. I circle my arms around his neck and lay my head on his shoulder. We sway as one to the music, completely lost in each other. Suddenly, I'm transported back to high school.

I let out a contented sigh as we dance. "I love you, Nick," I whisper. "I always have."

He stops moving, and my stomach flips. *Shit, I went too far. He's gonna kick me out.*

I feel his hand under my chin. He lifts my head and gazes into my eyes. "I love you so much, baby."

His lips crush mine as he picks me up. I wrap my legs around his waist, loving the feeling of his hands on my bottom.

He walks me over to the bed and lays me down. My mouth waters as I watch him strip down to just his briefs. And let's just say he's happy to see me!

He's always had one of the sexiest chests I've ever seen. I've never been a fan of the six pack. I prefer my man to be a teddy bear, and Nick fits that perfectly.

"Baby, I've been thinking about this for so long."

My heart swells hearing him say those words. "I have, too. I want you more than I've ever wanted anyone." *So much for that sleeping thing.*

Flames dance in his eyes as he removes my bra. He slides my panties down, stopping to tickle my feet. *Shit, I was hoping he'd forgotten how ticklish I am.* I giggle, which only serves to egg him on.

"Stop, please!" I beg breathlessly.

"That's not what I wanna hear right now, baby."

"Can't breathe! Too tickly!"

He laughs at me. I try to pout, but I'm laughing too hard. "What do you want then, baby?"

"I wanna be naked with you."

"That's all?" He smirks.

Heat spreads through my face. "Um, no." *Please don't make me tell you.*

"Then, tell me. You're in charge."

I giggle and whisper, "I can't."

"And why not? Where's the bad girl I remember?"

"I'm older now."

"And?"

"I can't say those things."

"Like hell. You're even hotter and sexier than when we first met. You damn well can tell me. I'll do anything you want, but you have to tell me."

"Make love to me," I whisper, throwing my earlier thoughts of just needing to sleep out the window.

"What? I can't hear you." He smirks at me. *Turd.*

"Make love to me," I say a little louder this time.

"That's my good girl."

He smiles at me as he drags his fingers across my breasts. It's been so long since anyone touched me, I forgot what it felt like. I love that Nick's the one doing it.

Being completely naked in front of him, I suddenly find myself feeling very self-conscious once more. Going from being confident to not is my silent curse. I cross my arms over my body, trying to hide myself.

"No, no, no. A beauty like you deserves to be not only seen, but worshiped." Nick scans me with his eyes, and a wicked smile spreads across his handsome face. "So beautiful, my sweet Holly."

Daring myself to be brave, I say softly, "Mmm, Nick. Please touch me."

"Where, baby?"

I look away from Nick and whisper, "My pussy."

"Mmm, yes, angel."

He gently spreads my legs and gazes at me. Instead of feeling embarrassed as I expect, I get even more turned on. I'm surprised that I like him watching me; that it feels even better than when he did it before.

"I've missed you so much. I can't wait to taste you again."

He moves his head between my legs, running his tongue up and down each thigh before setting up shop where I really want him. When I feel his tongue swipe up my pussy, I nearly fly off of the bed.

"Feels so good," I moan. I forgot how incredible his tongue is. When Nick sucks on my clit, my body quakes as I buck off the bed. "Oh, Nick!" I scream.

He doesn't stop as I writhe beneath him. I feel my body take flight as I explode into the strongest orgasm I've ever had. I never want this to end.

Except now, I want him inside me. Before he even asks, I tell him. "I need your dick inside me."

He flashes me a devilish smile. "That's my good girl. But first, I have a little surprise for you." He stands at the foot of the bed.

I watch as he removes his briefs, and his cock springs to full attention. Fuck, I forgot how sexy he looks naked. A pleasant surprise indeed.

Though, back in high school, I was especially shy and preferred to only have sex in the dark. I open my legs as wide as they'll go, eager to feel him slide inside me.

Nick lowers his body over mine, bracing himself with his arms so I don't take his full weight. I wrap my arms around him as I feel his dick slide inside me. My pussy's still wet from my orgasm, and he slides in with ease.

"Oh, Holly, you feel so damn tight. Sweet. Oh God."

A tear settles in the corner of my eye. "I love you, Nick." I need him to know.

"Mmm, love you, baby." His tone is filled with so much passion. The same deep feelings I've always felt for him.

He groans as he slides in and out of me. I rake his back with my nails, and he growls as I arch into him. I love the way his body blankets mine as I pull him closer. Our bodies move together as one. Two souls made for each other. His thrusts are slow and deliberate.

"Baby, I want this night to last forever," Nick says, his eyes locked on mine.

"Mmm, so do I." I smile up at him, realizing at that moment that I don't want to spend another day without him. Trying to deny my feelings for him or hide them is silly.

His thrusts get harder and deeper. I can tell he's close to coming. I pull him tight against me. I can feel his heartbeat against my chest as my legs start to tremble. My pussy begins to tighten.

"Oh, Holly, I love you so much," he growls as I feel him thrust one last time before he empties inside me at the same time I find my own release..

After we finally come down from the intensity of the lovemaking, Nick rolls onto his back and pulls me in close. I smile up at him as we lie together. The only sound in the room is our perfectly in sync breathing. I've never felt happier than I do in this moment.

He kisses my forehead as we lay quietly. I nuzzle his neck with my lips, eliciting a low growl from his throat. I lay my head over his heart. The sound of his heart beating has a calming effect on me, and I let out a contented sigh.

❊ ❊ ❊

I wake up alone the next morning. I can hear Nick in the kitchen. After the best night's sleep, well, best night period, that I've had in a long time, I bounce out of bed. When Nick sees me, he grabs me and pulls me in tight. He plants a kiss on the top of my head.

"What can I get you for breakfast?" Nick asks.

"I'd love a bowl of cereal."

"Lucky Charms or Cheerios?"

"Lucky Charms, please."

Nick grabs two bowls and hands them to me after he fills them with the cereal and milk. He pours two cups of coffee, and we sit down to eat. I can't keep my eyes off of him the whole time we're eating.

"Baby, I'm not some piece of meat," he teases.

I lick my lips. "I don't know about that. You have one hell of a delicious sausage."

"Holly!" He laughs.

"Oh, don't you dare. You know you love it."

Nick grabs me and twirls me around. I squeal as my feet come off the ground. He puts me down and looks down his eyelashes at me.

"Wanna help me with something?"

"Of course."

He flashes me a dangerous grin. "Come with me."

He takes my hand and pulls me to his bedroom. He strips and points to his bathroom.

I just blink, confused. "What?"

"I need help in the shower."

I shake my head back and forth. "No way are you seeing me naked."

He furrows his brow. "But I saw you last night."

"Yeah, but - "

"No, baby. No but."

"Come on. I'm not one of those perfect women that men love to see naked."

"The hell you aren't." Nick points at me. "You listen to me. You are the most beautiful woman I've ever seen."

I stare at the floor as my cheeks catch fire. "Okay," I whisper. "I'll shower with you."

Nick walks over to me and hugs me. "Only if you're sure. I never want to pressure you." I nod and remove my pajamas. I refuse to take my eyes off of the floor. "Look at me, baby." I lift my eyes in time to see a soft smile on Nick's face. "So beautiful."

Nick takes my hand, and we walk together to his bathroom. I watch as he turns the water on, giving it a chance to warm up.

He scoops me up and gently places me into the tub. He has a tub/shower combination that I love. He gets in with me, his eyes scanning my body. My cheeks are on fire again as he stares at me.

I shiver as the chill of winter in Pennsylvania washes over me.

"Come stand under the water, my love."

I smile and do as Nick says. The hot water feels amazing on my skin as I finally start to warm up. Or maybe it's because Nick's so close to me.

He grabs my shower puff that I bought at Target and squeezes some of my peppermint scented shower gel onto it. As he soaps me up, all I can focus on are his strong, calloused hands on my body. I sigh as my body relaxes, like all my inhibitions are washing down the drain.

I grab Nick's washcloth and squirt some of his body wash on it. I inhale, the scent of sandalwood filling my nose. I return the favor and soap him, spending extra time on his perfect package and his oh-my-god so sexy ass.

He pulls me against him as we rinse off. There's something so intoxicating standing here under the water in Nick's arms. I melt into him as he kisses me.

Nick breaks the kiss and gives me a serious look. My nerves go into overdrive. He must've realized how unattractive I've become. But, as usual, I'm overly hard on myself. That's not what he thinks at all.

"Baby, I need to know something." He caresses my face.

"Ask me anything," I murmur.

"Are we, I mean, um, after last night…?" He stops and just stares at me.

I smile softly. "Yes, we are together… If that's what you want."

Nick exhales loudly. "Sorry for being an idiot just now."

I tilt my head. "Why would you say that?"

"Because I got all tongue-tied."

I giggle. "Trust me, you do just fine with that tongue."

Nick's jaw drops. "Damn, naughty girl."

We both laugh as we finish up in the shower. After we're dressed, we head to the hardware store.

From the minute we open, we have a steady stream of customers, and the day flies by. After a quick cleanup, we head to my dad's house.

Chapter 6

❄ Nick ❄

Holly knocks on the door, and we hear her father call us in. Just as Holly opens the door, I take her hand in mine.

Her dad raises his eyebrows when he sees us. "Looks like I'm not the only one who's had some big news."

I look over, and Holly's grinning from ear to ear. My heart swells seeing how happy she is. How happy I've been able to make her.

"Now, I need you to get something for me," Holly's dad says.

"What's that?" Holly says.

"There's a box on my bed. Don't open it, just bring it out."

"Have a seat, Holly. I'll grab it," I say.

I come back out with the box, and I'm about to hand it to her dad, when he stops me.

"Go sit next to my daughter. I want you both to see this together." Holly and I look at each other with wrinkled brows. She shrugs. "Go ahead and open," Holly's dad says.

I rest the box on my lap while Holly takes the lid off. I look down and see a photo album. The cover is cream-colored with gold borders. Holly lifts it out of the box and starts flipping pages. She stops after the first few pages.

"Oh my god," she exclaims.

"What is it?"

"It's pictures of us, and there's a note. Is it okay for me to open this, Daddy?"

"Of course." I look at her dad, and his eyes are glistening.

Holly opens the envelope and starts reading. Tears stream down her face as she hands me the note. She walks over to her dad's chair and throws her arms around his neck while I read.

Dear Mark,

I've started this album of pictures of Holly and Nick. Please keep filling this up and give it to them as a wedding present when they get married. I know I won't be here physically to see it, but I'll be watching. Please give them both an extra kiss for me on their big day.

My love forever,
Alice

"Dad, you never told me Mom thought we would get married someday," Holly chokes out.

"She made me promise. I hope you understand."

Holly nods. "Of course I do."

"Nick, I hope this isn't too much for you," her dad says.

"Absolutely not. I've never stopped loving this woman." I tousle Holly's hair.

"Thank you," her dad says.

"For what?" Holly asks.

"I was having second thoughts about moving. I didn't wanna leave you alone. But now, seeing you and Nick together, I know you'll be okay."

"I will, but I'm gonna miss you. I'm glad we'll have one more Christmas here before you go."

"Actually, sweetie, I'm leaving after Thanksgiving."

Holly's mouth drops. My heart hurts a little that this is all going down so fast. "But your hip!"

"Honey, I'm okay to travel."

"You'll never be ready in time! What about the house? All your stuff?"

"I'm going to take what I need with me. I have a moving company to take care of the rest."

"But the house!"

"Sweetheart, I appreciate your concern, but trust me, I've planned everything. Heaven knows I've had plenty of time on my hands."

Holly laughs, but I see concern on her face. The worry. She looks around, trying to hide her tears. "I'll miss this house."

"Not if you want it." Her dad shrugs with a soft smile.

Holly's jaw drops. She just stands there, open-mouthed, as her dad chuckles.

"So, what do ya think?" I ask after a few moments.

"Oh, Daddy, I'd love to live here."

Looking at me, Holly's dad says, "And you?"

I point at my chest. "Me?"

"Do you wanna live here, too?"

"Well, um," I hesitate, unsure of what to say. Not that I don't have the answer. I know what I want. I just don't want it to be too fast.

"It's okay, I want you and my daughter to live here. Together."

"Then, I'd be honored." I put my hand out. Holly's dad accepts it and shakes it.

Holly sniffles, her eyes filling with tears. "Well, I still wish you'd stay until after Christmas, but I understand. I will, however, be cooking Thanksgiving dinner," Holly says.

With a wink, her dad says, "You better! Well, as long as you don't mind making a slightly larger meal."

"For your friends?"

"If it's okay." He smiles.

"Anything for you, Daddy."

"Thanks, honey. Now get outta here! The guys will be here for poker shortly." He laughs, and we join in.

After Holly packs some more clothes, we head back to my house. We're sitting on the couch when Holly lays her head on my shoulder.

"You remember that one weekend when your parents and my parents were both away?"

"Oh yeah!" I flash a sexy grin. *I'll never forget the night we lost our virginity together.*

"Not that. I was talking about the movie marathon."

I pout, pretending to be upset. "Jammies, pizza, popcorn, and movies?"

She giggles at my fake pout. "Yeah."

I smile. "Sounds like a perfect evening to me."

Holly makes it halfway through one movie before she's out like a light.

❄ ❄ ❄

"Rise and shine!" I shout from outside the bedroom. I hear stirring and footsteps. The door opens, and I'm greeted by the cutest sight I've ever seen. Holly stands there, hair sticking out in every direction. She wipes her eyes before she narrows them.

"How did I get in there?" I laugh.

"About halfway through the first movie, you passed out cold. I carried you to the bedroom and got you tucked in."

She looks at the floor and gives me a little giggle before blushing. "Oh god, please tell me I wasn't snoring."

She was.

Loudly.

"No, not a peep." I shake my head because I don't have the heart to tell her. I quickly change the subject before she catches my lie. "I thought we could hit the grocery store and get what we need for Thanksgiving dinner. Of course, breakfast first."

"Okay. Mind if I shower first?"

"Of course I don't mind." I go sit on the couch and wait for her. I try my damnedest to get the picture of her naked body out of my head to no avail. She comes out in jeans and a hoodie, hair up in a messy bun, and I can barely control myself. We head out to my truck, and I drive us to breakfast. After we finish, it's off to the grocery store.

"I don't know if one turkey will be enough, but let's go with this one," Holly says, pointing at the biggest turkey in the case.

"What else do you want to make with it?"

"Definitely need some creamed spinach."

"Oh, of course. I remember that being your favorite."

She smiles, and there goes my heart again. Like she didn't already own it anyway. "Cranberry sauce and stuffing, too."

"Do you want mashed potatoes?"

"Of course. You have to have mashed. And pumpkin pie!"

We get to the front of the store, and they only have self-checkouts open. I unload the cart while Holly starts scanning and bagging everything.

"Wow, you're a pro," I say in admiration of the perfect bagging she did.

"All those times we played Tetris. I can fit anything anywhere."

I laugh, and she joins me. *I know what I'd like to fit somewhere.* I groan quietly at myself. *Good lord, I'm a pig.* I chuckle. *No, I'm a dude, and she's hotter than hell.* I roll my eyes at the inner argument I have going with myself. *Stop it. Keep it in your pants.* This woman is making me lose my mind.

After Holly insists on paying, we load the bags in my truck and head home.

❄❄❄

The next morning, we get up early and head over to Holly's dad's house with all the groceries. After we unpack the bags, I stand and put my hand to my forehead like I'm saluting. "Put me to work, boss-lady."

She laughs, and I feel a twitching in my pants. I need to keep it together in front of her dad.

"Are you sure you want me in charge?"

"Damn right I do!"

She blushes and stares at her feet. "Okay. Then you get to clean out the turkey while I get the stuffing ready."

"Yes, ma'am!"

She rolls her eyes at me.

She gets the rest of the ingredients into the bowl and starts mixing the stuffing. I watch her hands kneading the ingredients together, and all I can think about is those hands on my skin. We finish getting everything ready and in the oven, then head into the living room.

Her father has the TV on as we all eagerly await the start of the Thanksgiving day NFL games. Her dad's friends arrive a little before kickoff. As dinner nears completion, Holly heads into the kitchen to finish up.

And, of course, being the amazing woman she is, won't let me help.

"I don't want the guys to think less of you," she says with a smile.

"I don't really care what they think, but thank you."

❄ ❄ ❄

Dinner was amazing, but I can't help but notice the sadness in Holly's eyes as she watches her dad enjoy the food. After I help Holly clean everything up, we head home so her dad and his friends can get what he needs packed. I can't help but wonder how my girl's gonna handle him leaving.

Chapter 7

❄ Holly ❄

"Daddy, are you sure you won't at least wait until after Christmas? What about all of our traditions?"

Dad looks between Nick and me. "You two need to start making your own traditions. Together."

I can't stop my tears from spilling over as Dad and I embrace.

"I'm gonna miss you," I barely manage to choke out.

"I'll miss you too, sweetie, but we'll still see each other." Dad turns to Nick and pulls him in for a hug. "You take care of my precious girl."

"You have my word, sir."

I watch as Dad climbs into the van he rented for the drive down to Florida. Nick wraps me in a side bear hug as we watch the van back out of the driveway. I wave until the van's out of sight. Tears stream down my face as Nick walks me inside.

Dad's house feels so different without him in it. "Oh, Nick, I don't know how I would have gotten through this without you."

"You'll never have to worry about that. You're stuck with me!"

"Good!"

❄ ❄ ❄

The weeks leading up to Christmas are hectic. Between increased business at the hardware store, me resigning from my job to takeover the store full-time, and packing up our houses to move into Dad's old house after some renovation, we've barely had a chance to breathe.

We're sitting in what's now our living room the morning of Christmas Eve. Nick gets up without a word and goes out to the garage. When he returns, he stands at the front door.

"Close your eyes," he commands.

"Yes, sir," I tease.

I can hear him moving around as well as some other noise I can't quite place.

"Okay, you can open 'em."

My eyes widen when I see it. I squeal as I jump up from the couch, racing over and giving him a huge hug.

"I love it! Thank you!" I stand gawking at the beautiful Douglas fir Nick just set up in the corner of the living room.

"I've been hiding it in the back of my truck."

"You're so sweet." I kiss his cheek.

Pepper gives us a bark and a tail wag. She's adapted well to living in a new house. Secretly, I think she likes me even more than she likes Nick, but that's our little secret!

"How about we decorate it today?"

I clap my hands and bounce up and down. "Oooh, yes please."

"And, of course, no tree decorating would be complete without this."

I give Nick a puzzled look, and he snickers while he turns on the TV. "Oh, yay!" I exclaim, bouncing up and down again when *National Lampoon's Christmas Vacation* starts playing.

"And tonight, we're gonna snuggle under a blanket and watch a certain marathon."

"Eeek! *A Christmas Story?*" I bounce even harder now. I can't help but notice Nick's eyes on my chest. I point at my eyes, and he laughs louder.

"I can't help it when you're bouncing like that." The brat in me takes over, and I make myself bounce harder yet.

Nick grabs me and tickles my sides. I'm laughing so hard I can barely breathe. "Santa's gonna leave coal in your stocking if you keep that up, woman!"

I stop bouncing and jut my bottom lip out. "You're a mean one, Mr. Grinch."

We're both in hysterics as we attempt to put the lights on the tree. After a few do-overs, we're finally ready to get the ornaments on. Once we're done, we put the boxes away.

"No tinsel?" I ask. Nick points at Pepper. "Got it," I say with a chuckle.

We grab some leftovers out of the fridge. We each make a plate and sit down at the kitchen table. Of course, Pepper sits between us, just waiting for anything to hit the floor.

After dinner, we take Pepper for a walk, definitely well-needed after all the leftovers we scarfed down. When we get back, we get in our jammies and settle on the couch.

Nick covers us with an oversized blanket. Pepper curls up next to us, and we watch a couple airings of *A Christmas Story*. When we're done, we head to bed. I snuggle up next to Nick while Pepper curls up at our feet.

Nick holds me tight. I rest my head on his chest. "You okay, my angel?"

"Yeah, why?"

"Well, I just meant with your dad being in Florida."

I look up at him and smile. "I thought this was going to be impossible to handle."

"But something changed that?"

"No. Someone. You."

Nick kisses the top of my head. "I love you, baby."

Nick opens the drawer in the nightstand next to the bed and pulls out a small box.

Tears fill my eyes as he gazes at me. I take a deep breath and exhale slowly.

"Will you marry me?"

"Oh, Nick, yes! I'll marry you!"

Nick slips the ring on my finger - a perfect fit. He leans toward me and presses his lips to mine in a fevered kiss. Tears of joy slide down my cheeks. We tear each other's pajamas off and spend the next hour celebrating. We're both so spent, we're barely able to get dressed before we drift off to sleep.

❄ ❄ ❄

I awaken Christmas morning and roll over to Nick's side of the bed. He stirs awake and greets me with a sleepy kiss. Sliding my hand under the covers and into his briefs, I slowly stroke his dick.

"Tryin' to solidify your spot on Santa's naughty list, huh?"

"Mmmm, you make me naughty."

Before I realize what's happening, Nick has me out of my jammies and on my back. I spread my legs wide, and he climbs on top of me.

I moan when I feel him slide inside me. We hold each other tight as our bodies writhe in passion.

"Mmm, you feel so damn good inside me."

"Oh, baby, I love that sweet pussy wrapped around my dick."

Still holding me, Nick rolls onto his back so I can ride him. I sit up straight, giving him a full view of my body.

"So beautiful, my love," he growls.

I ride him slow, never wanting this to end. When I can't take the pressure for another second, I increase my pace until we explode together.

I slide off of him, and lie in his arms. Pepper barks from the living room where she must have wandered when we were celebrating our engagement, and we both laugh.

"I think someone's ready to see what Santa brought her," I joke.

"Wait until you see what he put under the tree for you, baby," Nick says, a wide smile on his face.

"I already have everything I need right here. Nicholas Daniels, you are the perfect package."

The End

About Samantha Michaels

I live in Pennsylvania with my husband and our dog. I have loved reading since I was a small child and have now turned that into a love of writing.

In my free time, besides reading and writing, I enjoy spending time with family, watching TV/movies, and listening to my favorite hard rock bands.

Books By Samantha Michaels

Available Now

The Melody Of The Seasons Series
Rockin' Spring
Rockin' Summer
Rockin' Autumn
Rockin' Winter

The Rockstar Quadrilogy
Leather and Lace
A Second Shot At Love
Pet Shop Passion
Silent Angel

Standalone
Ten Days In Heaven

The Shooting Star Ranch Trilogy
Cowboys Don't Cry
Silent Screams

Social Media Links

Follow me on:

Instagram
@samanthamichaelsauthor

Tik Tok
@samantha.michaels.author

Website
https://www.samantha-michaels.com

Printed in Great Britain
by Amazon

30810034R00165